BAD INFLUENCE

ALSO BY CLAIRE AHN

I Guess I Live Here Now

BAD INFLUENCE

CLAIRE AHN

VIKING

VIKING
An imprint of Penguin Random House LLC
1745 Broadway, New York, New York 10019

First published in the United States of America by Viking,
an imprint of Penguin Random House LLC, 2025

Visit us online at PenguinRandomHouse.com.

Library of Congress Cataloging-in-Publication Data is available.

ISBN 9780593403167

10 9 8 7 6 5 4 3 2 1

Printed in the United States of America

BVG

Edited by Jenny Bak
Design by Lily K. Qian
Text set in Franziska Pro

The authorized representative in the EU for product safety and compliance is Penguin
Random House Ireland, Morrison Chambers, 32 Nassau Street, Dublin D02 YH68, Ireland,
https://eu-contact.penguin.ie.

For my sister, who reminds me
we all have nothing to prove

CHAPTER ONE

They say money doesn't buy happiness, but . . . doesn't it? I've been staring at my closet for twenty-three minutes and I'd be much happier if I had the money to buy something I actually want to wear to this event happening in less than three hours. Money pays the rent, money takes the tension out of my mom's shoulders, money pays for my little sister's activities. And most importantly, money will help me fulfill my filial duty to my parents as the elder daughter of immigrants and absolve me of future guilt when I leave one day for college.

This is the year everything's going to change. I can feel it. Or at least I can *will* myself to feel it.

I grab my secondhand Loewe bag and rush out of our apartment, determined to find a better outfit for today than what my sad closet offers me. The G train isn't far, and within a half hour, I'm inside one of my go-to thrift stores in Williamsburg. They sell a lot of clothes that scream '90s, like things you'd see from that movie *Clueless.* It's not fully my style, but if I match it with something I already own, I like what I can create. I scan the room. There's a rack with a lot of bright colors and it looks happy and inviting, so I start there.

Next to me, two girls are talking about their office drama. Their baskets are filled halfway with necklaces, earrings, multiple tops and shoes. I'm filled with envy. I don't need a basket because I'm pretty sure I can only pick one thing. *Focus on yourself, Charlotte.* There's no point in getting distracted by what the people next to me are buying.

By my third rack, I see something promising. It's a bright purple off-the-shoulder dress with sleeves, all one piece of delicate satin. It's stunning and perfect. I check the price tag, hoping the Korean money gods are on my side. They are not. It's eighty-five dollars. I check my wallet, wondering if what's inside somehow more than doubled. Nope.

At the register, I see the two girls checking out. One of their totals is more than two hundred dollars and I'm awash with annoyance at their happy laughter and the casual way in which they pay for their new possessions. I hang the satin dress back on the rack, squashing every ounce of envy that thrums through my body. I thank the woman at the counter and leave, empty-handed, ready to head to my second hope. I only have one hour before *Fall into Florals* starts.

This store is smaller, with less selection but often better curated. I take a deep breath, determined. Slowly, I look through each item of clothing, imagining it on me, paired with every piece I have in my closet. If I maximize the use of what I buy, I feel less guilty. I pick three tops, all under forty bucks, and go to the dressing room. The same thrill of finding that purple satin dress is missing, but I convince myself that a top is much more practical than a fancy dress. I settle on a red one with lacing on the hem and an oversized bow in the middle, and I'm pleased with how it gives my muted yellow pants some pop. It'll pair well with most of my shorts, too. Inside the fitting room, I dump out my bag of accessories to see what'll go best with my new outfit. I check the time before deciding on feathery earrings and a simple black headband.

With just enough time, I pay for my new top, rush back to the train, and make my way to Flatiron. It's at The New York Edition hotel, and, like most hotels, I've never been. But I was promised free food and a preview of the fall collection for some of New York City's trendiest boutique brands in (unspoken) exchange for posting to my Instagram stories. After checking in, the hostess, dressed in an all-black fitted outfit and heels that look too high to walk around in, leads us quickly and gracefully to the event area. Strewn across the space are different tables showcasing all categories of late summer and fall attire, each uniquely designed and decorated. Servers walk around with trays full of crudités, appetizers, and drinks.

"We're so happy to have you, Charlotte," the hostess says, walking with us. "Welcome to *Fall into Florals*. So, today we're showcasing our favorite boutique designers in New York. At this event only, everything is twenty-five percent off for our influencers as a thank-you for joining us. Just use this hashtag if you post to your stories," she finishes, handing us a sticker with the event hashtag on it.

I nod, looking around for familiar influencer faces. New York is probably the second-biggest pool of influencers, second only to Los

Angeles, and the proof is right in front of us. There are a handful of people I recognize: @LizzyBrawls, @GirlInTheCorner, @JulesJewels, @WooYoungOh, @AudreySena. I study their outfits and am in love with Audrey Sena's look. She's wearing a pink-and-orange crocheted bucket hat, a white fitted three-quarter-sleeve top, and baggy velvet purple pants. I glance at my own reflection in the dark glass panes, suddenly no longer appreciating my own wide mustard pants and new top. I look like a Heinz ad. The satin dress would've looked so much better.

I spend some time recording videos of the booths, tagging vendors and the hotel, taking selfies, and making small talk with a few of the influencers I vaguely recognize. I feel out of place and everyone else seems like they're friends. I wonder if they also think I'm out of place here.

One of them looks my way. "Hey, I love your top. The bow is so cute."

"Thanks!" I say too chipperly.

"Where's it from?" another one asks.

"Oh, it's vintage." Vintage is close enough to secondhand, right?

"Ugh, I knew it. Aren't vintage things the *best*?" the first girl says.

I nod, pretending to agree, and try not to fidget. Eventually, enough time passes where I feel like it's acceptable to excuse myself and wander through the booths. I try on a few plaid coats and oversized knits. Not much catches my eye until I notice a beautifully dark, leather baker boy cap. I've seen them everywhere, or versions of them anyway. It's the hat in all of Condé Nast magazines' "trendy fall accessories" lists. I feel like the only influencer who hasn't gotten the memo. It's the perfect accessory I've been looking for, and something I've been craving for my closet. This booth has three different colors: black, a caramel brown, and a Barbie pink. I try the black one on, and the seller offers to take a few photos for me.

"It's okay," I decline politely. She has no idea how uncomfortable giving her my phone makes me. The power they wield with the camera frightens me to my core. I will always and only do selfies alone or timed pictures when I'm posing.

"Do you like it? It's the last one in that color."

"It's perfect," I tell her. "How much is it?" It's habit that I ask. I already know I can't afford it.

"It's 325 dollars, with the discount."

I contort my features so it looks believable that I'm considering the purchase. I hold on to it for a few moments longer than I need to. Because not being able to buy things never gets easier. While the seller goes to greet someone else, I snap a few photos at an angle that looks like the hat is mine. The very definition of curated content.

I slip out while she checks someone out at the register and quickly walk through other booths. I'm about to try on sunglasses when I hear whispers behind me. There's a giant rack of coats between me and the quiet snickering voices, so I stop moving to make myself invisible.

"Honestly, I don't get what people see in her," someone says.

"She got big for no reason. Because her family has money and nowhere to spend it, so she just uses it on nice clothes and voilà, she's suddenly an influencer," a new voice says with a mocking tone. I catch a glimpse of her between coats. Her outfit is forgettable, but she has an intensely long fishtail braid.

"Hi, I'm Audrey Sena, and I *looooove* being authentic," the third one says, her voice dripping with sarcasm. She's wearing a cute LoveShackFancy dress.

They're all hovering over a phone that a blond girl is holding up, and I strain to see it in between the coat collars I'm peeking through. She's zoomed into Audrey's Instagram page.

"There are so many Asian influencers now. Aren't we the minority yet?" the girl with the phone says. She flips her thin hair over her shoulders with a look of disgust on her face. My hands feel clammy and cold. They have zero idea that I'm standing right here. Me, an Asian person. *Is this how everyone talks about us?* I wonder.

LoveShackFancy nods vehemently. "Honestly, just so much Asian *everything*," another adds. "Like, oh my god, did you guys see that Shake Shack is doing a Korean menu for their burgers? It looks gross."

Fishtail pretends to gag. "Seriously. They're taking up too much space. You know they're the ones who started Covid, right? People like her—" And that's enough for me to interrupt.

I step out from behind the rack and snatch the phone from the girl's hand before they know what's happening. "People like what? Asian? Seriously?" I feel like someone is scraping out my stomach.

It's clear she didn't know she was being overheard. A flicker of guilt flashes across her face but she replaces it with annoyance. "Give me back my phone," she says. "And sorry, who are you?"

LoveShackFancy snickers. "Oh, I know. An amateur influencer trying to find her 'space,' too."

Fishtail chimes in. "We were having a private conversation. It's not our fault you overheard and got all righteous." She's not much taller than me, but her long blond hair reaching her waist and her icy gray eyes make her feel more intimidating.

I toss the other girl her phone. "If you're going to be racist, do it in your bedroom so the rest of the world doesn't have to deal with your idiocy. And yeah, we're taking up space. It's about damn time, but it's not even close to the space you've been occupying." My hands feel shaky but I ball one of them up in a fist. The other one is holding my phone, recording this entire dialogue.

She leans in so our faces are too close. I make a face when I smell the garlic bagel on her breath and discreetly bring my phone higher up.

"No one can hear us, anyway. So yeah, annoying little know-it-all Asians like you *are* getting in the way. You, Audrey Sena, and the rest of you need to just back the fuck off. No one can tell you all apart anyway," she hisses. Fortunately, her whisper isn't quiet enough.

I stare at her with a small hint of a smile and pull back, showing her my phone. "And, stop." I wiggle my eyebrows, channeling confidence the best I can. "I wonder what the world will think when I blast this video, angled perfectly to capture your face?"

She looks stunned, shocked, and scared all at once. She stammers, glances around at her silent friends, then regains her composure. "You don't even know who I am."

"LilasLovers," I say, remembering what I saw when I grabbed her phone. "Really bad username, by the way. Are you trying to have online orgies?" She goes pale. "Find Audrey Sena and apologize. I'm going with you."

"Hard pass. And again, who even are you?"

"Do it, or the video goes viral. Also, you're in a compromising position so maybe don't be a ragingly rude human to me?"

She says nothing but scans the room with a cold stare. When she spots Audrey across the space from us, she stalks over. Her friends and I follow behind.

When we get to Audrey, I'm nervous though I pretend not to be. "I'm Charlotte," I tell her, extending my hand. "These girls were being racist jerks about you and got caught on video by yours truly. Now they're dying to apologize." I turn to LilasLovers. "Take it away." The entire ordeal is super cringy. She apologizes and begrudgingly mutters something about not meaning what she said. We all know she meant it, though.

LilasLovers is watching Audrey, waiting for a response, probably hoping she doesn't tell me to post it. After a moment, she says, "Uhh, hello?" She waves a hand in front of Audrey's face.

Audrey just stands there, intimidatingly stoic. Finally, she says, "People like you make me even prouder of people like me."

LilasLovers purses her lips, knowing she can't retort back.

"Sorry," she mumbles again. We all know she doesn't mean a syllable of it.

"Charlotte, want to look at that hat again?" Audrey says, turning to me.

I'm baffled; did she see me? Audrey Sena is talking to me. Me! "Sure."

LilasLovers grabs my arm as we turn. "Wait, I apologized. Now delete the video." She's desperate.

"The deal was I wouldn't post it, not that I'd delete it," I say, yanking my arm back. "A deal's a deal, but the content belongs to me and you have no right to tell me what to do with it. Now *you* back off." My whole body is sweating and I quickly nudge Audrey and scurry to another booth before LilasLovers has a chance to follow.

A server has a tray of tuna tartare nearby so we make our way over. I take a fizzy citrus mocktail from a different tray and take a long sip from it.

"Are you okay?" I ask her. More servers come by and I study my options, opting for a fancy mozzarella stick.

Ever so gingerly, Audrey puts down her deviled egg, dabs the edges of her mouth with a napkin, and looks at me. "Thank you," she finally says.

"It was no big deal," I say, but the vibe feels heavier than that.

"I heard her say the first part of it," she admits quietly. "Then I walked away. I've been getting a lot of messages like that lately. Ever since I started speaking up and being more vocal about supporting other POC creators, I've gotten some nasty messages and a lot of unfollows. I've turned off my DMs and disabled comments. I expected it, but it doesn't make it less shitty."

I stand there, staring at the tablecloth, unsure of how to respond. My mouth feels dry. When I feel really helpless or angry, I get numb and fumble, often becoming disassociated. When this happens, people think I'm insensitive. But I'm so crippled by the pain that I think my heart tries to rescue me by turning off. I don't know Audrey well, so I search my mind for anything appropriate to say. Anything at all. "I just feel like the world is moving backward sometimes," I manage to say. A beat later, I add, "I'm sorry."

"It really did mean a lot to me, what you did."

I offer a small smile. "Well, if you ever want to get back at LilasLovers, I have the video," I joke.

Audrey smiles back. "Thanks," she says, finishing off her deviled egg. "I think I'm going to head home now. It's been a long day."

I nod, unable to say anything consoling. "Totally," I tell her sincerely. To her back I say, "Bye."

Mindlessly, I find my way back to the booth with the popular leather caps before I head home. I try on the pink one this time. The seller isn't here at the moment, which is a relief. I know I can't buy it. I just wanted to see myself in it one more time.

CHAPTER TWO

I get off the R train and walk toward our apartment on the northern side of the Queensboro Bridge. Some people think we have money because we live in LIC, Long Island City, but we're lucky we got this unit when it was still rent stabilized, when my mom was pregnant with Jojo. The doorman gives me a nod as I enter.

"Hey, Teddy," I say.

"Finally Saturday," he says, lightly chuckling.

"*Finally*," I echo.

The elevator *dings* when it reaches the fourth floor, something that makes me a little nervous every time. Four is unlucky in Korea so all the apartments there have gotten rid of that number in elevators. When things don't work out for my family, which happens often, I always wonder if it's because we live on the fourth floor. If there's a Korean god, I imagine they're upset with us for moving to the States and betraying them by living on this cursed floor that doesn't even exist back in the motherland.

"I'm home," I call out. I don't have a chance to throw my backpack on the floor before Jojo jumps into my arms, as she routinely does, and throws her sticky arms around me.

"Sharty's home!"

"Char-lotte," I correct her while kissing her cheek. Joanna's three and a half, but when she was two, she couldn't pronounce "Charlotte" and would call me "Shart." It was a super-annoying stage and somehow, even with the tonsil ability to pronounce l's, the name stuck.

"SHARTY!" she screams louder, with the untainted glee only a toddler could have. I follow her into the kitchen, where my mom is trying to bribe Jojo into eating pancakes.

"How was book club?" my dad asks. "Steven was there, too?"

Steven, my best friend, would absolutely shame me if I brought him into my ongoing lie. So, I shake my head. "Nope. He doesn't read because he's barbaric." I wasn't great at lying at first, but two years of growing my profile and hiding it from them has improved my skills. My parents have no idea I'm an influencer. They're Korean parents. I don't need them asking all thirty of their church friends, "*Please pray for our daughter to let go of her worldly and ungodly desires of becoming an online celebrity!*" As long as I continue to do well in school, no one needs to know what I'm trying to achieve online. "And book club was good," I say, pretending to focus on my ice cubes.

"What book is it this time?"

My parents feel like opposites. While my mom focuses all her energy on Jojo, my dad never stops asking me questions about my life. My dad is affable, the type who everyone loves in any group setting. And the more emotive of the two. He talks slower than my mom, a result of not having grown up in the States. And unlike my mom, he moved here as an adult, so he's got a strong Korean accent and forgets conjunctions. My mom was born here and went to USC for undergrad. But marrying my dad was this whole thing since he comes from a poorer background, so her parents don't really speak to her anymore. How dare she get married to a class beneath them! They were appalled. So they never got around to liking him, which makes me sad, because he's pretty much the most likable person I know.

"No work today?" I ask, hoping he'll forget his question. I'm not paying any attention to him as he rambles on about his current contract. I need to think of a book he won't know about so he can't ask me any more questions.

"So I'll start again on Monday," he finishes. He tilts his head as if trying to remember something. "Ah, so what book you read?"

Damn. "The . . ."

"*Book of Dust?*" He smiles at me.

I shake my head, pretending to swallow water.

"The . . . *Tattooist of Auschwitz?*"

I gulp. Swallow.

". . . Nanny," I finish.

"The *Nanny?*"

"It's a book," I argue. I recall seeing it displayed through the glass exterior when I was walking past a bookstore in Chelsea last week. It looked creepy.

"Is that scary book? I've seen it around."

I exhale slowly, relieved. "Something like that. Mystery. Horror."

"Mmm. Let me know how you like," he says from over his shoulder. He's already walking toward the living room. For someone who can't speak English fluently, he loves his books. I think it's because he can read at his own pace, unlike the flow of conversations.

My phone vibrates and I see a text from Steven.

> **steven**
>
> what do you think jojo will want me to make for dessert tomorrow?

> pillsbury funfetti cupcakes
>
>

I grab a pancake from the table and fold it before taking a bite from it. My little sister grabs one too and imitates me. My mom shoots me a glare as Jojo now refuses to eat any of her cut-up pieces.

"I mean, this is the superior way to eat pancakes," I argue. "Sorry," I add sheepishly.

> carol-eemo is probably cooking
> a trillion things already

> she already started. brace yourself

Our families meet for dinners every Sunday, a tradition that's been ongoing since we were kids. Carol-eemo and my mom always say we're each other's families here in the States. They've been best friends since their twenties. We're supposed to take turns cooking, but most of the time, we go to Steven's place because his parents own a dumpling shop in Flushing, which basically means they're amazing cooks. Well, it used to be his parents' shop. Since last year though, it's just Steven's mom who runs the store. His dad is in Panama now with his new twenty-something-year-old girlfriend. If there's an "at least," it's that he left all ownership to his ex-wife so there wasn't much to battle over, including Steven.

I spend the rest of my day cooped up in my bedroom, wanting to refuel. I feel drained. Sad. Frustrated. And still angry. Why do I feel so tied to a world that doesn't even feel that real to me? I go, I try on things as if I can afford to buy them, and then I come home and lie to my parents. It's a world that will never accept who I really am. Even though I thought I wanted nothing to do with Instagram for the rest of the day, my hand eventually looks for my phone. I sit up on my bed when I see that my notifications are blowing up; I have almost one hundred new followers, so I scroll all the way to the bottom to the first notification. *@AudreySena has tagged you in a post. @AudreySena is now following you.* I raise the volume and watch intently.

"This is why community is so important, and why, more than ever, I'll continue speaking up. Taking up space," Audrey says, with so much intent. "Friends like Charlotte help me feel bolder in the face of a lot of hateful messages, and it's not always and only be-cause I'm Asian. But I also can't deny that some of it—a lot of it—is. People like to say, 'Well, maybe it's not because you're Asian . . . ,' but you know what? It is."

The greedy part of me is delighted with all these new followers.

I'm eating it all up. It feels like a small reward for being the Good Samaritan. Audrey Sena considering me a "friend" on Instagram feels like a next-level achievement in my online life. I check my DMs and see that Audrey messaged me her phone number. I text her immediately.

wow thanks for tagging me.

audrey

hope you're feeling better ?

I am, actually. And posting the
video was cathartic for me haha

Sometimes I feel like making a new friend is twenty times more nerve-racking than any conversation ever with a boy, no matter how hot. It's a different level of performance pressure. A different type of desire for approval, trying to be likable. We text back and forth for a while until my dad calls me to the dining table for dinner. I don't really have an appetite, though. Not after today.

"Char?" My mom's voice brings me back to the dinner table where Jojo is belting out a song I can't make out. She has noodles all over her hands and in between her fingers. Her utensils are nowhere to be found. As she throws pasta on the floor, my mom sighs, her small frame bending over to pick up the noodles.

"Huh?" I look up from my phone, trying to be present. "Sorry."

"Never mind," she says in Korean, waving me away.

I help pick up the pasta but my mind is elsewhere. I try not to think about the day's event but I can't help it. The longer I sit with that memory, the more it eats me whole. I replay the scene over and over again. *Asians like you. Taking up space.* The phrases shout at me inside my head, making me feel smaller and smaller. I ball my fists in anger and my knuckles turn white.

"Jojo." I look at my baby sister sternly. "No throwing food on the floor."

"Aigo, Charlotte, don't be so harsh with her." My mom speaks to me in Korean most of the time, and my comprehension is significantly superior to my speaking.

"Umma, she needs to learn. She'll be four in six months!"

When Jojo was born, my dad's physical and mental health was at its lowest, so my mom had to work extra shifts to help bring in more income. She wasn't around for Jojo's first two years and I don't think she'll ever forgive herself. Or my dad.

"She's still a baby, Seoyoung-ah," my mom says, using my Korean name. She plucks Jojo out of her seat and props her on her lap to feed her. I roll my eyes and head to my room.

At night, I have a hard time falling asleep. Every time I close my eyes I just see LilasLovers and her friends sneering at us. *Back the fuck off,* she'd said. I bunch up my bedsheets. Kick my feet out. Grab the bedside rails. Nothing helps, but eventually, my mind stops racing and my breath stops hitching and I spend the night in and out of bad, sweaty sleep.

By the time I'm up the next morning, I have over fifty new

followers, on top of yesterday. I go back to Audrey's post. A lot of people are on our side, urging Audrey to reveal the racist influencers. A user tags me: *@CharInTheCity is a reply video coming? we wanna hear your side!*

I've only done a few reply videos before. But for small things, like a question about where my shoes are from, or what my favorite coffee shop is. As a Korean American micro-influencer, I've definitely been on the receiving end of some creepy DMs, but not a ton of directly racist remarks. But I know it happens. I know it's there, lurking and waiting. Always striking. If not me, then someone else. This video is different. I feel nervous but I need to do this, and I know it'll help me move on. Hopefully.

I throw on a beaded top I stitched together and keep my pajama pants on. A bit of makeup and some blush and I'm ready. Deep breaths. I hit record and sit in the one corner of my room where you can't tell what the space looks like. It's got good light and nothing else shows much except a faux plant on my right and a framed acrylic painting Steven made when he was first going through his parents' divorce. Art didn't last long but he was trying many different hobbies to find the right outlet for himself, courtesy of the therapist's suggestion, instead of stealing windshield wipers from cars. I remember, clearly, the moment the painting became mine. He was trying to throw it away in the garbage outside our school, and he couldn't control his sobbing. He was rage-crying and I held him tightly and begged him to keep it. It was the only time I hugged him like that, so tight so he'd know he wasn't alone. We didn't say much after he calmed down, but he silently gave the painting to me, holding on to it by just the corner. I bought an eight-dollar frame from Michaels the next day and put it in my room. And we never spoke of that incident after.

"Hey, it's Charlotte Goh. A few of you asked for my response to Audrey's video, so I wanted to share my experience." I pause. Through the camera, I see the painting behind me. A canvas that's been lathered with black paint with streaks and splashes of gold. And a small bright yellow flower. I take a quiet breath and continue. "So yes, Audrey and I did encounter racism at the event we were at recently. I'm not going to call out what event it was because it's irrelevant and not the organizers' fault. I overheard three influencers saying anti-Asian things. I didn't know it was about Audrey until I snuck up on them. They showed no remorse because it was apparently my fault for overhearing when they were in the 'privacy' of their corner," I say. "So is it okay to be racist if you think no one's listening?" I pause again. "I'd like to assume that most of us know there's no space for racism and hateful words, online or in person." I shrug. "But unfortunately that's not the reality we live in. I'm not calling out the specific racist influencers on here, but if you're watching, let me answer my question for you. *No*, it's not okay to be racist in private, either. It's never okay." End record.

I include a content warning on my caption, and post. I go back to Audrey's post and respond to the user who asked for a reply video, letting her know it's up. In my attempt to not obsess over my reply, I flip my phone face down and change into a normal outfit for the day.

CHAPTER THREE

Since my mom rarely cooks, I love going to Steven's place. I guess in my mom's defense, she doesn't have a ton of free time in between taking care of Jojo and working. She's the manager of a large Korean grocery store in Queens and sometimes takes up extra shifts. Thankfully, she has flexibility and days she works from home on the computer. Jojo started at a local universal pre-K earlier this year and I think it's been good for my parents. Day care is a money-suck and UPKs are paid for by the government, so they definitely fight less. Though honestly, looking at Steven's family and my own, I'm not sure I ever really want to get married. More bills, more money, and a lot of sacrificing . . . all without the guarantee of a happy ending. Just look at Steven's asshole dad.

The only downside is how far Flushing is from LIC on the 7 train for an impatient toddler. We have a car but sometimes Jojo will fight to ride the subway. Today is one of those days, but she probably has five more minutes left in her before a meltdown. I miss when Steven and I could walk to each other's places back in Elmhurst.

"Appa, I want xiao long bao," Jojo says.

My dad looks down at her as we walk out of the subway. "Wow, Jojo, you know word 'xiao long bao'!"

She beams, loving the attention.

"But Carol-eemo is cooking for us today, so we get soup dumplings next time, okay?" Steven's mom isn't our actual aunt but knowing her since we were born basically makes her my mom's non-biological sister. And in Korea, everyone's an eemo.

Jojo pouts, wriggling her hand out of my dad's and making a run to their home. My dad can't run to catch up with her because of his joint pains so I dash after her, repeating that she can't cross the street without holding our hands.

We buzz in, and by the time we reach Steven's floor, we smell the aroma of various stews and rice lingering throughout the hallway.

"Door's open!" Carol-eemo shouts from the inside.

I lower my head in a quick bow of respect to her as we walk inside. "Annyeonghaseyo."

Steven does the same as he walks toward us, directed toward my parents, before wrapping Jojo in a hug.

"How's my favorite girl?" he asks, kissing the top of Jojo's head.

There's probably not a single person Jojo loves more than Steven. He's the only one who'll play *Paw Patrol* with her, the only one who will never tell her to stop talking, and the only one who dotes endlessly on her every time she approaches him. Sometimes, I've thought about how Steven would be as a dad. How much better he'd be than his own father, how loving he'd be if he had a daughter. I've even wondered if I'd be the mom. If we'd ever have a happy ending.

Thirty minutes of bustling conversation and aggressive plate setting later, we're all eating the myriad of dishes Carol-eemo has prepared.

"Seoyoung-ah, pass the jeon," my mom says to me, extending her hand to receive the kimchi jeon. It's amazing how flour and kimchi can form the best type of pancake ever. I don't speak a ton of Korean, but *food* is an entire language. Korean food will always be my favorite part of our culture, always the thing that draws us together. It's the language of sharing, a message of apology, a way to comfort, and to cook Korean food is the epitome of unvocalized love in our culture.

"Mmm, Steven-Umma, your cooking as always wonderful." My dad compliments her, dabbing the edges of his mouth with a paper napkin.

"Seriously! You don't have to cook so much every week, you know," my mom says, plating the rest of the kimchi jeon on eemo's plate and taking the empty one to the kitchen. It's always been interesting to me that Korean adults call each other "mom of insert offspring's name," like their own identities are irrelevant once children are a part of the picture. My mom just calls her "Carol," since they've been friends for so long, but when you aren't besties with someone, that's what it is and it's weird. I don't want anyone calling me my future kid's mom. I want to stay Charlotte Goh.

Carol-eemo waves her hand away, dismissing my mom's comment. "Somebody needs to make sure my Charlotte is eating good Korean food," she teases. "None of this instant food nonsense."

My mom rolls her eyes. "It's so much better than the instant stuff we had when we were kids," she argues. Our parents mostly speak in Korean to each other, but to us, it's more English.

Carol-eemo's pork and chive dumplings are the most popular, with everyone grabbing and reaching over each other to take multiple dumplings. Jojo half eats her miyukgook while the other half of the seaweed soup sloshes to the floor. My dad reaches over every few seconds to wipe her mouth while she avoids him and spills more soup. The whole hour eating is chaos, but our weekly tradition with Steven's family has often been my succor when shitty things happen. It's the best way to start a new week. It's my safe place.

Steven gets the ladle and refills my bowl with more miyukgook as I plate the rest of the sweet gamjajorim onto his. Braised potatoes are Steven's favorite side dish and a staple in their home. It's the language of many Korean families, this constant plating of food on each other's plates. I mimic my mom and take the empty plate to the kitchen, rinsing it with water and placing it in the dishwasher. The Changs actually use their dishwasher to wash dishes! My mom thinks it's heresy. How is it supposed to get all the crevices? That's what she always says.

I'm taking a quick close-up shot of my half-eaten soup when my dad breaks the comfortable silence. "Steven-Umma, gwenchana?" he asks. *Are you okay?*

It feels like we collectively stop breathing, even Jojo, who's looking up at Carol-eemo.

My mom is the first to respond. "Yeobo, of course she's fine." Steven and I are still sitting there, not breathing. "She's better than fine. She has us." My mom's a classic bulldozer. She insists we're all fine, that you can get through anything in life with grit and that therapy is a concept for white people. Who needs therapy when you have God?

Carol-eemo sighs slowly. "Yoonho-ya, get the dessert, would you?"

"I'll help him," I offer, reading the room. Their home is railroad style so the hallway to the kitchen creates enough distance. I can hear the adults talking, murmuring about Steven's dad and Panama.

Steven stands in front of the sink, his body looking uncomfortable and rigid.

"Wow, she made mochi?" I pretend to intently study the chewy powdered goodness.

"Yeah," he murmurs. He rubs the back of his neck with his hand, holding that posture for a minute. "She was craving mochi so I didn't make anything," he adds. Steven's detached as he says this and I wish I knew what to say to make him feel better.

"Can I try one?"

Steven shrugs. "Go ahead."

I raise the powdered mochi to my mouth and chew it slowly. "Oh, mmm. It's really good."

He doesn't say anything.

I dust the powder from the sides of my mouth. "But your madeleines are way better."

A small smile slips out. Steven plucks a mochi from the wooden tray where I've plated the dessert and bites it in half, letting the powder fall to the floor. "Guess we should head back in."

I grab his arm as he turns away. "Hey, are you good?"

He shrugs and holds the tray with focused hands. "It is what it is."

I follow him back to the dining table wordlessly, praying Carol-eemo's spirits are lifted a little bit. Just enough so Steven isn't hurting so much. The vibes still feel off.

"Um, Steven and I are going to grab bubble tea. Anyone want one?" Steven's still fidgeting and I know they're not done talking.

My mom has her arms around Jojo, whose eyes are fluttering open every few seconds in a futile attempt to stay awake. The adults shake their heads no and we make our way out.

"Good call," he says, shoving his hands in his pocket as we walk onto the pavement.

"Is she okay?"

The sky is casting a medley of orange and blues, even purple, and the night feels so promising, so different from how we all feel. He shrugs. "She hasn't been great."

I remain quiet, waiting for him to continue.

"She's been super moody, and I know she's not sleeping well. Your mom is the only person my mom told, I think."

"Still?" Steven's parents got divorced almost eight months ago.

He nods. "I told her to go to a therapist, that it helped me a lot, but she refuses to listen. She doesn't even like that I'm going to one, but she's letting me because she knows I'm at least not kicking random cars." He pauses. "Or stealing windshield wipers," he says sheepishly.

Eventually, we make our way onto Main Street and enter our go-to bubble tea shop. I scan the menu even though I always end up getting the same thing. "I'm not sure how much help my mom would be, honestly. Actually, talking to my dad would probably be more helpful."

"What can I get you?" the cashier says to us.

"Brown sugar milk tea with bubbles please," I say. "One hundred percent sugar for me."

"Hot oolong tea, no bubbles, no sugar," Steven says. "Yeah, no one in their church group knows. She just said that he moved to Korea for the time being because of business."

"I'll get this one." I insert my card into the reader. "Wait, but they run a dumpling shop."

Steven scoffs. "Exactly. Like, does she think people buy that shit?"

I shrug. "Maybe they do, it could be for research or something. Chefs do those inspirational trips."

Steven rolls his eyes. "Right, like my parents would ever do something like that. They'd argue that they're losing money when the store could be open."

We get our orders and I watch Steven sip on his bitter tea as I savor the sweetness of mine. We walk a few blocks quietly, comfortable in our silence. We're surrounded by the sounds of heavy Flushing traffic and the rustling of plastic bags as people head home after evening grocery runs. "Want some?" I offer.

He makes a face. "No thanks, I don't like sugar water."

"Tea snob." He offers his and I push it back. "Life is bitter enough for me, thanks."

This gets a little chortle from him. I'll take it.

Steven sighs loudly. "I wish she'd just *talk* about it. She acts like . . ." He pauses, searching for the right words. "Like it never happened."

We turn a corner to a street with more residential homes and find one that has three steps out front and make ourselves comfortable. Steven is leaning his back against the railing as he drinks his tea. I'm sitting with my legs sprawled out in front of me. "Maybe she thinks she's protecting you by not dumping it all on you." I think of how my mom might cope with something like this. I shudder at the thought. "Trust me, it's better than talking to you like you're the therapist."

"Well, she's not," he says bitterly. "The silence is deafening. Feels like the only time she talks is when you guys come over."

I lean my head on his shoulder. "I'm sorry. How's therapy been?" When Steven first started therapy, five months ago, he went every week and he was so surprised at how helpful he found it. But two months ago, he started only going every other week.

"It's fine."

I throw a small twig at him. "Anything else besides fine?"

Steven grabs a rock and draws on the cement, evading eye contact. "How's your quest to dominate social media?"

"Like I don't know when you're just trying to avoid my question," I say, throwing another twig at him.

He sighs slowly. "I'm thinking I'm going to stop going."

My joking grin disappears. "What? Why?"

"I mean, it's been five months. I feel pretty fixed."

"You sound stunted when you say that, Steven."

Steven turns his head away from me, with an irritated breath. "There's only so many times I can keep talking about the worst experience of my life, okay?"

I know the conversation is over. He's already mentally left the space of talking about therapy. So I nod. "Okay. But no one can *fix* us."

He stares hard at me.

"Like, we don't exist to be fixed or to be broken, you know? We're just here."

Steven looks up at the dark sky. "Can we change the topic?" he asks. His voice is quiet.

"Here's a distraction. I dealt with racist girls, made a friend—I think—and got all vulnerable on social media."

He looks at me with concerned attention. "What?"

I detail the events of that afternoon that I'm struggling to remove from my head. LilasLovers' cutting words and how I wish it didn't take up so much space rent-free in my mind. *Asians like you. Getting in the way.*

"What the *fuck*?" Steven runs his hands through his hair, tugging in frustration. He turns to me and holds my shoulders. "Are you okay?"

"Why shouldn't I be? It wasn't even directed at me."

"It was, though. We're a small community."

I flick a small pebble on the ground with my fingers, and it lands where the two twigs are.

"Char, you sure you still want to use social media after something like that?"

"Well, it wasn't related to social media, it was the fact that these white girls were upset that we were Asian influencers. And it hap-pened offline."

The familiar tension rises in my chest and it's not what I want to argue about right now. We've never really had any huge fights, but we both have an "agree to disagree" sort of approach when it comes to social media. I can't yell at Steven about his hatred to-ward it because it's personal. He found out about his father's affair through Instagram. A random model posted a picture poolside and his dad was in it, lounging in the background. There were more. A photo of him holding her waist in a swimsuit that barely covered her privates. Then a photo of them sharing a sundae together. He was wearing sunglasses and a cap in all of them, but it was obvious to Steven who it was. Steven never used social media that much to begin with, but when someone at school sent him that photo and asked if that was his dad, he deleted his accounts altogether.

He must not want to get into it either, because he stands up, wiping the back of his pants to dust off the gravel. He takes my hand and pulls me up. "Want me to beat 'em up for you?"

I laugh. "Yeah, could you?" I joke.

"Let me see the video," he asks, waiting for me to open up my phone.

It's been a few hours since I've opened Instagram and it's been a welcome relief. When I open my account to a flood of notifica-tions, it takes a moment for everything to sink in. "Oh my god."

"What?" Steven asks.

"My post went viral."

CHAPTER FOUR

I pause. "Do you know what that means?"

He looks at me incredulously. "Seriously, Char?"

"All right, all right. Look." I pass him my phone.

He turns up the sound on my video and I snatch it away immediately. "Sorry. I hate the sound of my voice. But look." I lean in to give him a closer look. "Over a thousand new followers."

"Can you tell who they are?"

I squint to get a better view of the profile pictures through the thumbnail. "Mostly Asians." I feel a wave of gratitude wash over me, a sense of digital solidarity.

"All from that one video?"

"I guess so."

As we walk back to his place, I try not to make it a big deal, not in front of Steven anyway. But it is a big deal to me. A *really* big deal. I'm still processing by the time we say our goodbyes and make our way back home. I'm *still* in shock when I'm in bed and my follower count has grown even more. And keeps growing every few minutes. All this in one evening.

I grab my phone from the nightstand and text Audrey.

I got a ton of new followers after that video.

like thousands.

Was that a weird thing to text? I don't want her to think I'm talking about what happened as a ploy to gain followers. Most times, yes, I'm trying to, but not this time. Shit, now I'm too deep in my head. Maybe I should follow up, tell her that I didn't mean it like that. I'm not trying to gain profit over her trauma. Shit, shit, shit. Before I can spiral further, my palm vibrates.

audrey

That's a good thing, isn't it?

yes yes yes but

sorry, i mean, i didn't do it for the followers

I know

Me neither.

Then she calls me.

"Hey," I answer, masking the surprise in my voice.

"Hey," she says cheerfully. "I'm not really a texter. And I try to be off my phone unless I have to be online."

I'm in awe of her boundaries. I could never. Two a.m. is my golden-hour social media browsing time. "Wow. What's up?"

"So . . . I got an invite for the MITI Gala and it came with a plus-one."

There's a pause and I hold my breath. The Most Influential Teen

Influencers is the gala of the year in New York for influencers in all categories under the age of twenty. I never thought I'd ever get invited. Or if I did, not this soon, anyway.

"Hello?" Audrey sounds confused.

"Hi," I answer.

There's a laugh on the other line. "Wait, so . . . do you want to be my plus-one?"

"*Oh*, sorry, *yes*, of course. I didn't realize you were asking me! I'd never get invited to that on my own," I joke. Well, it's not a joke because I wouldn't.

The MITI Gala is my best shot at getting brands to sponsor me so I can make money for our family but getting invited to it also feels like a reward, like proof that I'm entering the inner circle.

It's finally happening. I knew this year would be different.

"Yay! Perfect." Audrey sounds so chipper it makes me smile, too.

"Thanks for inviting me," I say genuinely.

"Want to go dress shopping together?"

And before I can think too long about how I can't afford a dress or what I'll tell my parents when I need a night out for an event they can't know about, I answer her. "Down."

I fall asleep that evening with various thoughts circling my head, but the loudest is the possibility of having made a real friend besides Steven. Who also happens to be a kick-ass influencer.

◆◆◆

Despite the adrenaline rush that I felt yesterday, a Monday at Roosevelt High feels the same: loud and empty all at once. High school is one of those things I hope is outdated by the time I have children, if I ever do. Or maybe it'll be an all-virtual school, so you actually focus on the learning part and not all the insecurities that come with uncomfortable, fake conversations in a decrepit building brimming with a bunch of hormonal teenagers. I gave up on making friends pretty early on, except Steven of course. No one ever really seemed to take any interest in me or thought I was fun to be around. It felt lonely at first, but it's not bad. I don't mind sort of drifting through school. No friends means no drama which means no emotional volatility.

During second period, someone taps my shoulder. "Hey, I saw your video," says Isabelle Yu. "Thanks for sharing. And sorry that happened."

I look at her, too stunned to speak. No one at Roosevelt High ever talks to me about my Instagram. Only to ask for my notes. I quickly recover. "Oh, thanks, Isabelle," I say, shrugging lightly. "Didn't expect to get so viral."

"Yeah, it's everywhere. Pretty dope," she adds.

"Thanks." I smile and face the board again.

I'm not excluded or bullied by any means, but most times, I move through the day quietly. But it's a one-off moment because no one else addresses it for the rest of the day.

I open Instagram under my textbook. Seeing my follower count up so high feels like a shot of adrenaline in my veins. It's an intense feeling of validation and I'm ashamed at how ravenously I consume the growing numbers. I want more. I'm distracted for most of the day after that, and finally, the school bell rings, signifying the end of another dreary day here. I walk past students creating TikToks, whose faces I vaguely recognize, silently judging them. I think a part of me might envy them and the ease in which they can make a fool of themselves in public hallways, so comfortable with the security they're able to provide for one another. But today, I get to have a semblance of that with Audrey. I rush out of school and head to Bergdorf Goodman. There's a sentence I never thought I'd say.

"What about this one?" Audrey holds up a shimmering gold floor-length dress against herself. She makes a face. "Too much?"

"No way. You have to try it on."

She grins. "Did you find anything?"

I found more than a dozen things, but it'll cost probably almost everything I've ever thrifted combined. I should go check out the sales racks but it looks sadder there and I don't want to. I shake my head. "No, not really. They're all too ball gowny. Or shiny."

She brings me a shorter pink dress. Tulle flowers form a high collar while the rest of the dress falls like a gentle balloon around the thighs. It is stunning and perfect in every way.

"This would look *so* good on you!"

I take it and hold it against me in the mirror. It's 695 dollars. "It's not *quite* my style, but yeah, it's super cute," I say, lying straight through my teeth.

I put the dress back on the rack as my heart shatters into a million pieces and we start walking aimlessly throughout the rest of the floor. Audrey suggests heading upstairs to their restaurant. Despite not being able to pay for anything, I'm having such a good time that I don't reject this idea, but I'm nervous. Food in this department store can't possibly be that affordable. Audrey links her arm around mine. "I'm always starving in the afternoon. Bergdorf's bar seating has good food, even though it's not the full-service menu. I'm weirdly obsessed with their Thai shrimp salad."

When we get seated, I scan the menu. *Okay. I can get the pea soup, I guess.* $7.50. Audrey orders the salad and a glass of champagne.

"You don't want?"

I shake my head. "I'm good, thanks."

"I think afternoon champagne makes everything better. I can go through life without alcohol, except champagne."

I raise my eyebrows at her. "Okay, now you're making me want to try some."

She laughs as she raises her glass and clinks it against my tap water. "Do you have any random obsessions?"

I nod. "Yeah, death."

She almost chokes on her drink. *"Death?"*

I start laughing. "Yeah. I think about death a lot, particularly if my best friend died."

"Who's your best friend?"

"Steven. It's not just that he's my best friend. He's kind of like one of my only friends?"

She smiles, but it's not a pity smile. "Now you have me, too."

I grin into my split pea soup. Steven was always more than enough for me. But if I'm being honest, it's different to have a girlfriend. I guess I just didn't realize how much I wanted it. My almost-eight-dollar soup was worth it.

When I get home, it's well past six p.m. Right on cue, my mom meets me in the kitchen.

"Where'd you go, honey?" she asks, with Jojo sitting on her hip.

I act focused on washing my apple. "Sorry, I meant to text. I had an after-school thing."

In my room, I look through the photos I took by the school's deserted playground to post to my feed, but it feels unnatural. Not the picture, but posting a photo as if what happened over the weekend has blown by. I throw open my closet and pick out an outfit. It's all one color, including my beanie. I even put on mittens to emphasize the color. I set my phone up on the shelf and time a few shots. Caption: *Yellow peril*. Sure, it's an old phrase, but it gets the point across. I share the photo to my feed and stories then spend my night dreaming of the MITI Gala.

CHAPTER FIVE

The rest of the week flies by in a haze of endless scrolling for inspiration of what to wear to the gala and keeping up with basic school assignments. In the midst of poring over retail sites, I also forget about a quiz and get a B minus, which I'll need to make up for somehow. By the time Saturday morning rolls around, I'm still no closer to finding a dress but we're now six days away from the MITI Gala. I get goose bumps just thinking about it.

My mom comes into my room without warning and I sit up and throw my phone under my covers, as if she can see what's on my screen.

"Umma!" I shriek. "You can't just barge in."

She looks at me, eyebrows raised. "I didn't *barge* in, Char. I came to ask if you could take your sister to dance class today."

I drop my shoulders. "You can't take her?"

She sighs. "No, I have to go to the store. I won't be home until the evening.

"Can't Appa take her?" I ask, already knowing the answer. I know he doesn't like doing things like that anymore. He used to love it but the last few times it somehow always ended up with my parents fighting in their bedroom once Jojo was asleep. My mom called him things like *lazy, useless, dramatic*. He called her *cold, insensitive, unavailable*.

My mom looks at me like I'm her only hope and it fills me with guilt. I know at some point she gave up on him. She never asked again after the third fight in a month.

"I guess I don't have much going on today," I finally tell her. She squeezes my shoulder and smiles. Once she leaves, I sigh in anticipation of another morning I'll have to spend at Jojo's dance studio. She and her class of ten preschoolers have been practicing for their annual recital for what feels like an eternity now. It's sweet that she loves seeing me at her practices, but at this rate, I'm never going to find my dress.

I help Jojo finish her eggs as she goes on about her dance performance ad nauseam. I slap a supportive smile on my face. "Hey, Jojo, where do you want to eat after?"

"Chanson!" she says, pronouncing it "chan-sun." She's obsessed with their Messy Croissant, which is just an insanely decadent chocolate pastry. It's a should-be-rare treat that she begs for every week.

"Jojo, pick somewhere new this time."

"No, Chanson!" She pouts.

I look at her sternly. "Jo."

"It's okay, Char, go to Chanson, here's my credit card," my mom says.

Jojo claps with glee, delighted at the thought of chocolate pastry.

"Mom, you can't just keep giving in to Jojo all the time." I mutter quietly enough that Jojo isn't paying attention.

"She's always hungry after practice and needs to eat anyway." My mom stacks the dirty plates scattered around the table.

"Do you know how many options there are around there that don't cost nine dollars a pastry?"

She sighs and rests her hand on the side of the plates. "Char, it's not the end of the world, okay? You don't need to worry so much about this. I said it's fine, and it's fine. End of discussion." The water starts running as she soaks the plates in soap, and Jojo and I go to get ready for our day.

By the end of Jojo's class, I feel a headache coming on from zooming in on too many photos and outfit inspos on my phone. The door pushes open with a loud bang against the wall as ten children come running out, ballet slippers skidding across the floor.

"Did you see my twirl?" the familiar and overly excited voice says to me. I squint my eyes when she practically shouts into my ear.

"I saw your pirouette, Jojo," I lie. "Now go get changed if you want to get your pastry."

At Chanson, I'm determined to be present for my sister, and to try to take the gala out of my mind for even a few minutes, but I get a text.

Steven

Did you go to Jo's practice today?

Steven never forgets her schedule. I smile at my phone.

lol yeah

we're at chanson!

you?

I'm nearish

Should I swing by

Ok, I'm swinging by. Don't tell Jojo

Gonna surprise her!

To give Steven time to come, I annoy Jojo by taking extra long picking out my pastry.

"Come on, Sharty! You're taking too long," she whines, pressing her tiny hands onto the glass as she eyes her Messy Croissant.

I smirk to myself. "Okay, okay. I just can't decide if I want the macaron or tiramisu. You want to help me pick?"

"The tee-ra-mee-shoo!" she says slowly, trying to correctly pronounce it.

"Good job, Jojo. Okay, tiramisu it is. Do you want a drink?"

She shakes her head, content with her portable milk cup. She waits for me at our table, her chubby little legs dangling happily from the chair. After getting our pastries, I gather some napkins, plastic utensils and two iced lattes and sit across from Jojo. She watches intently as I cut up her pastry into smaller bite-size pieces. I see Steven walking toward us and hide my smile to not give anything away.

"Guess who," he says in a deep voice.

Jojo's body jumps in the chair and she squeals as she frantically tries to pry the fingers from her face. "Who?"

"Your favorite monster!"

I shake my head, grinning at Steven's stupid "monster" voice, which Jojo knows by heart now.

My little sister squeals again with glee as she flips her head around and wraps him in a hug with her chocolaty fingers.

"Here," I say, handing him an iced latte as he sits to join us. I felt a twinge of guilt buying so many things here, but if my mom said it's not my problem to worry about finances, then fine, I guess it's not.

Except, it is.

We share the tiramisu and I update him on the event invite. And that I need a believable excuse to be out of the house that night.

"So what's your genius plan?" he inquires.

I fidget. "Honestly, I have no idea. Care to help?"

Steven shakes his head. "No way. I don't want to get involved in this. And lying to your parents about it? I don't think it's worth it, Char." We're talking quietly so Jojo doesn't hear us.

"Steven, it's not the end of the world if I lie once, okay?" I tread gingerly because I know it's his pet peeve. Liars. Like his dad.

He shrugs. "It's not once, though."

I chew on the sides of my mouth. "Well, I'm doing this to help my family."

Steven takes a long swig of his latte, maybe to prolong the silence that follows. I watch him as he sips. Slowly.

"What? Just spit it out."

"Char, we're at an overpriced bakery. You just spent almost forty bucks on pastries and coffee. Outside looking in, doesn't seem like your parents need financial help."

"You don't get it. My mom spends money we don't have. Meanwhile, she keeps saying she's going to open the next big Asian grocery chain or something. Or buy an apartment in the next booming location. It's like a toxic trait of hers, trying to make it big but not actually being able to get there. And then she spoils Jojo when we can't afford to. Then she needs more money, so she takes on more work and gets burned-out and angry at my dad for an injury that wasn't his fault and so on and so forth. It's a vicious cycle."

Steven looks at the tile floor beneath us. "So if you didn't think your parents needed the money, you wouldn't be trying to become an influencer?"

I shake my head. "No, of course not. I don't *like* this world, Steven. It's just the fastest and most lucrative option for a sixteen-year-old."

He hands me the last piece of the tiramisu cake on a fork. "If you say so."

"I do. And I mean, I wish my mom wasn't like this . . ." I take a deep breath and pause before continuing. "But if she's not going to change, maybe I can take the load off a little."

"Well, I just don't see it ending that well, Char. And eventually, your parents are going to find out. That's inevitable. And with all the racism stuff, are you sure you're going to be okay? The world's already shitty, why add the online world to your real life and expose yourself to even more shittiness?"

I raise my eyebrows at him. "Steven, I've got it under control. And it's not all bad, all right?"

He sighs, knowing I'm not going to change my mind about this.

He claps his palms together lightly as if to reset. "Okay, so when's the event?"

I let out a breath. Talking about social media always feels dicey with Steven. "Next week. And I honestly can't wait. It's going to be so cool."

"Thought you don't like this world," he says teasingly.

I clamp my lips shut for a moment and then say, "Just trying to have a good attitude about everything. Fine, I'll admit, it feels pretty rewarding to be finally going to these fancy events after two years of being a nobody influencer."

"I hope there's at least some good food."

I grin. "I'll try to sneak you out a pastry."

"Nah, I make them better."

"Touché."

On the subway ride home, I turn to him, trying to keep my balance on the moving train. "So you're really not going to help me out? I need a good excuse for why I can't be home that evening."

He rolls his eyes. "Of course I'll try to help. I'll let you know if I think of anything."

The subway comes to a halt and I grab Jojo's arm to keep her from falling on the grimy floor. "*Thank you*. I mean it."

He gives me a nod, making himself comfortable on a seat and placing Jojo on his lap while I go back to my phone, searching once again for the perfect dress.

CHAPTER SIX

At church the next day, the sermon is aptly about lying, and the entire time, Steven is nudging me and making sarcastic faces. When the pastor's finally done talking, I escape outdoors and grab a coffee from the cart across the street.

Steven materializes next to me. "You felt so guilty you bolted out of there?" He gives a small chuckle.

"Oh come on, I was falling asleep. He talks for way too long."

"Can you make that two, sir?" he asks, leaning into the window of the cart.

We grab our coffees and loiter outside the church. "I'm making jjigae for dinner," I announce.

"Nice. What kind?"

"Doenjang jjigae."

Steven stifles laughter.

"Don't say anything," I warn him.

He holds up his hands in defense and silently sips his coffee. "Your doenjang jjigae is the best," he says, nudging me again.

A proud spark comes over me and I shrug. "I know." Doenjang jjigae is the only dish I know how to make, and every time he and his mom come for dinner, they always expect it. My parents feel embarrassed and beg me to make something new, but who has time to learn a whole new dish? Besides, they usually prep Korean barbecue, and nothing pairs better with grilled meat than doenjang jjigae.

"I'm bringing dessert."

"Homemade?"

"Of course."

Moments like these, I struggle with the right words to say to Steven. Since he bakes as a form of therapy, I always wonder if he's not in a good place when he does . . . like he's trying to escape, heal, or distract himself and the result happens to be something delicious. So, I can't be too happy because that feels so fucked-up to grin with glee at the delicious baked goods that's the result of a teen dude trying to be emotionally healthy. I'm relieved he found a way to handle it, but I just wish he wasn't hurting so much.

"Did you make it already?" I ask him. We're walking down 23rd Street together.

He shakes his head. "Nope, not yet. Why?"

I look into my half-empty coffee cup. "Want me to help?"

"*You* want to help *me* make black sesame white chocolate chip cookies?" He gives me a suspicious grin and it's then that I notice how tall he got recently. He's almost a head taller than me now.

"Oh, come on, it can't be that hard if *you're* doing it," I joke.

He shrugs and grins at me. "Okay, I'll bring everything over tonight, then. We can make dessert for everyone."

I feel relieved, knowing he hasn't already made the cookies.

After a beat, I look up at him. "Are you okay, though?"

He nods. "Just trying to do more than nothing. The house feels so slow and stagnant lately."

"You know you could just call me if you feel bored." Steven never wants to be a burden to anyone. He doesn't realize he could never be a burden to me.

He bumps my shoulder as thanks. "So where are you headed until dinner?"

"Greenpoint to go to some thrift stores to find a dress."

"For the party?"

"Gala," I correct him. "And yes. Want to join?"

"Definitely not. But we can go to the subway together."

Later, I'm walking around Brooklyn with my phone tightly clutched in my hand, opened to the image that mirrors the look I'm going for. I enter the first thrift shop on my map of today's drop-ins and rifle through each rack, carefully but swiftly. I've done this a hundred times before. I know which shops in Brooklyn highlight a more vintage-clothing-only look versus the ones with a hodgepodge of furniture, accessories, and clothes. And if Brooklyn offers nothing for this dress, there are tons of other places on the Lower East Side and even some in Queens that I can check out after.

I go into focus mode where I'm aware of how little I'm blinking because I can't miss anything if I'm looking for the perfect ensemble, head to toe. Here and there, I glance at my phone to track my time. If I don't, I could get lost in the clothes and accessories for hours that could turn into a whole weekend. I feel nervous and I hug my tote a little tighter. Not wanting to miss another amazing dress like the purple satin one, I actually brought my debit card with me, the one that has all my savings from years of Lunar New Year money, birthday gifts, and petty cash I got for odd jobs. If I got mugged, today would be the one day it'd suck really badly.

One rack looks promising and I walk over, my pace slightly slower, feeling hopeful at the number of beautiful dresses hanging there, squished in between two columns stacked with purses. There are tons of nice-looking outfits, but that's all they are. Nice. It's not *perfect*, and for the gala, I know I need to find The Dress. An hour later, I'm walking toward a new spot on my map. I'm running out of time. I speed up my process, swiftly looking through racks and accessories on shelves. Nothing again.

There's a starred place on my maps, one that I've been wanting to visit but I haven't let myself because I don't want to go home crushed. That shop showed me that thrift stores can also be unaffordable. It's only two blocks away, and when I turn the corner, just the sight of the store excites me. I walk in and the air feels different somehow. More promising. Here I take my time, carefully sifting through each designer dress gingerly, not wanting to harm any of the delicate fabric.

Then I see it.

I grin in spite of myself. My intuition is spot on and there's no better feeling. It's like I can't feel my feet anymore and I'm just floating off the ground as I slowly make my way closer to the dress. It's the most stunning dress I've ever laid eyes on: a strapless, peplumstyle emerald-green dress from none other than Christian Dior. And I know I need it.

"Stunning, right?" the store owner asks. She has white hair and wears colorful earrings.

"It's gorgeous."

She takes it out of its casing. "Try it on," she says, leading me to the fitting room.

I feel like I can't breathe as I step into it. Not because it's tight, but because it's completely magical trying on something so delicate and beautiful. Like it can't possibly belong to me. Once zipped, I turn 360 degrees, loving the way the dress spins with me. It's a perfect fit. The fabric feels heavy but in a regal way, and it's structured so it doesn't drag or lose shape. I look in the mirror and gasp. I feel more beautiful than I ever have before. It's too long, but our local Korean dry cleaners would be able to tailor it for me.

Finally, I let myself look at the price tag. I close my eyes for a quick second as I flip the tag over, hoping, just maybe, that it's in my budget. Of course it's not, though. At 375 dollars, it's almost 80 percent of my savings. All on one dress. My heart drops to the floor. I can feel the spicy tingles in my nose as my eyes water. I pull myself together.

It's for the MITI Gala.

I shouldn't. I know I shouldn't. But I think again about that purple satin dress I let go of. How I settled for a crop top that made me look like ketchup and mustard. The leather cap I couldn't buy.

Everyone else has second homes or designer bags. I don't know how long I'm in that fitting room for, but eventually, I force myself to change back into my boring clothes. But this dress could change everything. This is the gala that could solidify my career and help my family, and my outfit will need to play the part. It's an investment, right?

"I'll take it," I tell the woman at the register. It's the same person who helped me initially.

"I knew you'd like this one. It goes so well with your skin tone, too," she says.

"Thanks," I say, smiling politely. I try not to overthink what she just said. I guess green goes with . . . yellow? Would this dress not look good on white people? I sigh. *She was trying to say something nice, just move on*, I tell myself. I have bigger things to worry about right now.

I insert my debit card as I let go of years of saved-up money for this dress. But I'll make it worth it. I thank her and rush to my final stop: the dry cleaners by my building.

The bell hanging on the door rings as I push it open. "Hello?" The ahjusshi who owns the cleaner pops up behind the table. "Annyeonghaseyo," I say, bowing.

"Why are you all sweaty?" he asks gruffly in Korean upon seeing me.

"I ran here from the subway stop. Ahjusshi, can you make this dress shorter?" I throw the big dress on the counter and his eyes can't hide his surprise.

"What are you doing wearing something like this? Do your parents know?" He's nosy like most older Koreans.

"Nae, of course they know." I try to maintain eye contact to not raise suspicion.

He looks at me through wide-rimmed glasses like he knows I'm lying straight to his face, but he just grunts.

After measuring me and deciding how much to hem, he tells me to study hard and not have too much fun. He has hemmed and tailored a lot of pieces I've thrifted over the years and I'm pretty sure he knows this is a secret from my parents. But besides the old-man commentary, he's actually really good to me. He barely takes any money for the tailoring and sends me home with rice cakes he keeps in his freezer. "Hobak injeolmi," he says, handing me a rice cake square. "Defrost for ten minutes before eating. Eat more, too. Be healthy," he says, with that same gruffness.

I bow to him again. "Gamsahabnida." I wave and begin running home. I'm already late to start my jjigae before Steven and his mom come over.

"You seem to be in a good mood," my mom says, smiling. She reaches over me to grab the spatula as she prepares a few banchan side dishes for the table. "Which is rare when you make jjigae," she teases. The pork belly is defrosting next to us.

"I didn't realize you thought I was such a grinch," I joke.

"When you're cooking? Yeah, you are."

I roll my eyes as I finish putting the rest of the chopped potatoes into my boiling soybean paste stew. It's probably one of the easiest Korean dishes to make, only second to miyukgook, which is literally just boiling seaweed and meat in water, but I still take my time, careful to not ruin the steps I've memorized by heart.

"I'm almost done, maybe that's why I'm happy," I answer. The guilt circles inside me and I ignore it.

The doorbell rings as I raise the fire on the stove.

"Just in time," my mom replies, walking out of the kitchen.

I insa to Steven's mom, bowing a respectful forty-five degrees. "Annyeonghaseyo."

She rubs my back lovingly and I warm at her touch. Carol-eemo always feels like a second mom to me—a more affectionate one.

"Need help?" Steven asks, peering past my shoulder to inhale the aroma of the stew.

I push him back with my elbow gently. "Nope."

"So," he whispers while our moms are chatting, "I've been thinking."

"About?" My eyes are focused on all the vegetables dancing in the boiling water.

"*MITI*," he whispers even quieter. He's being totally sarcastic, the way he's saying it, and I burst into laughter.

"This isn't *Mission: Impossible*."

"Oh, it's not?" he says teasingly.

"Okay, maybe close. So what's your big plan?"

"You'll know when I mention it at dinner."

"You're annoying, you know that, right?"

Steven nods gleefully and I'm relieved that he seems to be

having a good day. Ever since his dad left, it's like a light went out in his heart, and though it sometimes comes back in the most childish ways, like this joke, when it does, it makes me so happy. Even though I don't know how to express that to him. "Don't spend all your energy on jjigae, you still need to be my assistant for the cookies."

"I know this recipe by heart, don't you worry."

Halfway through dinner, Steven leans over and whispers something into Jojo's ear and she covers her mouth with her hand and giggles. She giggles at everything, but I can't help but want to know what he's saying to her. I shoot him a glare.

"Come on, Jojo, tell the grown-ups," he insists.

"Steven and Sharty is going to Kings!"

Everyone looks up, puzzled. He whispers in her ear again.

"Kingston," she repeats confidently.

I stare intently into the small side dishes to avoid eye contact.

"You're going where?" Carol-eemo asks in Korean.

"It's for our AP Lit class. It's that all-day trip and we get back the next day. Damn it, I left the parent consent form at school. Char, did you bring yours?"

I look up and open my mouth then close it again. And open it again. "I, uh—the form—I." Clearing my throat to buy an extra second, I continue, "No, dang. I left mine in my locker." Under the table, I kick Steven gingerly just in case I accidentally hit someone else. When I know it's him based on his reaction, I stretch out my toes a bit and pinch his skin hard.

He kicks me back and we're even. But I'm grateful. Anything

that pertains to school or school events is a yes for them.

"What's the trip for?" my dad asks.

"Something about old white authors in Kingston." Steven says this with a casual confidence that doesn't create more questions, thankfully.

We offer to do the dishes as the parents go lounge in the living room with coffee and Jojo watches a show on our small TV. Steven's bringing me the plates from the dining table and I'm soaking them and getting started on the water cups. A few minutes later, he joins me and rinses the suds from the glasses I hand him.

"Really, old white authors?"

"It worked, didn't it?"

Steven Tetris-places all the clean dishes and cups in the dishwasher (aka our dish rack) as I turn to the pots and pans.

"It did. What if they asked for names?"

He grins. "I would've probably been like, 'Char, what did Ms. Carter say again?'"

I shake my head. "Well, assuming all that's left is to make a fake parent consent form, I guess I'm all clear to go."

"You don't sound as excited as you should be after all this work you put me through."

"I *am* excited, but also a little nervous, I guess."

He's quiet and I look at him through my periphery.

"I hope it's worth it, Char."

And I know he's not just talking about the gala. "It will be."

Steven methodically prepares all the ingredients and lays them out on the kitchen counter. There's not a ton of space next to our rice cooker and stovetop, but everything is arranged like in a cooking show. "Here, put these on." He hands me a pair of disposable kitchen gloves, like the ones Carol-eemo uses when she makes kimchi. He kneads the dough that he premade while I put on the gloves.

"Can't we just mix it with a spoon?"

"Yeah, but it's more fun this way." We dust some flour on the counter so the dough doesn't overly stick and start mixing in white chocolate chips.

"Gentle, gentle!" Steven grabs my hand instinctively and shakes my wrist so my fingers loosen up. "Like this."

When the dough is finished and he sprinkles a bit of sesame powder and *lightly* mixes it in, the sweet smell of cookie dough is too much for me to resist. I quickly grab a tiny bit and eat it. Steven pokes my ribs. "Hey!"

"Oh, come on, like you never do this." I turn around to shove some dough into his mouth and it's only when we're face-to-face that we both seem to realize how close our bodies are. He draws back, but still not enough for the vibe to disappear. A shyness kindles and dances between us. I open my mouth to say something and close it when nothing comes out.

Steven clears his throat. "Okay, fine, give me some of that dough," he finally says, grinning. I feed him some of the mixture on my glove and focus back on scooping the rest out onto the trays. Before anything can happen between us, we both go into the living room and join Jojo on the couch while the cookies bake in the oven.

CHAPTER SEVEN

Throughout the week, I post regularly on my stories and feed to build up momentum leading to the MITI Gala. It feels like muscle memory to me now. Like my body knows to wake up and open Instagram. On a particularly bold Wednesday night, I post a story I've been thinking about since my thrifting day on Sunday. It's a photo of me in the red Heinz top, one I took before the event started. I write a caption that's maybe as honest as I can be right now, tag the thrift shop I got it from, and within ten minutes, Audrey texts me.

audrey
Omg I didn't know you thrifted the
cute top you wore that day?!

yeah! lucky findddd

I love it!
I'm so bad at thrifting. Teach me!

I don't tell Audrey that it isn't a choice for me or that I have massive impostor syndrome going into the gala. I'm not telling *anyone* I thrifted my gala dress, but that first event was lower stakes. Still, I'm a little proud. For once, of all the clothes I've thrifted before and posted, I was honest about where I got it from. In a way it's like honoring the clothes, which deserve it. The cherry on top is the follower count of my profile that keeps growing. I got thirty new accounts since the story about my *Fall into Florals* outfit, and I go to bed that night with a sense of validation. I know this will be worth it. *There's good in this*, I think.

The next day, Steven and I spend our free period in the computer lab, drafting up a fake parent consent form, which doesn't take long with all the resources available online.

"Don't let anyone see you," I whisper.

"You whispering makes it all the more suspicious. And no offense, but no one cares enough to snoop."

"Okay, true."

"Aaaaand, done." Steven hits Print.

As we walk out of school together, I look carefully at the sheet, rereading each word, double-checking for spelling and typos, anything that hints that this is fake. Not that I think my parents would even read it that closely.

"It's pretty good," I admit, not catching any issues.

"Right? Should we go into business together?"

"What kind of business?"

"The kind that makes fake parent consent forms for students to get away with things they shouldn't be trying to do anyway?" he says with his goofy grin.

"Not very lucrative."

"About the same success rate as making it big on Instagram?"

I roll my eyes at him but he throws his arms around me and smiles sweetly. "I'm glad you talked about your vintage dress."

My eyes go round. "So you *do* read my Instagram!"

He shrugs. "Just here and there, when I'm extremely bored. But good for you."

I glower at him jokingly. "Thank you."

I feel a surge of confidence boost through me all the way home, but when I open the door to my apartment, a heaviness replaces it. I sense it instantly when I see the lights are all turned off at four p.m. In the early fall, it's late enough that our home feels dark and hollow, and it sucks the light out of me, too. I already know what I'm going to walk in on in the master bedroom.

It's always the late afternoon when my mom gets like this. When the reality of her goals unrealized hits her. My dad, my naive dad, considers it healthy to have dreams, hopes. I consider it a burden.

I rush to the kitchen and grab my favorite mug, the one I'm *always* holding when she wants to talk about her troubles. I rub the ceramic Band-Aid decorating the exterior, willing it to make my soul feel lighter, less pained that I can't do more for my family. Sometimes, I'm already home when the mood hits her. I can always sense it in the way she calls my name, so I ask for a minute and quickly put a cup of Korean coffee mix into this specific mug.

I was walking through Greenpoint with Steven a few years ago and there were vendors lined inside a market. Steven bought a seven-hundred-piece puzzle of baked goods and I bought this mug. I often think about the ceramicist who sold it to me. She overheard me telling Steven I couldn't afford to spend thirty-eight dollars on a mug but I was unable to let go of it. She lowered her voice and told me she functions on a sliding scale and that I can pay however much I'm willing and able. It felt like such a New York moment for me. I always wonder if more people cheat her or if they respect her system. I hope it's the latter and that she's still selling her art.

I pour a cold cup of coffee into the mug before making my way to her bedroom, anxiety pressing on me like a stack of rocks.

"Umma? You okay?" I can't ignore her even though I want to sometimes. I have a hard time focusing on much else until I talk to her and help her feel better.

My mom rolls over to face me from the bed. "Oh, you're home. Come sit, cheotjae ddal," she says. *My first daughter.* These are the days she's expressive. Usually the only days. "Your dad's joint pains flared up again, did you know? He had to leave work because of it and he went to the doctor." This is why she probably had to work that shift last week. There's a pregnant pause and fear wells up in me.

"Will he not be able to work at all anymore?"

My mom nods. "Not as much, anyway. Maybe something from his desk if he can find work." She sighs slowly and sits up. For the next twenty minutes, she goes on and on about what we could achieve—buying a building in this one part of LIC that isn't developed yet, or in deep Brooklyn that we could afford if we save up enough, if we work harder, spend less. She always has so many ideas—none are realistic. My fists are in balls by my sides. She doesn't realize she's the one who should spend less, not us. She's the one dissatisfied with her life, not us.

But I don't say anything to crush her spirits. I don't dare let her know how I really feel. It would kill her. Or maybe it would kill me, if I couldn't make her happy.

"Seoyoung-ah, you know Evan's umma bought that building in Elmhurst a few years ago? The price went up by almost two hundred thousand dollars!" Her eyes are sparkling as if she's imagining herself with the same plan. Not acknowledging the big difference—that Evan's dad left his family with enough life insurance money to invest when he passed.

These are moments my mom talks more than ever, when she's sharing what we could become. "I'm going to meet with her sometime to talk about it more," she continues. "It'll take a few years to get the money together, but once we do this, it'll definitely get easier. We'll have passive income, Seoyoung-ah, and we can move to a bigger apartment one day."

I nod a few times, feigning interest. "Sounds perfect, Umma."

"Jojo will have more space to run around."

I force a smile, hiding what I want to say. *Is our family not good enough for you? Why do you need so much?* I just want us to be stable, to be comfortable and not trying to "make it." *We have enough, we're okay,* I want to tell her. But deep inside me, a part of me I sometimes hate, I want to make it all possible for my mom and dad. So they can finally rest. So she can finally say she did it. Then maybe I can stop trying so hard, too.

She squeezes my hand as she pushes herself up off our bed to go prepare dinner. I remind myself that my mom isn't looking for an answer from me. She just wants someone to listen to her pipe dreams. I stay on the sofa alone as I hear the sound of spatulas and ladles in the kitchen. My chest feels like it's been tied up by a thick rope and I can't untangle it. My mom's unhappiness is the one ache in my heart I've never been able to numb. As I take the last sip of coffee, I stare at the painted words inside: *refill as needed*. If only it were that easy.

At dinner, my dad's quieter than usual. My eyes follow his arms that disappear under the table. My gaze drops to his fingers, gingerly massaging his knees. My poor appa. I wish I could make his ailment go away and bring his vivacious energy back. My mom is silent, too, so I wonder if they got into a fight. Ever since Jojo was born, they haven't really fought in front of us, not in that loud obvious way, anyway. It's like my mom became a whole new kind of mother when she was born, because prior to that, I saw them fight too many times to count. I'm glad, though, that Jojo will hopefully be saved from witnessing it. It's scarring. I bet the silent treatment in front of kids can be equally scarring, but maybe less memory-searing.

"So, Appa," I say, twirling a fork around my spaghetti, "you find any good vinyls lately?" He claims to be a vinyl nerd and bought a janky record player last Christmas. My mom was pissed, and for months, anytime he played it, she'd sort of storm around the house, angrily doing dishes, slamming doors, and sweeping really vigorously.

His creased eyes light up at my question and he looks at me, smiling. "Actually, I recently got hands on a *Rarities* album from 2006. Looks vintage. Very nice."

"The Beatles?" I ask.

He nods. "Want to listen?"

Jojo interjects by slamming her small hands on the table. "Put it on, Appa, put it on!"

"No." My mom's voice is firm. And cold.

I see my dad's spirit wither again, but he doesn't say anything.

"Why not?" I ask.

"Dinner time is family time. We need to be talking and sharing, not listening to music or watching shows."

"Umma, watching TV and listening to background music is—"

"Umma said no," she repeats in Korean.

No one says anything back.

I turn my attention toward Jojo. I read that children may not understand fully but are very perceptive about vibes. Joking and chatting, I try to lighten the mood, at least for her.

Toward the end of a somewhat quiet dinner, I slip my dad the form. "This is the parent consent form for Kingston." I open and close my fingers under the table to give myself something to actively focus on. For how many times I've lied to my parents, it hasn't gotten much easier.

My dad scribbles his signature on the line and passes it back to me. "Sounds fun. You sleeping there?"

"Yeah!" I know I sound too excited.

they signed the form :D

steven

Nice. Got mine signed too.

why?

Man if you murdered someone,

you'd be caught so fast.

ohhhh right doi. lol

👍

Are you excited?

i am actually!!!

not that u care but I

found THE perfect dress

Haha. Send pics.

Wait. I did NOT mean

that in a weird way.

omg you pervy perv

hehe i will

There's a corner of my bed where my stuffed owl sits. It's the corner I escape to when I'm stressed and I'm sitting here now, knees tucked, chin resting. The Most Influential Teen Influencer Gala is tomorrow and there's an overwhelming sense of determination building inside me. I need to help our family.

◆◆◆

The next morning, I'm going through my daily stories scrolling and I see Audrey's: It's a snapshot of her morning face with no makeup, coffee in hand, smiling. It feels genuinely unfiltered, not unfiltered as a brand. There was an immediate sense of trust when I met her at the event last month, like she was already someone I knew. I post a picture of my latte and pastry from Chanson last week.

My mom and Jojo are out for the day at dance class. I get into the kitchen and my dad is sitting in the dining nook with his newspaper and a cup of boricha. He's the only non–coffee drinker, always preferring his Korean barley tea.

"Hi, Appa. Do you want a croissant?" Trader Joe's mini croissants are a staple in our home.

He nods. "Seoyoung-ah, how did you sleep?" His eyes smile as he takes a sip of his tea.

I shrug. "Okay."

"Excited for your trip today?"

I inhale a deep breath and let it out quietly. "Yep. Very." I *hate* lying to my dad. He's so trusting, that's why it's so shitty.

"You get some fresh air, okay?" He beckons me over just so he can plant a kiss on my head.

"Is your knee okay, Appa?"

It's his turn to sigh. "It'll be okay. Don't worry about me, okay?" he says in Korean.

"But are you and Umma okay?"

His smile never reaches his eyes. "Yes, yes, Seoyoung-ah, no worry, okay? Be happy? Umma and Appa really okay."

He's desperate for me to not peek into their cracks. I manage a nod and head back to my room to pretend to pack. The event starts at five p.m., so it's just enough time to leisurely gather everything I'll need for my outfit and slowly head toward the venue.

After saying goodbye to my dad and texting my mom, I pick up my dress from the cleaners, take the E train into the city, and wander around, on the lookout for a restaurant or café. There's an Italian place on the corner with a white awning. I step through the doorframe where a hostess in a tight dress greets me.

"Hi, how may I help you?"

"Um, hi. Could I please use your restroom?"

She makes a face that's supposed to resemble pity. "So sorry, but our restroom is for customers only."

"Oh. Okay. Thanks."

She smiles with her lips, but she's just waiting for me to leave.

There's another restaurant one block over, but I've lost the confidence to ask.

I find a nearby Starbucks, a spot that I really *don't* want to get ready in, but I also know that the bathroom there is not restricted to paying customers. Reluctantly, I pull open the door and squeeze in through a throng of patrons waiting for their orders and find my way toward a different line—the one for the bathroom. I'm seventh, which isn't that bad, considering it's free for anyone in New York.

Twenty minutes later, I'm up. I panic, knowing I'm going to be here for a long time, but also knowing there's four new people who have shown up to line up behind me. I turn around to the man directly behind me. "Um. I'm going to be in there for . . . a long time." I pause and he says nothing. "Sorry!"

He shrugs.

The bathroom floor is wet in certain spots, and I avoid stepping in them, unsure if it's urine or water. I gingerly change into my outfit as carefully as possible, not wanting to step on the floor in socks as I lift one leg after the other and pull off my pants. In a hopefully record-breaking seven minutes, I'm in my outfit and the first layer of foundation is on my face. A vicious knock comes at the door.

So much for the shrug. "One sec!"

As fast as I can, I apply some eye shadow on my lids before another knock comes for me. *Forget it.* I sweep my belongings into my plastic bag and open the door. It's not the same man I talked to and there's only one bathroom. "Seriously?" A girl one head and a half taller than me has her hand on her hip. "This isn't your bedroom."

We lock eyes. "Yeah, no shit. Sometimes, you just end up needing to get ready in a bathroom, okay?"

She rolls her eyes and pushes past me. "Whatever."

I finish the rest of my makeup on an outdoor bench with my handheld mirror and it's not too difficult, given how many times I've done it in the subway before. And even though there's dried bird poop next to me and my hair is pulled into a bun so tight my head already hurts, I feel like royalty. The dress has a bit of shimmer to it, and the bodice is a different shade from the rest of the dress and hugs me just right at the waist. Thick layers of eyeliner and chunky gold knot earrings give my delicate princess vibe a modern twist, just the way I like it. I toss the plastic bag into a nearby garbage can and walk confidently toward Lotte Palace.

CHAPTER EIGHT

"Deep breaths, Char. You got this," I say to myself. But as I get closer and closer to the venue, my hands are shaking and my confidence is disappearing. I squeeze them together, willing them to calm down. I want to fit in so badly tonight.

I see the Lotte New York Palace Hotel from the end of the block and I watch as influencers I recognize make their way past the red velvet ropes and into the lobby. I tell myself that I belong here, too. One more deep breath and I walk past the main entrance and stop by a giant mirror to do some touch-ups on my face. As much of a pain as it was to get ready in a Starbucks and then outside, I'm glad I didn't do it here. Audrey and I agreed to meet by the main entrance, and I scan the area, looking for her.

"Charlotte!" a voice calls from a distance. I look and see Audrey waving and rushing toward me with a big smile on her face. I feel a wave of gratitude wash over me as she comes over. We made plans to have a sleepover at her apartment after the gala, which to her is just for fun but for me is lifesaving.

"Wow, I *love* your dress," I tell her. She's wearing a beautiful sequined blush dress that falls to the floor, trailing behind her just enough to turn heads in awe. She looks like an actual celebrity. Her hair is up in a chic high pony and she has a graduated diamond necklace on with matching earrings.

"Thanks, I got lucky with such an incredible design team."

"Whose is it?"

"Celine. Look at you, though. You look like a modern but vintage Barbie. Whose is yours?"

"It's Dior," I tell her. "Custom vintage."

"Ugh, I knew it. Custom dresses are the best, aren't they? It looks so good on you."

Okay, so maybe it's not *really* custom but tailoring is technically custom. Today I just need to be royalty, even if I have to lie to Audrey. But as Audrey links my arm with hers and we walk toward the ballroom, guilt washes over me. I know she wouldn't have judged me at all if I told her I thrifted it. But I would've judged myself.

I push it out of my mind and focus on tonight. In front of the main room where the gala is taking place, a sparkling black step and repeat is propped up and influencers are having their photos taken. When it's our turn, photographers flash their cameras as Audrey and I wave. We stand in front of the backdrop, posing in different positions next to each other and it's a moment I want to hold on to forever. It feels every bit as glamorous as I imagined it to be as we stand side by side, shoulders slightly slung back, turning with our backs to the camera. The tension I had building up in my chest disappears and I'm pumped with excitement and endorphins by the blinding lights and the special treatment. This is probably why so many celebrities end up depressed. How do you even come down from this high? Everything else pales in comparison. I already don't want to leave.

We make our way inside. The ballroom looks incredible, decked out in romantic and dreamy centerpieces with dim lighting. The bar is creatively curated with fifteen different mocktail options and hot beverages for the chilly early evening. I order an espresso mocktini and Audrey gets a virgin mojito. She takes some photos of me at the bar and we snap some selfies before posting them online. Surrounding us, everyone is doing similarly. My drink is beautiful, with a few coffee beans as the drink topper and a sprinkle of sparkling sugar on top.

The energy is loud and electric, and the coffee from the mocktini has my blood buzzing even more. Most people are standing and chatting, and there's a photo-booth line that's insanely long. I see the party guests using Instagram Live to show everything in real time, which I remember influencers doing last year because I obsessively followed anyone who would show me a glimpse of it.

And now I'm on the other side. It feels surreal.

After we sit at our assigned tables, I open Instagram and am shaking with nerves to see if I got more followers since coming to MITI. More than *fifty* new followers. I try not to grin like an idiot but it's hard not to. As I look around me, I feel like I've finally been accepted into an exclusive club I've been working toward.

As the opening speaker greets us, everyone at my table cheers with our mocktails. One of the girls introduces herself as Lena Spencer and the other two are influencers I follow, @SwanGomez and @TanyaLB. We exchange usernames on Instagram and make small talk about where we go to school, what we want to do one day, and vacation plans during break.

"I'm actually trying to be an actor," Audrey reveals shyly. "Well, eventually, anyway."

"I could really see you as an actress," I tell her encouragingly.

"I've had a few auditions," she admits, "but none that worked out." She shrugs. "I'll keep trying, but it's sometimes embarrassing, putting myself out there so much and not having anything really stick."

"Yeah, but you did it with social media," Tanya points out. "Just keep being bold."

"It'll stick one day" Swan adds, smiling as she runs a hand through her sweep of thick brown hair.

A guilty part of me is surprised at how kind these influencers are. Isn't the world of social media supposed to be full of fakers and cyberbullying? People always say it's only glamorous on the outside, that the shit that goes on behind the scenes is not worth selling your identity for. But everything I'm experiencing tonight has been the perfect happy glitzy glamour I've been dreaming of. Maybe people say that because they're jealous, the way people do when they see a huge house they can't afford. So many Korean ahjummas are like, "Who needs that kind of space?" while they're probably thinking, "I'd *love* that kind of space."

We pick from a dinner menu of filet mignon, fish, or vegetarian before an assortment of side dishes and appetizers and more mocktails grace our table. Halfway through my branzino, someone walks up to Audrey, who's making her way through her vegetarian dish.

The person introduces herself as a reporter from *CLIMB*, a high-caliber digital magazine about people in leadership roles and executives and how they "climbed" their way.

"Audrey, I wanted to talk to you about your recent experience, if you're open?" the reporter says.

"Sorry, could you clarify what experience you're alluding to?" Audrey asks.

The reporter, dressed in a black pencil skirt and a semi-sheer blouse, clears her throat. She looks uncomfortable. "In one of your recent videos, you shared some of your thoughts about the rise in anti-Asian hate crime. Is this something you're open to speaking with me more about?"

Audrey puts her fork down and folds her cloth napkin. "Sure."

I sense Audrey knew what the reporter was referring to from the beginning. She folds her hands together on her lap, as if to compose herself. "I think the first step is to address it head-on and call it for what it is. There were influencers at an event who were being racist, openly and directly, about me."

The reporter nods. "Yes, absolutely. You're right." She looks down at her heels, probably to hide the blush of shame.

Audrey softens up and relaxes. "Actually, I wouldn't even have known about it had it not been for my new friend, Charlotte." She gestures toward me and the reporter gives me a small smile.

"Charlotte Goh, right?"

I nod, my heart thumping. *She knows me!*

"I watched the video you posted, too. It was really moving."

"Thank you."

"How did you feel, overhearing that?"

My lips purse inadvertently. "Not great. I mean, it sort of lit a fire under me to get more out there and not be so afraid to speak out publicly. I guess it's a form of reverse psychology, if the psychologist is a racist."

Audrey stifles a laugh and chimes in. "It might've been eye-opening in the ugliest of ways for Charlotte, but it wasn't a first for me. There's a reason I turn off direct messages and sometimes even comments for periods of time. I've been messaged, texted, and emailed some nasty things from all sorts of people in this world. It'll never stop, but the least we can do is keep speaking up."

The reporter drags on the interview longer than necessary, and by the time she leaves, Audrey looks at me. "Mocktail time?"

"Absolutely."

At the bar, more girls flock to Audrey, trying to snatch a minute of her time. I knew she was a big deal, but I didn't realize how big. I watch her from a few feet away, politely exchanging hellos and giving hugs to others when appropriate. She's genuine in every interaction, addressing each acquaintance or friend by name. I'm in awe of the way she exudes a level of humility and confidence, while the innermost part of my heart craves the attention she gets. Maybe one day I'll get there, too.

"Piña colada, please?" I ask the bartender. "And a Cheeky Craze for my friend."

A guy slides into a barstool on my left. And I know him. Everyone knows him. It's Alan Travis Smith, influencer turned actor. I saw one of the movies Alan was in—a rom-com about a girl who's trying to win him over. It was probably his biggest hit and his popularity grew massively after that.

He's attractive in that mysterious way, with broad shoulders and toned arms. His eyes are grayish-green and his long lashes emphasize the depth of his features. I want to say something but nothing comes to mind. His presence feels overwhelming, in a way, like you can't turn your attention away. I'm starstruck and I realize that some people are meant to be actors. When he gets his drink, he pulls out a flask from his jacket and pours some into his glass. When we lock eyes, he discreetly offers his flask to me and I shake my head no. Alan raises his drink to me and I mimic him, but there are no words exchanged.

When Audrey escapes her fans, I hold out her drink and she looks at me gratefully.

"Thanks. Ugh, wish it was spiked." I consider telling her that Alan has a flask, but I don't. "Hey, one of the girls is having an after-party at her place. Do you want to go?"

I nod. "Sure." I hop off the barstool, and as we head back to our table, I turn around to see if I can spot Alan again—purely out of curiosity—and see that he's already looking directly at me. We lock eyes before I avert my gaze and ignore the goose bumps rising on my skin.

Audrey and I spend the rest of the gala together, wandering

around tables, admiring decorations, getting our pictures taken, and meeting other influencers. We even speak to a few more reporters, all about similar things, and with each interview, I feel more confident talking about the incident. No, we didn't get physically assaulted and no one was harmed, but it was still a racist attack and it's still worth discussing. And all throughout the evening, my follower count increases.

Too soon, people start trickling out and heading to the after-party at Lizzie Chen's apartment. We wait outside to grab a cab even though I'm not ready to leave yet. I don't think I'll *ever* be ready to leave. I remember this night last year, telling myself that everything looks better online, that the event can't be that perfect, but I was wrong. Tonight has been a dream and I'm devastated that it's already ending.

Lizzie's apartment looks like a showroom for the rich and famous. It's a three-story penthouse of a tall building near Grand Central and the elevator opens up into her foyer. There's a DJ already going, and snacks and drinks are lined up throughout the kitchen. It might be my first legitimate after-party (or any party, ever), and I take it all in slowly. Girls and boys are snug on the long sofas, a few are lingering outside on the balcony with their coats on, and the rest of the party seems to be upstairs, where it's the loudest. I can feel the bass reverberating through the apartment. The view of the Chrysler Building is the backdrop of the enormous living room.

I can barely hear Audrey as we take our coats off and toss them on a chair that's been long buried by other coats and bags.

"What?" I shout over the music.

She points up. "Upstairs!"

I nod and we weave through people to make our way up a spiral set of wooden stairs.

At the top of the steps, as I try to push past a few others, a guy turns around and rams into me, his drink cascading down my dress. At first I think it's water, but the smell of liquor wafts up my nose and I make a face. *Thank god* it wasn't a colored drink. I can't even imagine how much it'd cost to get a stain out of this perfect dress.

The guy holds my elbow. "Shit, sorry," he says. It's the same green-gray eyes that belong to Alan Travis Smith. "Oh," he says, recognizing me, "hey."

My annoyance of an almost-stain and the stench of alcohol all over me dissipates too fast. "Hi," I say, smiling. There it is again: goose bumps.

"Sorry again." He grabs cocktail napkins from the bar a few steps away and brings them back to me. "I'd help you, but—"

"Nope, I got it," I say, laughing awkwardly as I take the napkins. "Thanks," I add as I dab as much as I can off my chest and the tops of my boobs.

"You know Lizzie?" It's loud and he leans in so I can hear him. He smells like boy (in a good way) and beer.

I shake my head. "Friend of Audrey's."

He puts his hand on my lower back. "Do you want me to get you a drink?"

I shake my head again. "Nope, I'm okay!" I look around for

Audrey and spot her on the upstairs terrace outside. "I'm going to go join her," I say, but our eyes stay locked on each other for an extended beat.

Before he has a chance to respond, I squirm through a few people near us and join the group of girls outside.

Audrey waves at me as I join her. I didn't know being seated outside could feel so cozy under the heated lamps. "Kinda lost you there for a bit," she teases knowingly. My cheeks flush pink. She introduces me to Lizzie and the rest of the guests lounging around on the outdoor sofa.

A few of them have changed out of their fancy dresses and into casual clothes while others are still in their ball gowns. My eyes drop down to their "casual" outfits—all brands I recognize with even more expensive bags and accessories—and I fail to tame my insecurities at the leggings and Target shirt in my purse. Even my thrifted Dior dress feels less special than it did an hour ago. I wish deep down more than anything that I just *didn't care*. No, actually, I wish I had all of what they have and was cool enough to not care. That it didn't matter to me who wore what. How truly liberating it must be for people who actually just don't give a flying fuck. I hate that I have expectations I can't meet. The same ones everyone else seems to have so much more easily. Even the easiness of their friendship with one another seems out of reach for me.

"—at my uncle's place, in Newport," Lizzie is saying. They're talking about spontaneous weekend trips they could take together.

"That would be amazing!"

"Oh my god, or that spa upstate in the Catskills?"

"I've been there. It's super cute. Could even be a day trip. We have a place nearby."

I recognize Audrey's voice, but everyone else's blends together as the group drones on about places they've been, places they plan to go to, weekend homes they have scattered throughout the East Coast. They're talking about dates they're free. I have nothing to add, and I muster up whatever fake energy I have to smile and share in the excitement while my insides hate me. Every minute I stay seated on that sofa feels like I'm prey in an open field, waiting to be caught. Or maybe they already know that I don't belong here. I stand up too fast and the blood rushes to my head and the group falls silent.

"S-sorry," I stutter. "Got really thirsty all of a sudden."

"For water or for something else?" a girl says jokingly.

"More like some*one* else!" another girl adds.

I feign laughter and go back inside. In such a big apartment, there must be one unused space somewhere. I go downstairs and see another set of stairs and go down those, too. There's a garden terrace and I open it, satisfied to see that it's empty. Finally relaxed, I sit down on the fake grass and lean my head back against the door, letting the chilly fall air slap my face freely.

"Knock, knock," a voice says some time later.

I manage to move my eyeballs to the side to confirm the familiar voice, but I know who it is.

"Can I join you?" Alan asks.

"Are you following me?" It's a lame attempt at a joke.

Alan grins as he sits down a few feet away from me and mimics my pose, resting against the glass pane. "Why are you being all loner-ish?"

After a full day of trying to fit in and say the right thing, I'm tired. And there's no point even trying to fake it with a celebrity. He can probably sniff out posers easier than dogs can sniff out food. In the quiet darkness, I don't even have the energy to mask it anymore. "I am."

"You are?"

"A loner."

"Pft. I don't buy that."

I shrug. "You don't need to."

He takes a long, slow sip of his drink. An impulsive desire washes over me. "Can I have some?"

Alan passes the cup to me. "Not even going to ask what's in it?"

I purse my lips. "If it'll help me feel better, then I'm game." I stare down into the brown liquid sloshing around the red Solo cup. There's not much left, so I down the rest of the drink in one big gulp.

"Whoa," he says.

My throat burns. My insides suddenly feel like lava and my face contorts into itself. "Oh *god*, what's in this?"

I hand him back the cup and he seems shocked while registering that it's now empty. "Can't believe you just chugged my entire cup of whiskey. It's a good one, too."

My mouth yearns for a chaser. "That was disgusting."

"Whiskey isn't really meant to be chugged like beer. Here." He hands me a soda and our fingers graze each other as he passes the can to me.

Within minutes, I start to feel relaxed. I can't see any stars above, thanks to the lights of New York City, but the sky looks so heavy it feels like I can touch it. A few minutes of silence pass between us.

"Hey." A gentle hand holds my elbow.

I turn my head to face him. Alan's voice sounds even better right now.

"That was kind of a lot of whiskey. Are you going to be okay?"

My cheeks feel rosy. I nod slowly, probably unconvincingly. We make small talk and I'm aware that his eyes never leave me. I talk about Jojo and he talks about his movies. He talks about his most recent filming in Ireland, and I listen, but his voice feels far away. It probably wasn't a good idea to have my first drink ever around a guy I barely know, in a stranger's home, but at some point, things suddenly start to get really hazy . . . and then blackness envelops me.

CHAPTER NINE

I'm not sure how much time passes after that, but when things become clearer, I'm slouched on a sofa and someone's hand is on my knee. I'm about to freak out when a familiar voice tilts my chin up and hands me a cup of water.

"Come on, Char, you need to hydrate."

Audrey. The room comes into focus around me, and I'm mortified and grateful all at once. I down the full cup of water and my body feels like it's slowly coming back to life.

"Can I have another glass?" I croak.

Audrey stays put and someone tall walks past me. I can only make out jeans, but I think it's Alan. Two more cups of water and I'm able to sit up.

"Ughhhhhh." I groan and rub my eyes.

"Ah, alive again," Audrey says jokingly.

The music is still loud upstairs and we're in one of the many bedrooms in this apartment. Disturbing moaning comes from the next room and I make a face. "See, this is why I'd never throw a party."

Alan smirks. "You mean you don't want people staining your bed?"

"Ugh." I bang on the wall. "Keep it down."

Audrey bursts into laughter and the moaning stops for a moment before it continues, slightly more muffled this time. "Glad to see your energy is back."

"How long have I been out?"

Alan reaches over and hands me another cup of water. "You passed out on the terrace so I found Audrey and she dragged you to this room. We came in like fifteen minutes ago to check in on you and force you to drink water."

"Thanks for resuscitating me." I hang my head and rest my forehead on my knees, still in disbelief that one gulp of whiskey could do this to me.

"Do you feel okay?" Audrey asks.

"I feel fine now, but I don't know how I fell asleep so fast."

"Low tolerance, girly," she answers.

Alan's seated in a chair across from the bed. "Was this your first drink or something?"

"Yep. And likely my last."

"You say that now," he jokes, "but just you wait."

I shake my head. "I *will* wait. How much of the party have I missed?"

Audrey shrugs. "An hour, tops. A lot of people are still around."

"Speaking of which, the party is waiting for me. See ya," Alan says, throwing up a peace sign before he heads out. "Feel better."

I wave and look at Audrey. "When do you want to head out?" I ask.

"Not feeling it?" she asks.

I put my hand to my head sheepishly. "Guess I'm not as sober as I thought."

Audrey nods, understanding. "Totally. Let's go."

I swing my legs over the bed. There's a lingering headache from the whiskey. "Hey, thanks," I tell her before we leave the room. "Seriously."

She waves her hands at me like it's no big deal. Shame washes over me and I vow to not be so reckless again. The DJ's still going and people are on the pseudo dance floor.

"Where's Lizzie? I feel like I haven't seen her. We should thank her before we go, right?"

Audrey practically shouts in my ear above the noise. "Oh, she left with Austin hours ago!"

"Left her own home?" I'm shouting back.

"Yup." Audrey smiles mischievously. "Back to his place."

We say bye to the girls Audrey was hanging with, whose names I can't remember right now, and without saying bye to Alan. He's nowhere to be found. I wish I could've found him and thanked him, too. The crisp air feels so good after the heat of fifty-plus bodies dancing and shouting.

Audrey's apartment isn't as grand as Lizzie Chen's but it's a lot nicer than anywhere I've lived. Her living room is large, and colorful paintings line the wall. Despite the size, it feels warm and inviting, full of color. She shows me to the room I'll be sleeping in.

"Wait, is this your parents' room?" I look around at the terra-cotta-colored rug on the floor, the lamp with a face for the stand, and a Baccarat crystal vase with fresh flowers. It's perfectly designed.

"No, I live alone."

"Wait. Is that legal?"

Audrey laughs. "Yeah, I'm nineteen."

"*Oh*." The surprise catches me and that's all I say. The Korean in me immediately thinks about college. Is she a part-time student? She's never mentioned it, and it feels wrong to ask.

"Your apartment's beautiful," I tell her, changing the topic. We're sitting in her living room and my toes feel cozy against her white furry rug.

"I feel lucky to have it. My parents live in Vancouver, but we got this place when I transferred here for high school."

"You must miss them. And Vancouver." I look around, seeing how spacious it is when you live for one and not for four, like my family. It feels pristine, if a little melancholy. The chaos of a three-year-old's trail is nowhere to be seen and no newspapers from an old-fashioned dad are scattered throughout the apartment.

She looks around, as if sensing my emotions. "I do. A lot."

"I'm sure. What do you miss the most?"

"This trail I hiked a lot at Deep Cove in North Vancouver. The Quarry Rock hike. Some of the best memories of my childhood were from there." Her smile is sad and it makes me want to hug her.

"With your parents?"

Audrey brings up her knees and tucks her toes under a pillow.

"Yeah, but, man, it was not easy," she says, shaking her head. "I felt *suffocated*. And I mean like, screaming into a pillow, walls closing in on me sort of suffocated. I couldn't handle it. And it wasn't me being dramatic, which my ex-boyfriend kept saying it was."

"That's why he's an *ex*," I add, raising my eyebrows.

"Exactly," she says. "I learned later they were anxiety attacks. I felt like the world was pushing me down; I couldn't focus on anything anyone was saying to me and everyone's voices would become muffled. Stuff around me became blurry and I'd sort of lose my footing. It was hard to tap into my five senses and point out what was reality and what was in my head."

I nod slowly, letting her continue.

She sighs. "Anyway, it just became clearer that I needed space away from my parents. And they agreed, after finally seeing one of my attacks. They kept saying I was overreacting and it took some time for them to believe me. But eventually, they came around."

"Kudos to them, though, right? I mean, at least they eventually believed you."

"Yeah." Audrey's voice gets really quiet. "But I hurt them a lot."

"I'm sure they didn't *want* to let you go."

She looks at me with an expression I recognize: she feels seen. "Yeah. I always visit for holidays and stay for a long weekend. And honestly, it's pretty accessible since Vancouver isn't too far on the plane, so at least there's that."

I want to tell her everything about my family, about the pressure I feel to help my parents and to make sure Jojo doesn't feel the burden I've grown up feeling. But she doesn't know that I'm in this for the money and I'm not exactly proud of it. Especially around someone who doesn't need money. Her oversized two-bedroom place in Manhattan is bigger than our apartment in Queens, and it's all for one person. I do see her. But I can't expect her to see me.

We retire to our rooms for the night since we're both exhausted from an eventful day. And I think I'm still a little drunk.

When I wake up the next morning, the world feels still. No one rushes into my room to jump on me before I've opened my eyes, and there's no TV blasting in the living room. The rustle of newspapers is absent. It's peaceful and I bask in the quiet, stretching out my limbs and snuggling up in Audrey's comfortable guest bed. The room is a little chilly but the down comforter keeps me warm. Nothing feels cozier than having your face be cold while the rest of your body feels like it's roasting by a campfire. I open my phone in bed, and my heart beats faster. When I see hundreds of new followers, I kick off my covers and do a happy dance on the mattress. It almost makes lying to my parents worth it. Validates it, sort of. Can I be this hungry for fame?

I hear faint music coming from outside the door, which means Audrey must be up. I step into the fuzzy slippers she lent me and join her.

"Morning," Audrey says, while folding an omelet.

"She cooks!" I say.

"Yes, she does. Can't always be eating out!"

"Smells delish."

Audrey plates the eggs and some fresh berries for me and I pour us juice from her fridge. It feels like the perfect morning after an eventful night.

"I'll make us pancakes," I offer.

"But I already made us breakfast."

"Please? The Korean daughter in me is screaming about being the worst guest ever."

Audrey laughs. "Fine. But only because I understand the treachery of being an empty-handed guest."

"Plus, my pancakes are bomb. Steven taught me."

Seventeen minutes later, I add matcha pancakes to our half-eaten plates. Steven claims that his matcha soufflé pancakes are the fluffiest. Something I love about him is that he never tries to be anyone else. All his pastries have an Asian spin and he wouldn't dare bake without that. It's the essence of who he is.

"Wow, this is impressive," Audrey says, eyes wide and mouth full of sugary matcha fluff.

The long vibration of an email takes me out of my thoughts and I pull out my phone. It takes a moment to recognize what I'm reading, but when I see it, I can't believe it.

"Audrey. I just got my first sponsorship."

She squeals with me and we look over the email together.

"Wait, I love Ryokan Homes," she says. "I've done work for them in the past and they're really great. I use all their storage products in my bathroom and pantry."

I read through the email in detail, noting the products that they'll send me, and at the bottom of the email: two grand for a story and a post on my feed. *Two thousand dollars.* The thin hairs on my arms and neck feel like they're rising. This is what I've been working toward for two years. As I expected, the MITI Gala was the stamp I needed to prove my status as an influencer. So maybe I have LilasLovers to thank for the sudden growth in my brand. And Audrey, of course. Every time she posts a photo of us, I get more followers. It's like secondhand fame.

"When did you work with them?" I ask.

"A few years ago. They were the first brand I ever worked with after dropping out of college. It confirmed that this was the path for me."

I can't mask my surprise. "That's so cool. Your parents didn't threaten to disown you?" I joke. Maybe not all Asian parents are intense.

"Oh, no, they definitely did. They're still not happy about it, but when I keep telling them how much happier I am, it's hard for them to keep pushing me to go back to school. I promised I'd consider it later, but right now, it's just not for me."

"You're living the dream, Audrey. You worked so hard for it, too. Is it weird to say that I want to be you when I grow up?"

She laughs and I join her, but I'm not joking. Audrey's life is my goal, except maybe the living alone part.

"You're starting to live the dream, too," she says encouragingly. "Ryokan Homes is truly amazing and so good to work with."

I want to tell her it's so much more than I could have dreamed and that I hope it only goes up from here. But I can't share that without divulging my desperation. So I shove in some more pancake to keep my mouth shut and I smile.

This is just the beginning.

CHAPTER TEN

After a lazy morning taking more selfies with Audrey, I walk home from the subway station at Queensboro Plaza. I press my ear against the door of our apartment, listening. I can hear Jojo stomping around and my mom chasing her, telling her to use gentle feet for our downstairs neighbors. I push open the door and immediately Jojo jumps into my arms and nuzzles my neck. It's only been a day but her loud footsteps and sticky, sweet smell is like a missing puzzle piece to me.

"Sharty! Missed you."

"I missed you, too, Jo," I say, putting Jojo back down. "Hi, Umma."

"How was the trip, honey?"

"It was fun! I learned a lot. I mean, Steven and I learned a lot. We all had a good time."

My mom smiles and doesn't press further, which I'm grateful for, mostly. If she cared more, would she ask more questions? I should be happy.

"What's Appa up to?"

I know from the way her head hangs down and she runs her hand through her hair that she's not happy with him. "Your appa is *always* ill, Seoyoung-ah. Always. I'm so sick and tired of it," she says in Korean.

I bite my lower lip so as not to take anyone's side. "Is he . . . okay?" My eyes instinctively look to see if Jojo is listening, but she doesn't seem too bothered.

"Of course he's okay. He's fine, but he's always sick. Always!"

After she walks away, I bend down to Jojo, who's working on her coloring book on the floor. "Jojo!" I whisper loudly. "Aren't you happy Appa can be home more? He gets to play with you!"

Jojo smiles sweetly up at me. "Yay! Appa and Jojo can color!"

I spend the early afternoon playing with Jojo. Eventually, my mom settles in near us on the sofa, but she's completely focused on something else. She's on her laptop, brows furrowed together in concentration. When I peer over her shoulder, all I see is a bunch of numbers on an Excel spreadsheet. Her shoulders look smaller, too, like she's lost weight recently.

I get up and quickly make myself a Korean coffee from the kitchen, stirring the mix into my mug, feeling drained already. When I rejoin her on the sofa, she doesn't seem to even notice I'm here. "Umma. Do you want some?" I offer her my cup, but my mom shakes her head. I thumb the ceramic Band-Aid. "Will we be okay?"

She shrugs, offering no alleviation from my worries. "I need to work more." She rubs her eyes and blinks rapidly, like she hasn't been sleeping much. When Jojo turns around to face us, I raise the volume on the TV. I don't want her hearing these things.

"I'll work, too," I tell her. "I'll get a job, Umma."

We've had this conversation before, so I already know how it'll end. In peak Korean mom vibes, she wants me to only focus on school. She doesn't get that I can do more, doesn't see me as an asset to help our family. She vehemently shakes her head and shoots me a death glare. "Goh Seoyoung, you stay put inside school walls."

"Please, let me. I can do both. I promise."

Maybe I can put this whole influencer thing behind me and get an actual job. Or maybe I can do both. It feels nice, to think I won't have any secrets. But the tease of the easiest two thousand dollars I'll ever make lingers in my mind.

"Don't even dream about it," she says in Korean.

"Umma—"

She stands up, ending the conversation. "I need to call the store. Watch Jojo?"

"Where's Appa?"

"Sleeping or something," she says, before walking away. Her footsteps are quiet and I slink back into the sofa as a wave of desperation falls over me. There's no point pushing back. I reread the content of the email. Two thousand dollars.

steven

You back?

where did you sleep????

It wasn't lost on me that I didn't know what Steven's plans were for last night. Maybe a part of me didn't text him at the MITI Gala because I didn't want to know. For once, I didn't want to feel bad about someone or something and I wanted to be selfish. I'm feeling like a jerk about it now, though.

> At a friend's.
>
>   oh???? who friend
>
> Nosy mcnosy over here
>
> So you're back?

Maybe Steven doesn't want to tell me because he slept over at a girl's place. But who? I don't think there's anyone Steven's close to besides me that's a girl. And even if he *did* sleep at a girl's place, who am I to say anything about that?

>   im not nosy . . . just being a good best fren
>
>   yep im back
>
> Haha. At Bobby's from youth group.
>
> WHYYY are you so curious?
>
> See you tonight then?
>
>   hahah o
>
>   yep c u

I send Steven two pictures from the gala. One of me and Audrey and one of just me.

> Who's the friend? 😊
>
>   Omg

Haha just kidding.

You guys look great. That dress

looks good on you.

I wonder if there's a rule about best friends. Like if at some point you're destined to end up together, however briefly, or if you could maintain the platonic best friendship forever. Or maybe, if there are no romantic feelings, you just drift apart. Steven and I, we've never talked about what would happen if we caught feelings for each other. There's comfortable flirting sometimes, but the kind where even the flirting feels like a joke because neither of us would cross the line beyond harmless teasing here and there. I never thought too deeply about him. Or at least I never *let* myself. And I don't think he has ever, about me. Because neither of us are willing to risk our kinship for something more that could tear us apart.

The contract with Ryokan Homes says that I won't be paid until I post, so I spend most of the day brainstorming the post and planning it out since the items are slated to arrive soon. As I continue to share content from MITI, I methodically go through each comment, replying to the kind ones, liking the emoji ones, then going through DMs and responding to each question, each compliment. It takes up my entire day, and even though my head is dizzy from staring at my small screen, I feel exhilarated. Audrey and I text throughout the day and she sends me her best tip: *Don't accept sponsorships with brands that feel off from your honest self.* I repeat that to myself multiple times as I manifest to the universe for more partnerships. The high engagement grows my following, but it's not easy to ignore the trolls.

Yellow trash.

So much ~korea~ content she should just be an "influencer" there 🤣

Ur content is boring

Anyone else think her vibe is not a vibe??? Lololol

Yes and also anyone else think shes totally fake?

Def and her content is just not good lolol

Bruh just be a student not an influencer ur gunna ruin ur life

And so many more. Half of which are grammatically incorrect. I shouldn't be offended by idiots who can't form basic sentences. But I am. I stop myself from looking through them. Learn to delete messages before I look because I can already tell from the first two words who the haters are. Learn to allow Instagram to filter the comments. My dad pokes his head in through the door to remind me to get ready for Steven's.

"Already?" I ask.

"Seoyoung-ah, not already, it five now," he says, before closing my door behind him.

I look at the clock. It *is* almost five p.m. I didn't get to my history assignment or even respond to text messages. I remind myself to do these things later tonight.

When we get to Steven's place, the smell of Carol-eemo's food feels so familiar. Even though there are five dishes cooking at once, I know exactly what's for dinner. Sometimes, walking into their apartment feels more like home for me than my own. I give Carol-eemo a hug. "Annyeonghaseyo," I tell her. I grab the water glasses and help set the table.

Today, Carol-eemo is happy. It's rare to see her this excited since Steven's dad left them. She scoops pa-kimchi from a big plastic container into a bowl. Seeing her with the food-prep gloves on as she gently transfers the scallion kimchi makes me ache with love for her. She's in her element, lovingly feeding a large family, something I know she always wanted. I know they tried for a long time to have another kid, but it never worked out, even with two pregnancies.

Steven's in his room and I knock, then push open the slightly ajar door. "Why so secluded?"

He turns around, grinning. "Sorry. Got distracted. My mom forced me to help her with the million things she decided to cook up for you guys tonight and I was in the middle of researching a new recipe. Or rather, a new spin on a recipe I want to try. Anyway, I finally got my time back, and then you barge in," he teases.

"I did not *barge* in. What's the recipe?"

"Secret. But it includes misugaru."

Steven looks so mischievous as he says this, like multigrain powder is a suspicious ingredient in food. I grin and join him. He scooches over on his computer chair to make room for me so we're sharing a seat.

"I love misugaru. Is it a donut? Pandan cake? Dalgona sponge cake? Mille-feuille? Lemon curd tart?"

He laughs and covers my mouth with his hand. "Stop naming everything I make. And a lemon tart with misugaru would be appalling. I'm making a mochi muffin infused with misugaru powder and sesame."

"Ooh, I can't really imagine that taste but I love mochi. And muffins. And misugaru."

"It's even better combined. Anyway, do you remember my mentor from last summer?"

I turn my head to him, and because we're in one chair, he feels really close to me. I don't think he notices because he's too into pastries right now. "The mentor from that culinary school?"

Steven nods. "Yeah. He's getting kind of big now and said he could hook me up with small jobs and opportunities here and there if I wanted. Just for experience and even a little cash." He's so excited about this, I can tell. His smile is so big it reaches his ears, and he keeps wildly gesticulating.

I squeeze his arm. "That's so cool. And it's just the beginning. I bet everyone will want to work with you once they meet you."

Steven grins. "And taste my pastries."

I nod. "Exactly. Then you're going to get big, too, and forget all about me. I can feel it," I say, grinning back.

He shrugs. "I'll try not to forget you."

I close my eyes and shake my head, pretending to be understanding. "It's okay. You go fly. I'll be singing Taylor Swift's 'Stay Beautiful' while you go be a star."

Steven raises his brows. "Okay, now you've lost me."

I push our chair back and stand up. "Ugh, never mind. I'm starving. Carol-eemo cooked up a storm. Why's she in such a good mood?"

Steven swivels around to face me directly. "She found a vacation deal online. She used the word 'unpassable.' "

"Whoa. What kind of deal?"

Steven grins big. "Some island in the Caribbean. I forgot where. An all-inclusive place for fifty percent off. She's *insistent* on going."

"*Wow.* I don't even remember the last time your mom went on vacation."

"Same."

"When are you guys going?"

"You mean when are *we* going?"

Before I can respond, he prods us out into the hallway and to the dining table. My parents and Carol-eemo are already seated, and in Korean, I can make out the bulk of the conversation. They're talking about dates . . . the weather . . . a beach?

"Wait, what's going on?" I butt in.

My dad matches the smile on Carol-eemo's face. "Steven-umma found great deal online for trip to Caribbean. Aruba! We never been and she wants to make it family trip."

Jojo looks up from her miyukgook, seaweed stuck on the sides of her mouth. "Let's go! Trip!"

My mom shakes her head at Jojo. "We'll see, honey."

"Aigo, gajago!" Carol-eemo says, nudging my mom aggressively. *Come on, just go!* My mom is hard to convince but she smiles and assures her in Korean that we'll try to make it work.

Most of dinner is Steven's mom talking about Aruba and this all-inclusive resort, about how she made sure it's not a scam. There's nothing Asians hate more than being the victim of a scam. Because we put so much stock in our intelligence, if someone can manage to deceive us, it's a knock on our knowledge and our pride.

Later, during the car ride home, my dad is the first to bring it up. "Yeobo, we should go," he says, turning to Mom, but she's facing the window. "What do you think, Charlotte?" My dad looks at me through the rearview mirror.

"I mean, it sounds nice. Is it really a good deal?" I sneak a glance at my mom through the reflection in her window. Her gaze looks stone-cold and heartless.

"Just because it's a good deal doesn't mean we can afford it," my mom snaps.

I shut my mouth, not wanting to be caught in a cross fire.

She says to my dad, "Dangshini don beoneun geotdo anijana." *You're not even the one making money.*

I want to tell them that I'll make two thousand dollars soon and that it's just the beginning. I want to tell them I can take their stress away, so please stop fighting. But instead, I lean back in my seat, too scared to get in her path. The rest of the car is silent and the only movement I can make out is my dad repeatedly rubbing his knee. I'm worried that even the drive from Flushing to LIC is becoming hard on him. The tension is so loud, heard by everyone but Jojo. I pull out a book from the backseat pocket and distract her before she can pick up on the fight between our parents. I envy her as I read *Llama Llama Red Pajama* and see her smiling face. To be so loved and to know no pain, to get to blithely be whatever you want to be, say whatever you want to say, without having to read the room. I'm desperate that she stay this way as long as she can, as long as I'm around to shield her.

The package from Ryokan Homes is in the mail room when we get back and I sneak it in behind everyone else. That evening, I stay up late, snapping pictures of a keepsake box, a jewelry organizer, and some other chic room-storage solutions. I meticulously draft my caption, editing and editing again. It takes hours, but when it's done, I schedule to post in the morning. When I finally close my eyes, I think of the two thousand dollars and having it multiply, so much so that we can go on this trip, that my mom doesn't need to attack my dad for not being able to work, that I can continue upholding my sister's joy of being little.

I go to bed hoping I can do all this without getting caught, and dream about the relief I would feel lying on an expansive beach under the Caribbean sky.

CHAPTER ELEVEN

When my Ryokan Homes sponsored post goes up, it's hard to describe how I feel. It's like the inkling of what I'm working toward, but only an inkling. I hate how much I lack gratitude. I've always been astounded by how so many Americans are easily proud of themselves. In Korean households, there's always something to improve upon. I remember in middle school when I got a ninety-four on an essay, the bare minimum score you need to get an A. Instead of praising me, my mom said, *There's a low A and a high A. You got a low A.* Never mind that the actual letter grade is exactly the same. So whether it's been ingrained in me or maybe I already had the gene of never enough in my DNA, the post is up and I'm hungry for more. Ravenous, really.

During free period, I settle in my seat and take a deep breath. It helps me mentally prepare for the online world, for the shifting of my identity. I scroll through the comments and likes, replying to users, answering their questions, until my eyes land on a name that catches my breath and I read his comment. **@AlanTravisSmith** Love this brand. Big fan. There's a message waiting for me in my direct messages.

Your first sponsored post, yeah?

It's good.

> thanks, and lol at you
> helping the engagement.

Just trying to help you live
your best life! 😎

Is it working?

> ill let you know what RH says

Are you free this Friday?

I know he knows I've seen his message, but I close the app. Free period's over anyway. Even though I don't respond all evening and throughout the next day, Alan's message lingers in my mind. I can't believe he DMed me. Doesn't he have like a movie premiere to be at? I don't even want to be thinking about him, but I can't help it. I know I want to see him again. There's no way we'll end up actually hanging out, though. He's a freaking celebrity. Maybe he regrets sending me that message. I text Audrey to see if she's free, and thankfully, she is. The second the school bell rings, I head toward her apartment. She's filming content in her living room and her space is set up like a mini studio. The walls are decorated with red paper lanterns, bunnies, and dragons, and there's a small marble table decorated with delicious-looking mooncakes. Audrey sees me eyeing them and hands one over to me.

"I have a lot more." She quickly grabs some from the kitchen and brings them over.

"You're half Chinese, right?" I ask her. I already knew she was Korean, but I feel like so stupid for not realizing this sooner. Even after having followed her on Instagram long before we were actual friends. Just goes to show how little information you actually retain despite hours of scrolling online.

"Mm-hmm. My dad's side. I'm doing a sponsored post for this bakery before Mid-Autumn Festival this Friday."

"Wow, that's pretty cool, getting to post stuff like that on Instagram."

"It's nice, yeah, and always sort of becomes a reminder to my followers that I'm not fully Korean." She laughs a little as she says this.

"I'm sorry. I also didn't realize. Does that bother you?"

Audrey's sitting on a stool behind the tripod where the camera's set up and puckers her lips before shaking her head. "No. Not really, anyway. Sena is a popular enough Korean name, so I get that's why most Asians think I'm just fully Korean."

I'm sitting across her on a comfortable chaise chair. "Do you have a Chinese name?"

She shakes her head again. "My mom won the ongoing mixed-race battle of the middle name." She laughs. "I have this friend who's also half, but she only has two American names as her first and middle to keep it neutral because her parents wouldn't give in."

"I guess since my parents are both Korean, our middle names being Korean was the one thing they actually agreed on," I say. "Mine's Seoyoung. Do you ever feel pulled into one culture stronger than the other?"

She smiles. "Ooh, I like that name. Um, yeah, sometimes I do." She lowers her body to look through the camera. "You look good there.

Hold on." Audrey snaps a few candid photos of me and I make a few attempted goofy faces at the camera to up the mood. "Cute! Yeah, there's a lot of guilt that comes with it, which sucks. My mom and her whole family are in Canada, but my dad's side is still back in China."

"So I guess you just mostly see your mom's side, huh?"

"Yeah, it's almost like the frequency of hanging out with my maternal grandparents has exposed me way more to Korean culture. And I'm not blaming them or anything, but I feel bad sometimes that my dad hasn't been able to expose me to his part of the family as much. And he's not really one to force his story and experiences on me, and my mom kind of is? So naturally, I speak more Korean, I eat a lot of Korean food when I go home, and my grandparents also keep pinning Korean values on me."

"Kinda makes me feel bad for your dad." My voice is quieter than Audrey's and I hope I didn't say the wrong thing. Half my interactions with people end up with me crossing my fingers that I didn't offend someone.

"Well, these types of things help. I called my dad the other day to ask about the Mid-Autumn Festival and he was explaining a ton of things. It was pretty cute, he was so happy," Audrey says, laughing as she adjusts the lens on her camera.

I help her take photos and stage some food and decorations celebrating good food and an abundant harvest. "Do you celebrate Chuseok, too?" Chuseok is the Korean fall celebration, and it takes place on the same day or weekend as the Chinese Mid-Autumn Festival because they're basically the same holiday.

"Oh god, did I not mention? I'm heading home tomorrow for a week. My mom always makes me come home for Chuseok because it's a huge deal in my family."

I give her a small smile.

"What about you?" Audrey asks.

"Steven's mom always hosts Chuseok dinner. I've never made traditional foods or kimchi or any of that at home before."

"I *hate* helping my grandma and mom prepare everything. You should come with me to Vancouver and take my spot," she says, laughing. "You're lucky."

I think of Audrey in her home, buzzing with a large family spending all day cooking together. It feels so different from the solitary apartment she lives in here in New York. Another half hour later, we're finished with the photos for Audrey's sponsored post and are lounging on her sofa with green tea.

"So," I say, staring into my patterned teacup, "can I ask you something?"

She perks up. "Sure."

"What's Alan like?"

"Alan . . . Smith?"

"Mm-hmm."

Audrey goes from lying down sideways to sitting up, cross-legged, grinning so wide it's like a lemon wedge is stuck in her mouth. "*Why?*" she asks playfully.

I roll my eyes. "It's not like that. Just curious. I guess he intrigued me."

"Intrigued you? Do you *fancy* him?" Audrey giggles and I actually get genuine butterflies when she says that. Not because of Alan, but because of her. Because I can't remember the last time I sat across from a girlfriend, laughing about a boy. Can you miss something you've never had?

"Okay, truth? He asked me to hang out."

Audrey literally squeals. "What did you say?"

At that, I bite my lower lip. "I . . . didn't respond."

"You just left him on read?"

I nod. "I panicked."

"Well, that's fine. I mean, honestly, it probably makes him want you more, as cliché as it sounds. I know that wasn't your intention, but dang, playing hard to get, huh?"

"Oh my god, it's not like that. It's just . . . I don't know. It's been a while since I've had a thing with anyone and even then it was barely anything."

"What's Steven?"

I wave my hand in the air. "That's totally different. He's family."

Audrey comes closer and squishes next to me on the cushion. "If you say so," she says lightly. "Okay, show me the message."

I give her my phone and we scroll through the short conversation and there's more squealing as she drafts a response on my behalf and we wait for Alan to respond.

"I doubt he'll reply that quickly," I tell her.

"Just you wait. I did some good texting work there," she says with a teasing voice. I'm about to come after her and she tosses me my phone and jumps off giggling.

> **Don't really want to wait until Fri. Tonight work?**

"Oh my god, Audrey!" I'm baffled and laughing. Within minutes, just as Audrey suspected, a DM from Alan is waiting. We open it together.

> **Feeling spontaneous huh?**
> **I'm down! Let's kick it.**
> **Where do you live?**

"Not ready to tell him that," I say.

"In case he might kill you?"

"Yeah, social media is full of creeps."

> **New York** 😄
> **you?**

> **LOL**
> **Same**
> **How about I pick you up at**
> **Bryant Park then, by the fountain?**

"Pick you up! He definitely thinks this is a date," Audrey says.

"Is it?"

"I mean, he didn't ask you out, but *he* probably thinks he did. This is why I hate teenage boys."

"Wait, so does it make it a date then?"

"It's confusing. Either ask you out directly or just hang out casually. This whole 'let's kick it' and then 'I'll pick you up' is bull." Audrey's looking at something on her phone before she turns it face down and sighs in exasperation.

"Something wrong?"

She rolls her eyes and shakes her head. "It's fine. Just this dumb white brand that's trying to unwhite itself, but we're all boycotting it."

"Are they trying to apologize to you?"

"No, not really. They just don't want to be canceled." She sighs. "Anyway, did you respond to Alan?"

"Just about to," I tell her as I type out my response. She must sense my nervousness because she squares her shoulders to face me.

"Don't worry, Char. Just be yourself! He's not that big of a deal. Just a teenage boy," she says jokingly.

I smile and nod. "Right. Just a teenager."

Thumbs-up.

Lol, I like that you write thumbs-
up instead of sending the actual emoji.

4 p.m.?

4 p.m.

♦♦♦

At 4:05 p.m., I'm walking up the steps and I can see Alan standing in front of the fountain. There are a few girls standing near him who won't stop staring. One of them gets out her phone to take a picture. So much for just a teenager. He has this energy to him that draws me in. I'm mesmerized by his blasé charm that I wish I had. Most of us are out there trying not to care and massively failing. But when I look at even the way Alan is standing, leaning comfortably against the edge of the stone fountain, I can't believe that he's ever cared what others thought of him. In my psychoanalysis of him, I haven't moved from the steps and we lock eyes. Neither of us smiles and it feels like a silent competition of who'll break it first.

Eventually, he does when he breaks into a big grin and waves for me to come over.

"Why were you just standing over there?" he asks.

"I was studying you."

Alan raises his eyebrows and I notice his face. He's objectively handsome, with thick eyebrows and a big smile that makes you feel good and kind of shy at the same time.

"Studying me? What'd you learn?" His tone is a mix of comfortable flirting and friendliness.

"That you're nice to look at," I say, with a smirk. "So why'd you pick Bryant Park?"

"It seemed like a creeper-free decision," he says, leaning in.

"Oh, stop," I say, nudging him away. I can smell peppermint from his breath. It's intoxicating to be this close and I'm shocked at my own intense attraction to him.

"Really! So if I were to say, 'Let's meet at this corner on the Lower East Side and eat at this hole in the wall,' would you have been down?"

"Yep."

"You're a liar!" He nods his head toward the exit of the park and we begin walking out.

"I would have!" I say stubbornly.

"Fine. Next time, then." Alan leads us down the steps with a light hand on my lower back. It sends tingles up my spine.

We wander the area and head over to a Japanese bookshop. Upstairs I browse the manga section, each book delicately wrapped in a plastic seal, tightly locked for the reader who'll come to own it.

"Are you into manga?" Alan leans closer to me, studying the cover the way I am. He smells nice, like a cologne I smelled once from a magazine. Sometimes, when I see an issue hanging out in our lobby mailbox and no one claims it, I'll take it home. When no one's home, I like to rub the sample perfumes on my arm. Besides not having money to buy luxury perfume, my mom would never stand for it. She'd say kids should smell like soap or sweat. Another reason Alan's not just a normal teenager.

"No. I just like to study the drawings."

"Really?"

"Yeah. They're always so expressive, full of wanting and de-termination. I feel like I know the plot just by the cover and the character's expression."

"Oh yeah? What's this one about?"

I trace the girl's eyebrows, fiercely arched while the rest of her body hangs low, like a runner getting ready to sprint. "She needs to win someone, or something, back. Something she thinks has been taken from her." I observe her jet-black hair, how well it fits her expression, how it adds to her deep-seated rage. "And she doesn't want any help from anyone. She's controlled by nothing but her determination."

"Sounds like a sad life," he comments, taking the manga from me. "Let me try."

"Go for it."

"She definitely looks pissed, so I'll give you that. Her little brother's been taken captive by the enemy clan and she seeks vengeance on his behalf. She'll go disguised as a warrior into their territory, bring back her little bro, and come back to her village a hero."

At this, I laugh. "More creative than me, guess this is why you're the actor."

Alan slides the manga back into its shelf and we make our way to the small café on the same floor. After deciding to share an egg salad sandwich, we sit across from each other and Alan hands me my half of the sandwich. The sharing aspect of this meal makes it feel like we're a *thing* or something. A few people turn to look at us, or rather, him. I wonder if people think we're dating. I hope they do.

"You're not really a talker, huh?"

I finish swallowing. "I can be if I find the person interesting enough," I joke. "Just kidding. I guess it's a little intimidating hanging out with you."

"Oh yeah? Why?" He's grinning in that boyish way.

"Oh, come on. You know why. Even the girls by the fountain were taking pictures of you."

"It's more fun with you." He shrugs. "I'm still hungry. Wanna do an early dinner?" he asks. "Can you eat more?"

I can feel the heat rise up to my cheeks. "Always."

The restaurant he takes me to is fancy, with leather booths and a lot of people in suits. It's one thing to be at an event with other teen influencers, but Gabriel Kreuther is meant for people older than us, people who have enough money to comfortably grab a weeknight meal at a restaurant with dim lighting and servers dressed in all black. I look at Alan, whose calm demeanor makes me think he sees this establishment like any regular burger joint, and not a place known for overpriced food with small portions. The hostess leads us to an intimate booth table, and I thank her as she pulls out a cloth napkin and places it on my lap. No one's ever done that before.

"Do you usually eat at places like this?" I ask him. I immediately regret it, hoping I don't sound too judgy.

"Only for something special," he says with a wink. He actually *winks*. And I'm appalled at myself for blushing at it.

A server at the restaurant recognizes Alan and sends over free appetizers. The manager approaches us shortly after. She's dressed in a black pantsuit with pointy white heels.

"Welcome to Gabriel Kreuther," she says, with one of those big perfect smiles dentists have on their office posters. "Thank you so much for joining us today, Mr. Smith."

"Of course. You guys have the best food. And Alan is fine."

I force a few smiles while repeatedly telling myself not to fidget.

"This is my friend, Charlotte." Alan turns his body halfway toward me, including me in the conversation. His hand is lightly around my waist and my whole body tenses. I have to stop myself from wishing he'd hold me tighter.

"Nice to meet you. And thank you for the appetizers," I say, even though they weren't really for me.

The manager and Alan exchange a few more pleasantries and soon we're left alone again.

"Does this happen to you often?"

"Yeah, it's happened a few times," he says, with a humble laugh. "I guess by people who've watched the few movies I've actually been in."

"Any more in the pipeline?" I ask. There was one movie where he played an aspiring boxer that Steven and I watched together. I thought Alan looked pretty good in that movie, but Steven rolled his eyes and told me it was unrealistic and no kid our age was that strong.

He nods cryptically. "A few, but I haven't figured out what I want to commit to yet. A lot of them involve traveling since movies are rarely shot in New York. It's always a good time, if a bit tiring."

The rest of our dinner is him sharing about his acting life and me listening and following up with more questions. Our conversation doesn't get too personal, but there's a comfortable rapport between us and somehow, three hours go by. The sun has set and we get the bill, only to realize we've been comped by the restaurant altogether. We express thank-yous to the manager and step outside. I'm relieved because I wasn't sure how I'd ever be able to afford what we ate.

"I guess it's almost fall, huh?" My thin dress is meant more for the earlier half of the day and the evening breeze sends a shiver through me.

Noticing, Alan takes off his jacket and wraps it around my shoulders.

"No, it's fine, really."

"I'm not even cold. Just take it," he insists. He puts his arm around my waist lightly and I tense up again, reveling in this boy-girl touch. I know it sounds cheesy, but this moment, it feels like a perfect New York evening, except for the fact that I barely know the guy and he's actually a famous actor and people who recognize him are staring at me and younger girls are shooting daggers, as other bystanders, not so surreptitiously, get their phones out for a few pictures. Besides the teenage paparazzi, it feels ordinary: this walk, his hand on my waist, the breeze on our faces. Like everything high school promised me but never came through on.

We're on the 7 train together from Bryant Park because Alan insisted on taking me home. "You really didn't have to."

"I really wanted to."

I'm standing despite the many open seats because I'm an MTA germaphobe, and when the train lurches to a stop, Alan holds me firmly and closer to him. "This was fun," he says in that way that makes me blush.

I nod. "I had fun, too, even though I don't know anything about you."

A grin unfurls across his face and he lets go of the subway bar to hold my hand with his free one. We must look like we're about to do some sort of dance with our bodies so closely touching and hands intertwined like this. My body feels like I'm being injected with adrenaline.

Suddenly I'm reminded of the first time Steven and I held hands when we were twelve. I almost lost my balance while we raced, and he grabbed my hand before I fell. It made us awkward and shy, even though it was just to help me.

This feels different. Like Alan's really trying to romance me. I push Steven out of my mind.

"What do you want to know?" he asks. Whether it's the consistent movement of the rickety 7 train or merely the train as an excuse, Alan's face is close enough to mine that I know he ate a mint from the restaurant. I can smell it on his breath.

"Why'd you ask me to hang out?"

"I wanted to see you outside of a party and an event."

"Why?"

I know I'm fishing for compliments, but I can't help it. It's this ugly part of me that wants to be told that I'm wanted by someone tiers above me. I am really curious, too, though.

"Because," he whispers, and then he leans in and kisses my nose. "You seem different," he says, and then he kisses my chin. "Unique," he whispers, kissing my neck.

I'm frozen and probably shaking, I can't tell. My body feels weak against his light kisses and he's too good at this and I can't say anything. It's going to happen. And Alan has no idea.

"Go on," I say quietly.

"I want to get to know you even more," he says, and then it happens. My first kiss. Ever. His lips are soft against mine and he tightens his grip on my waist, pulling me in closer. I can feel him against me and I consider sitting on the subway seat just so I can keep myself from falling. He tastes like mint and he untangles his hands from mine, bringing them up to my back and taking me in deeper. When we pull apart, my head is spinning and I can't think straight. I hope I didn't suck.

"Yum," I tell him, and it's enough to make him burst into laughter.

"*Yum?*"

"I don't know why I said that," I say, but I match his grin.

"You're yum, too," he says.

The walk from the 7 train to my apartment building is too fast and I stop a block away, lest the doorman see me and bring up my mystery boy in front of my parents. "I'll take it from here."

"Can't I drop you off at your door?"

"No, absolutely not. We're from different worlds."

"Yeah? How so?" He leans against the brick wall and crosses his arms in amusement.

"My parents are Korean parents. Strict Korean parents. Yours aren't. Got it?"

Alan grins again, shaking his head. "I've just barely met you, but I feel like I've known you my entire life. And then I feel like I don't know anything about you and need to know everything as soon as possible."

I stare at him incredulously, shocked that any guy would ever say something so gross and cheesy and romantic to me, much less a celebrity.

"Can I kiss you again?" I ask with a lilt. My insides are screaming. Never have I flirted like this, with this ease, with this much control.

Alan leans in, kissing me like he's done this a thousand times, with the skill of a seasoned kisser. I memorize his movements and am aware of his hands cupping the side of my chest. I pull his hand downward, back to my waist, back where it feels exciting but safe.

He looks at me playfully. "Can I see you again?"

I nod. "Soon."

"I'll text you?"

I wave before I turn the corner and disappear back into my normal life. Teddy's not at the front desk today and I'm relieved. No one at home questions my whereabouts, but I tell my mom that I've eaten dinner already and I rush to my room. After locking my door, I lie on my bed, sprawled out, breathless, remembering every moment from the subway until just a few minutes ago.

I can't believe I had my first kiss. And with a boy I just met. Who happens to be a movie star.

I smash my face into a pillow and *scream*.

CHAPTER TWELVE

The next afternoon, I'm sitting on the stairs outside school, still thinking about my date with Alan.

I've always gone through life with bouts of feeling content enough to not complain, and yet also anxious, but this is something else. Everything feels hazy and I feel drugged up on Alan. If I couldn't still feel the tingle of our kiss on my lips, I would've wondered if it even happened. Most of school passed by in an uneventful blur. During lunch, I was surrounded by the clattering sound of trays landing on plastic tables in the cafeteria. Everywhere around me, voices buzzed loudly, talking about upcoming exams and gossip. I've always wondered if other students really feel excited about these convos, or if there's anyone like me, forcing themselves to fake joy in these group settings while not finding anything particularly interesting about them at all. Well, most kids are different from me, since they actually have groups. But just this one morning, a small part of me wished for friends so I could tell them about my first kiss and answer questions like "How *was* he?" or "OMG, how did it happen?"

I think of telling Steven, but he's at a club meeting and my gut tells me he wouldn't be super thrilled or ask me those questions anyway. I don't know why but it feels weird to talk to him about it. Something like a mix of nervousness and guilt.

The entire rest of the day though, through my classes, through my free period, I can't focus. It's not so much that I'm deeply in love with Alan; it's more that I did something simply because I wanted to, with no regard for consequences. It's a concept so novel for me, it's almost *wrong*. Kissing a boy in a dark corner a block from my apartment? No one would suspect or expect this behavior from me. It feels like a secret treasure that I've unearthed, a pleasure meant only for me.

Suddenly, Steven materializes next to me. "Hey," he says.

"Hi," I say. "How was your meeting?"

"Same old. What's up?"

I don't know why, but I feel so awkward. Like the kiss is still on the tip of my lips, and Steven can see it. "Not much," I say, trailing off.

"Why are you being weird?"

I grab my backpack and swing it over my shoulder as we head out. "Ugh, you think you know me so well," I say.

Steven looks at me pointedly. "I do know you so well."

I kick a stone in front of me and it rolls to his right foot. "Yeah, but do you ever think maybe I don't *need* to tell you every detail of my life?" The energy between us shifts immediately.

"I wasn't asking you to, jeez, Char."

By habit, we wordlessly head to the same café we've been going to after school for the last five years. It's a mundane walk with not many restaurants or stores—mostly filled with construction zones and half-blocked roads.

"Did I do something?" he asks after a while.

His question makes me feel so bad. I shake my head. "No. No, sorry, just a long night. Didn't sleep a ton." I should tell him. It's obvious to him something's on my mind.

We make it into the café and create enough peace to order two matcha lattes—one with extra milk and syrup for me and one with no syrup for Steven.

Steven and I tell each other everything, right? I sip on my drink for a long time to find an excuse for the silence. "I, um . . ."

He looks at me with a puzzled expression. "You . . ."

"Never mind." I take another sip of my latte.

"You sure?"

I know Steven doesn't pry, but I want him to. It feels weird to dish this out first. Or maybe it's that I don't want to dish it to him. But a secret this big feels even weirder for us.

"Um, I had my first kiss."

His expression reveals nothing. He looks like he's staring at a painting he's seeing for the first time. Deciding whether he hates it or loves it or simply doesn't care for it. The need to read his mind feels overwhelming and it feels like an eternity goes by as I wait for him to say something. This is unchartered territory for us. We've never discussed *kissing other people* in our friendship before.

"Oh. With who?" he finally asks.

"Alan Smith." I swipe my tongue back and forth against my bottom teeth as he processes this.

"Like, from that bad movie we watched?" He looks unimpressed.

"I don't think it was bad. But yeah, him. I met him at the MITI Gala."

"Well, congrats," he says.

"Congrats?"

"I mean, what *should* I say?"

My lips purse in thought. "I don't know." I stare at the space between us.

"Yeah. So, congrats."

"Thanks, I guess." I know I shouldn't expect him to ask me more questions like a girlfriend would. He looks as uncomfortable as I do. It's always been our world, not necessarily romantic, but still, just us. And our parents and Jojo.

Steven fidgets with his drink. "So are you dating Alan?"

"Uhhh, no. I don't think so, anyway."

He nods and doesn't ask anything more. Us trying to talk about this is a collision of awkwardness and it feels so unnatural and I hate it. I'm desperate to change the topic. "My matcha latte is too milky," I comment, making a face at my drink.

Steven takes it from me and tries it. "Here," he says, giving me his. "Mine's better."

We exchange drinks and finish them in mostly quiet. But it's gotten comfortable again. The reliable silence that we've always had.

"Guess what?" I ask, changing the subject.

"Did you kiss a second guy?"

I open my mouth, then close it.

He tries to smile big at me. "I'm joking!"

The awkwardness is palpable. "Ugh. Not funny," I say, nudging him with my foot. It's a pathetic attempt to move past the most awkward "joke" he's ever made. "*Anyway*, I got my first paycheck as an influencer."

"Whoa. That *is* a guess-what." He's relaxed again, leaning back against his chair and I'm relieved we're back to normal.

"Thanks." I open the cup and shake it to loosen the ice.

"Congrats, Char. Really. What are you going to do with it?"

"You already know what I plan to do."

In our culture, it's customary to give the first paycheck to the parents, as a silent thank-you for all that they've sacrificed in raising us. I think it stems from our inability to easily communicate what we're thinking, and how uncomfortable and disingenuous verbalizing our thanks can be. So instead, we give them our first paycheck. However many days or weeks of hard labor, the first experience of the ugly grind of life, and the measly reward of it goes to the parents as a silent way of saying, *I understand. I can't imagine doing this for forty more years. Thank you for suffering for me.* If we were to say those things out loud, there'd be an expectation of an equally sentimental, touchy-feely response back. Instead, we just dutifully hand over the paycheck, however small, however grand, and bow our heads. Our parents take it, while first insisting they don't need it. But they must, because it's how everyone finds equilibrium in our roles.

"How are you going to give them a lump sum with no proper explanation?"

"I'll think of something," I say, anticipating the relief I'll create on my parents' tired faces. It's not so much that giving them my earnings makes me happy on a personal level, but it makes me feel fulfilled. Less burdened. I don't know how much money it'd take for me to feel *completely* unburdened, if it's even a weight I can lift with just money. But at least now I can try.

Dinner feels tenser than usual, despite Jojo's normal chatter. I think my parents fought before I got home, probably stemming from the trip to Aruba. She babbles on and on about preschool, the things she learned about fish and whales and other sea creatures. She shares her newfound knowledge with total awe and glee, the confident brag that toddlers often have: Did we know that the ocean is home to 94 percent of all life on earth? None of us knew and she finds immense pride in that. It reminds me that all humans, no matter how young, have an innate desire to contribute to society. It gives us a sense of purpose, a sense of life lived well, because otherwise we'd be walking nuisances on earth, contributing to the already growing mound of waste, and not even the recyclable kind.

I swallow my bite of Korean popcorn chicken that my dad bought from the H Mart in Queens. The sweet, tangy, and sticky sauce is one I've never had recreated in any other cuisine. It feels uniquely Korean, despite the countless variations of ways chicken is cooked all over the world. It's what I love about food in general. There's no other way culture can be so strongly expressed without words, except through food. I'm still looking into my bowl when I get my parents' attention.

"I have something for you guys."

When I look up, they're both waiting for me to continue. They avoid looking at each other. I pull out the envelope with cash that I withdrew from my bank account on the way home and slide it across the table.

"What's this?" my mom asks.

The white bank envelope just sits there on the table before, finally, my dad reaches for it and counts its contents.

"Two thousand dollars?" He's mostly shocked, with a bit of a contortion in his eyebrows that shows worry.

I shake my head quickly, before his concern can take over. "I won an essay contest."

"What kind of essay contest?" For once, my mom seems skeptical.

"About being Asian American. It was for all of New York and New Jersey and the second-place prize money was two thousand dollars."

"Second place?"

"Yeah. The first-place prize was three thousand, but someone else got that." I try to act bummed. I wasn't sure if they'd believe me if I said I got first place. It seems too far-fetched, seeing as I've not shown much interest in writing before this point.

"Seoyoung-ah, spend on something you want. Why give to us?" My dad places the cash back in the envelope and slides it back to me.

"Just take it," I tell them. There's an urgency to my voice. "Maybe it can be for Aruba."

My dad shakes his head. "We don't need, Seoyoung-ah."

"Just take it," I say again. "Please."

My mom takes the envelope and looks at me tentatively. "Are you sure?"

I nod and give them a reassuring smile before turning my attention to Jojo, whose mouth is stained with the red sauce from the chicken. I offer her some green beans and she takes them, only to chuck them across the table. She bursts into giddy laughter.

After dinner, I retreat to my room. I'm about to text Steven to let him know how giving the money to my parents went, but another message pops up on my phone first. And instantly my lips tingle, as if remembering the kiss. Seeing it, I can't help but think about romance movies, with scenes where the main character and the love interest share a moment that can only happen at the right place and time. One has to be in a certain mood and the other happens to show up, interrupting it yet also sealing it.

Alan Travis Smith

Bored?

yes

Perfect. Wanna hang?

Again with that "hang." But I'm still down. Maybe Audrey was wrong and movie stars just use the word "hang" a lot.

where?

I have reservations for two at Okdongsik.

In twenty-two minutes

A moment of hesitation. I saw him twenty-four hours ago. Is it too soon?

Twenty-one minutes

thumbs-up

◆◆◆

The small alleyway-style restaurant with bar seating is crowded with servers and customers but we're shown to the remaining two stools at the counter. The smell of dweji gomtang penetrates my nostrils and permeates throughout my body as if I'm already eating the rich soup. Alan also orders two servings of kimchi mandu, the only other entrée on the menu.

"It's strange this place only has dweji gomtang. You said getting reservations here is hard, right?"

"Not as hard as when it first opened. They have the best pork bone broth I've ever had."

I laugh at this. "Have you had a lot?"

Alan looks at me, jokingly offended. "A white guy can't have his full share of pork gomtang?"

I laugh again. The way he says "gomtang" is so bad, like "ghome tong."

"The g and t should be lighter in emphasis. Almost like you're whispering them," I tell him. "Or like you're sick and can't put much strength into enunciating." I pronounce the words again for him and he follows.

"Gom. Tang," he says, quieter this time. He whispers them into my ear and it's now the most romantic broth I'll ever know.

"Close enough," I say, smiling.

Finally, our food arrives. You can tell when a soup's been simmered for a long time. People are always talking about how to cook a stew in twenty minutes, thirty minutes or less, but it's never the same. They should caveat that when they share the recipe. *Hey, try my kimchi jjigae recipe. It only takes thirty minutes! But! It won't taste anything like one that's been slowly cooked for three hours.* You know how good a soup is when you take that first spoonful and it's not a jam-packed richness. The intensity of the flavor grows with every slurp, one subtle spoonful after another. That's how you know it's been simmering for hours. This is how Carol-eemo's food tastes to me.

"How'd you find this place?" I ask.

"A friend of a friend's publicity manager brought us here last time, so it's my second time." He waits a beat and then: "It tastes better this time with you."

I finish chewing on my kimchi mandu and take a long slow sip of my hot barley tea.

"Does that actually work?"

"What?"

I gesture at all of him. "The cheesy clichéd comments."

"You tell me," he jokes. "Is it working?"

I have to drink my tea so I don't lean in and kiss him immediately. It's scary how I already feel this intense pull toward him. I barely know the guy.

I put my cup down and shake my head. "Not in the slightest," I lie.

"What works with you, then?"

"I guess knowing a Korean restaurant that actually tastes Korean is a good start."

"You don't like other Korean restaurants?"

The clanking of the brass chopsticks against the matching brass bowls creates a symphony that calms me. It's like lunch with a side of sound bath.

"No, not most of them, anyway."

"How come?"

I think about a particular memory I have from many years ago. "When I was young, we took a trip to Korea. The one and only time I went. We ate at this restaurant that served traditional Korean food—nothing fancy, just gook, bap, and banchan. Soup, rice, and side dishes. It was a small, no-frills place, and it was so good. No restaurant in New York has given me that sense of authentic Korean food, no matter how many different places I try."

"Must have been one incredible place."

"I don't think it even was. I think, also, Steven's mom's cooking spoiled me. If she opened a restaurant, it'd taste something like this."

Alan nudges me. "Who's Steven?"

I blush at the lightly jealous tone in his voice. He smirks, knowing this. "He's, um, a family friend. My best friend."

"Ah. My competition?" he asks with a confident grin.

I shake my head. "No, it's not like that."

Alan shrugs in that boyish way. "I'm up for it," he says mischievously. "So, Steven's mom . . . She makes gomtang a lot, too?"

I bite my lower lip, unable to stop myself from smiling a little. Alan's charming, I'll give him that. "No. I meant her food would taste like it was cooked for hours, like you could taste the jeong."

"Jeong?"

"It's like a Korean sentiment, like warmth, loyalty . . . attachment."

"Why's it Korean? Non-Koreans feel that, too."

"It's not just Korea. Other countries have their 'jeong,' too."

Alan gets his tea refilled as I work through my fourth cup. "Where else?"

I shrug. "Sri Lanka. China. Japan. A lot of places . . . just not America."

Alan laughs like I've said the funniest thing in the world. "Is that your personal opinion or a fact?" he asks.

I'm mildly offended but not sure why. I give him a look.

"It's both. 'Jeong' is a term that's akin to love and serving and attachment, but it's rooted in acting from collective social responsibility, something America doesn't have. The States are based on an individualistic system, whereas Korea focuses on collectivism. And 'jeong' stems from that."

Alan *hmms* softly at this and finishes the rest of his two mandus.

"Are you close with your family?" The question comes out of me before I think twice about it.

Alan looks a little surprised at the question, rightfully so, and ponders on it while he swirls the tea around in his cup. Finally, he shakes his head. "I wish I was, but it's impossible to be."

"Why?"

"My parents hate each other."

A slow groan releases out of me even though I wish I could stop it. "I get it. I never want to get married."

Alan looks at me. "Don't you want to try to do it better?"

I shake my head. "I don't want to take the risk of ending up in an unhappy marriage."

"Well, then, you could get a divorce."

"But that won't just cancel out all the unhappiness. Plus, it's not that easy, right?"

He shrugs. "Yeah, I guess so. My parents are super conservative and care a lot about their public image. They'd rather be miserable in private and perfect in public. But that's why I can never be close with them. I'm too busy trying to pretend like I don't notice their failed marriage, and being goofy and trying to make them laugh."

"That sounds exhausting just thinking about it."

"It is."

Alan hangs his head for a moment, and I have the urge to hold him, but I don't. Instead, I pat his back twice before bringing my hand back to myself.

"It's like a burden you can't ever get rid of," I say quietly, knowing too well what that feels like.

"Exactly. Dang, are your parents miserable, too?" he says lightly.

I smile. "Yeah. But I don't try to make them laugh. I just focus on my sister."

"So are you close to them, then?"

"Not super close, but not *not* close? We just exist as a family." My mind goes back to the envelope of cash that I gifted. I don't share this particular burden with Alan, though, because no matter how much we might understand each other, I can't shame my parents like that to someone else. Making them look almost pitiful to someone who's never met and who never will meet them. "I just feel uncomfortable sometimes."

Alan gently puts his arm on my back, rubbing it in circles. "Yeah," he says, leaning his face closer to me. "I know what that feels like." He dips his head lower and kisses me, just like that, like we've done this a hundred times before. I pull away after a few kisses because we're in a Korean restaurant and I can't bring myself to have excessive PDA in case there are Korean mothers around (since all Korean moms know each other).

After a while, Alan says he has to get back home, and I don't let myself be bummed about it. I try to focus on my food until we get the check, but I'd be lying if I said my body didn't want more.

CHAPTER THIRTEEN

I spend most of Saturday morning in bed, texting with Alan, whose name in my phone is now changed to ATS. For whatever reason, it feels more approachable than his full name. Despite all the kissing, I don't feel close enough to him to change his name to just "Alan."

ATS
Ugh, Robert and Lenora are both paying
way too much attention to me

> poor boi your parents love u too much
>
> also of course your parents' name
>
> are bob and lenora

Tbh wish they'd love me less lol
It's too much. I wish I had a
sibling to share the burden

> eh . . . mine is 3.5 so not really
>
> helpful in that dept haha
>
> but i get it. they just want
>
> an outlet to focus on before
>
> blowing up on each other

And I hate being that outlet

We stop at a few places to pick things up on the way over to Steven and his mom's for Chuseok, so that my mom feels less bad about barely contributing to the inevitably large spread we all know Carol-eemo spent days preparing: a Korean dduk shop for various rice cakes, a liquor store for wine, and a butcher shop for fresh meat.

When we finally arrive, everyone exchanges celebratory Chuseok greetings and huddles around the table with disposable plates and wooden utensils. It's a large group today because Steven's aunts and uncles are here, too. Steven's mom isn't close with her siblings and their respective families, but twice a year, on Seollal (Lunar New Year) and Chuseok, everyone gathers together at her home. This is the first time they're coming since Steven's dad left, who, although he sucked in the end, acted as the buffer between the siblings.

The table is covered in galbi jjim, since Steven loves braised short ribs; japchae with extra glass noodles because Carol-eemo knows I don't like the vegetables; pajeon; sweet rice cakes; fish stew; steamed Korean vegetables; and a refreshing giant bowl of cinnamon rice punch for dessert. Her younger sister brought steamed crab and fancy roe, which find their homes on an adjacent plastic table that's been brought out from the closet. Wines and non-alcoholic drinks fill the rest of the table and people begin helping themselves.

"I knew you'd be in here," I say, sneaking up behind Steven in the kitchen. I look past his shoulder and see him methodically cutting a large rice cake square into pieces.

"First time making yakshik, but it smells really good, right?" He looks at me proudly.

"Smells delicious." The texture looks perfectly chewy and bouncy, and the smell of the sweet rice is irresistible.

"Here," he says, passing me a bowl of pine nuts. "You do the honors of garnishing it."

"Can I just film you doing it?" The rare times Steven is baking for holidays are when I feel like I can take photos or videos of him in his element. Otherwise, it'd be like filming someone trying to take care of their mental health. I want to capture this moment of him preparing dessert for his family. It's something we can talk about when we're fifty and successful.

But he shakes his head. "Come on, Char, just help me instead?"

"Okay, okay. *One* picture."

He groans and I snap three quick photos while he garnishes, before finishing the rest with him.

When we return to the living room, Carol-eemo's siblings comment on how much we've all grown, especially Jojo, who couldn't talk well the last time they saw her. I nod politely, smile, and try to slip away.

"It's funny how much you hate being doted on by my aunt and uncle," Steven jokes. We're seated side by side on a mini sofa in a side nook since there are too many adults tonight. Admittedly, it's a nice change of pace to focus on our own food and not solely on Jojo tonight.

"Do *you* like it?" I scoop a chopstick-full of white rice and dip it into the braised short rib marinade—the best combination of savory and sweet. "I just don't think anything good can come from multiple adults giving you focused attention like that."

"Not particularly, but I don't hate it the way you do. You'd avoid most human interaction if you could," he says with a grin.

"You're not wrong. Not you, though."

"Or Jojo," he adds.

"Or Audrey."

And then he say a beat later, "Or Alan."

My body tenses. I purse my lips, opening my mouth then closing it again. "I guess," I finally say, shrugging.

He doesn't respond, so eventually, I'm on my phone, scrolling through my usual stories and feed. We turn on a movie and the background noise is comforting. I stand up to get seconds of the soup Carol-eemo made and ask if he wants anything.

"Nope." His tone is casual but he sounds off.

When I'm back, I'm balancing my phone on my thigh as I lean over the low coffee table for a bite of my jjigae when Steven suddenly pushes the table forward while repositioning himself on the sofa. My soup swishes out of the bowl, splashing my phone, pants, and the floor.

I blot the soup on my pants and shoot him a hard glare. "Dude, what is the matter with you?"

He looks at me right back with an intensity that I can't read. "Can you get off your fucking phone for like a *minute*?"

I lock my phone and put it face down. "*What* is your problem?"

"You don't even know these people, but you obsess over them for hours. And now you're hooking up with someone you don't even know? What's *your* problem?"

Steven's voice is so contemptuous that it makes me stop breathing. Despite our disagreements, he's never sounded so cold. This evening just went from chill to rage in one second.

"Just because you don't know them doesn't mean I don't know them. They're my friends, Steven. And, not that it's any of your business, but we're not 'hooking up,' " I say.

His eyes are still drilled into me and my soul feels bare.

"Why can't you just be happy for me?" I ask him. I stop breathing, waiting for his answer. Wondering what he'll say.

"You don't even know him, Char. Or what he wants. You're being naive."

Tears prick the edges of my eyes as Steven turns my most exciting memories into something ugly. Maybe I want him to tell me not to date him. Maybe he's jealous. Or maybe it's all in my head and Steven's never thought of me that way before. "I do know him, Steven. Just because I have a life outside of you, doesn't make it bad. Or wrong." My voice sounds angrier now.

Steven shrugs. "You think you can trust someone you just met? Suit yourself," he says, with a nonchalance I know he doesn't have. He leans back into the sofa, like he's over this conversation. Over me.

Well, *I'm* not done. "You're being an asshole."

He looks at me, like he's deciding whether he wants to get into it. "And you're spiraling."

"What?"

"You're obsessed with followers, you're never not on your phone, you're ignoring people when they're right next to you. And now you're dating someone you met online? Spiraling. It's not going to end well, Charlotte. I'm just saying."

I clench my teeth. "Well, *don't* just say."

Steven scoffs and it enrages me.

"You point fingers at my life and you think I'm doing it all wrong, but you know what's pretty damn obvious to me? That you quit therapy."

That's when he glares up at me. It's rare that Steven gets like this. Even more wordless than usual, his stare's so icy you feel pierced, his entire body emanating anger so much your whole body tightens. I hit him too hard where it hurts the most, but I can't help myself. He hit me, too.

"And you clearly shouldn't have," I add, making myself one level shittier.

"It's so fucking exhausting being your friend, you know that?"

My breathing evens and we look at each other like that for some time, each of us waiting for the other to say something, anything.

"Thank god Alan's normal. Thank god he's the opposite of you."

And the second I say that, I wish I could take it back. But it's too late. Steven gets up without a word and doesn't come back for the rest of dinner. Eventually I can hear him laughing with Jojo in the other room and making pretend monster voices. I envy the way he's able to compartmentalize, to laugh like that. Neither of us really yells or throws things when we're angry . . . sometimes I wish I could have emotional outbursts, but it's not in my DNA. I'm physically unable to move that quickly, to yell and scream. I clamp up, my body sweats, and I'm frozen, stock-still, as the rage and pain course through my body until words that pierce come out quietly. And tonight, I know it was bad. My dad knows something's wrong and he comes in twice to check in on me. I pretend to have a headache and he doesn't buy it, but he prevents my mom from coming in and lecturing me to join everyone else.

"Let her rest," he tells her in Korean, ushering her out of the small space.

The car feels cold the entire way home even though it's only the end of September, and I'm convinced it's because my mom spends the duration of the ride home shooting death stares at my dad. Their tension feels like it's taking all the fluid out of my body, like I'll shrivel up and collapse any second now. By the time we get home and Jojo is down in her room, I'm in the kitchen, quietly making myself a hot cup of herbal tea. Sometimes I feel psychic, the way I sense things before they're about to happen. I stand still, silently stirring my tea with the teabag. And then I hear my mom's voice. It's a little muffled but I can still hear her pretty clearly. "Perks" of thin New York walls.

"Did you have to say that in public?" she says in Korean, clearly exasperated.

"It wasn't public, we were with our friends." My dad sounds tired, like he's on the verge of giving up.

"It *was* public," she practically hisses. "They're not our friends; they don't even like Carol that much. You just love to talk about how injured you are."

I take a few steps closer to their door and through the tiny crack I can make out my dad situating himself into the armchair.

"You think I like feeling like this? Do you even think about how I feel? Not being able to work and function the way I used to?"

"Why else would you go around parading to everyone that you can't do anything because of your knee? I've always known you were lazy, but you're even more useless than I thought. That's why you're dying to go on this trip. An excuse to continue and do nothing with your life, nothing for our children." My mom's voice is barely audible, but her tone is so sharp and cold that I know instantly where I get my ugliness from. I want to barge in there, to tell them to stop fighting, that I'll make more money for us to comfortably go on trips, to not worry so much about the future, but I just stand there feeling helpless.

I'm not sure who I side with. It's not fair that my mom has to work more because of my dad's injury, but it's not my dad's fault that construction equipment fell on his legs and wrecked one of his knees forever. I just don't want them to fight all the time. They continue their quarrel but I retreat to my room, careful to not let my parents hear any movement outside their door.

you ever wish you could just disappear

ATS

All the time. What happened?

> parents are fighting again
>
> and someone told me it was
>
> exhausting to be my friend

Asshole

If we lived next to each other,

I'd tell you to come outside

Take you out for some ice cream

I smile when I read that last message. No one's ever been this forward with me, wanting to take me places, texting me back, texting me first. A lot of people at school make out and do much more and keep it casual, but I'm positive Alan has no idea that he was my first kiss. It's not that big a deal anyway and I don't want to put any pressure on us. It's nice, the way things are right now. Fun, flirty. It's always so easy with him, not like being with my family. Or even Steven. But I don't know how he really feels about me. If it's just me, or if there's anyone else. We never really talked about it but maybe we don't have to. At least not now.

> do you think im exhausting?

I hate myself for asking this.

No way

Had the best time the other night 😉

Def not exhausted 😃

But also def down to be exhausted 😉

I send an eye-rolling emoji and scroll through Instagram, interacting with users, replying to comments, deleting unwanted messages. I know Alan wants more; it gives me a sense of power, his desire for me. Nothing like I've known before, but it's hard, without the certainty of what we even are.

                                                          me too

    Free tomorrow?

                                                    definitely

We agree to text again tomorrow, and I go to bed that night feeling slightly less shitty.

CHAPTER FOURTEEN

My phone buzzes next to me, waking me up from too short of a sleep. When I look at my phone, I see it's a call from Audrey.

"Hello?" I say, trying to be as alert as I can be at ten in the morning. I love that she chooses to call people instead of texting. She's an influencer with the soul of a 1950s woman.

"Oops, were you sleeping in? I'm baaaack. Miss me?"

I rub my eyes. "Yes, *duh*," I tell her, laughing.

Audrey updates me about her short trip home and invites me to hang out with her friends later today.

I sit up. "What time?" Because we celebrated Chuseok yesterday, we're skipping Sunday dinner today so otherwise I'd be home doing nothing. First Alan, now this. My life feels like it's expanding.

"There's a new pop-up brunch thing that Lizzie wants to go to, and she got a reservation for all of us."

I squeal, proof that Audrey's influencing me, and agree to meet her there in an hour.

◆◆◆

Thirty minutes of throwing everything out of my closet and trying to repurpose clothes later, I'm in the Lower East Side with Audrey and her friends. They don't seat till everyone's here so we're waiting outside, off to the side to avoid the crowd. Once Swan arrives, we're next in line.

"Hi," the host say. "Name for—"

I look up the same time Steven stops talking. We both freeze. The girls are watching us staring at each other.

I recover first. "Um, hi."

He still doesn't say anything. Finally, he clears his throat. "Name for the reservation?"

Lizzie chimes in to give her name to him. He shows us to our table wordlessly. When we're seated, he returns to his post and takes the next party behind us.

"Do you know him?" Swan asks.

I nod and look at Audrey. "That's Steven."

Audrey's face lights up. "Oh! I thought he was like an ex-boyfriend or something with the way you guys looked at each other. Steven's your best friend, right?"

I laugh lightly to ease the mood. "Yeah. We, um, got into it the other night and haven't talked. It's not a big deal, though," I say, assuring myself more than anyone else.

No one presses further because no one's interested in "just friends" gossip the way you would be if we were in a situationship. But even though the conversation moves on, I can't take my eyes off Steven. Since when did he start working here? Why did he never mention it? So he has a job. It's not like this is some secret place or some weird thing to be doing for him to keep it from me. Then again, I'm at a pop-up with friends that I didn't tell him about, so maybe it's normal. But it feels so off and tense that it's hard to care about the drinks and beautiful pastries that come out ten minutes later. When I focus back in on our table, Swan is rolling her eyes and cursing in Spanish.

"Yeah, they asked me, too. Last week. Me cago en su madre," she says, muttering under her breath.

"Who asked you what?" I say. "Sorry, I was distracted."

"By your cutie friend?" Lizzie says with a tease in her voice.

"Ha. It's not like that!"

"Right," she says. "Anyway, I was talking about Lavish & Pearly."

Audrey turns to me. "It's that brand that I mentioned last week, remember?"

"Oh, the white one?"

"Yeah. They've literally reached out to all of us now, promising a lot of money and wanting to be more diverse, blah blah blah."

"Aren't they trying to do it right, then, by asking you guys?" I tread lightly, unsure if I'm asking the wrong question.

Swan shakes her head vigorously and her lush brown hair bounces back and forth. "No. They did all these 'I stand with AAPI' and 'I stand with BIPOC' posts and statements, but they were caught stealing artwork from Asian designers and putting it on their own clothes. Now that a bunch of individual designers banded together and came out with the truth, they're in trouble and trying to salvage themselves."

"Yeah. They got all this backlash and now they're trying to be like, 'No, no, really, we support Asians! And POC! Look at all our influencers!' Except, no one is accepting them," Lizzie adds.

"Well, they haven't asked me." I shrug. I try to make it a joke but it hurts. Seems like anyone that's anyone got asked and I am irrelevant.

"Let's keep it that way. They're not worth your time," Audrey says.

It's stupid, but I still want an invite. In some ways I feel like I'm finally a part of this world now, but stories like this remind me I'm still new. I'm not famous enough to be seen by this white brand.

We're halfway through our meal when my phone vibrates in my pocket. When I see who it is, I nudge Audrey subtly.

"Look who's calling," I whisper so only she hears. She makes an ooh-la-la face.

I roll my eyes and answer. "Hello?" I keep my voice down so I don't interrupt the other girls' conversation.

"Hey, where you at?" Alan asks.

"Lower East Side."

"Where? I'm nearby."

I mention the pop-up and ask what time he wants to meet.

"Soon?" His voice is flirty and I smile, just a little.

"How soon?"

"I'll come pick you up now."

"I'm with friends right now."

"On my way!"

"Alan!" I hiss loudly. I cover my mouth but it's too late. The other girls look up at me, mischievous grins on all their faces.

I look at my phone, but he's already hung up.

"Who was *that*?" Lizzie asks knowingly.

"Um, I think I have to head out soon," I answer. A sheepish smile forms on my face.

"To meet your *lover*?" Swan adds with a smile.

I wave them off, desperate to change the conversation. The girls ask me too many questions about Alan and I answer each one with a shy amount of detail. I can't deny that I enjoy talking about boys with my new girlfriends, but I'm definitely not used to it.

In a record-breaking twenty minutes, Alan shows up. I see him enter, looking right at us. He approaches the host stand and my heart drops. I can only watch as he tells Steven he's with a table that's already been seated, and Steven turns his head. It feels like slow motion, the way Alan and Steven are both staring at us. At me. I press my palms against each other, nervous.

Alan grins and waves at us. "Ladies," he says grandly. "They're *my* friends, too," he says to me pointedly. "You never mentioned who you were with." He turns his attention toward Lizzie, Swan, and Audrey. "Would you ladies mind if I stole Charlotte away?"

The girls roll their eyes and nudge me off the seat, laughing.

"Take her," Lizzie says good-naturedly.

"But be good to her," Audrey warns.

"Oh my god. You guys." I bite my lower lip, feeling uncomfortable and also . . . kind of giddy. We say our goodbyes and head toward the exit.

At the door, Alan holds my jacket open, and when I turn to put it on, Steven's right there looking at me. Instantly my giddiness is gone and replaced only by discomfort.

Alan waits for me to lead the way but I just stand there, immobilized. I'm acutely aware of his hand on my lower back. I can tell Steven is too when his eyes slowly drop to Alan's hand.

"Alan, this is, um, my Steven," I stammer. "I mean, my *friend*. My friend Steven."

Alan makes a *hmm* sort of sound and extends his hand. "Hey, man. I'm Alan, nice to meet you. You work here?"

Steven shakes his hand with a slight nod.

Alan leans in closer to Steven. "Hey, if you need a better gig, let me know. I can hook you up. Pay would be better than this place."

Shame absolutely covers me like a fire blanket. My cheeks feel hot and embarrassed. I don't know for who. Maybe all of us and this horrible clash. "Um, I'll text you later?"

Steven gives him a bitter smile and looks at me. "Don't bother."

I grab Alan's hand and drag him out before he does anything else to emasculate my best friend.

"Did you really have to say that?" I ask him when we're out of earshot.

Alan looks at me with innocent confusion. "It was just an offer, Char. Don't get worked up about it. Please?"

"It was dickish. And you know it."

"Come on, I was just playing, okay? Maybe I got a little jealous." He holds my arms in his hands. "I'm sorry, I just wanted to steal you for myself."

I shouldn't like hearing that as much as I do. But this attention he keeps giving me makes me feel . . . like one of those confident people you see in magazines, like a celebrity who knows she's a big deal. I give him a reluctant smirk and he knows I'm forgiving him.

"I came straight here from the airport," he says.

"From where?"

"Toronto."

"Whoa."

"I wanted to see you."

We walk around the Lower East Side, talking and flirting for some time, and Alan eventually asks if I want to stop for food. His arm is casually around my shoulder and it's another dreamy afternoon with him where life feels unreal. We settle on a hole-in-the-wall Chinese restaurant and pick five dishes to share. When it all comes out, there's barely any room left on the table.

"We may have overordered," Alan says.

"Doubt it." I dig in first to the plate of steaming baby bok choy, relishing its cute smallness.

He swirls a chopstick full of chow mein and lifts it to my mouth.

"Um, what are you doing?" I ask coyly. I reach over and grab a piece of garlic-marinated eggplant.

"Being cute. Is it working?"

I shake my head. "No," I say, laughing. I push his chopstick away and playfully guide the swirl of noodles into his mouth.

He grins and opens his mouth. "You feeding me is cute, too." I don't fight the smile that forms on my face.

But in a moment that feels like it's straight out of a rom-com, his phone that's sitting between us buzzes and jolts us out of the moment. My eyes dart down out of instinct.

> **Sylv**
>
> Had fun last night
>
> I'll be in nyc next week. C u @ your place?

I immediately wish I hadn't read it. I turn my attention to the eggplant.

"That was just a friend," he says, in a rushed way.

I shrug. "Sure."

"Are you mad?" he asks.

I shake my head. "We're not exclusive or anything." But does he want to be? I wish I knew exactly how he feels.

"Right . . . but you know I like spending time with you, right?" Alan's hand finds mine and he rests them on my leg. Goose bumps shoot through me even as I will them not to.

Deep breath. *We're not anything serious, just having fun,* I remind myself and bring myself to the present before I can spiral. I smile at him and squeeze his hand back. "Yeah. I know."

He inches closer to me, crowded table be damned, and whispers into my ear. "Mmm. You smell good."

"Better than this egg drop soup?" I joke.

He lowers his head and plants a kiss on my neck. "Way better," he murmurs.

My shoulders rise and I wriggle out. "Alan, not here," I whisper, half laughing in awkwardness.

"Why not? It's been too long."

I shake my head and peel his hands off me. "We're in an *Asian* restaurant. The ancestors are watching."

"So, no hands while inside this restaurant or any restaurant?" Alan asks as he sits back and twirls noodles on his chopsticks.

I feel taken aback by this question. "I'm not answering that!"

"I'm just trying to get a sense of what's allowed," he says, wiggling his eyebrows. The thing about Alan that I've come to appreciate is that he never really takes anything seriously. I can feel angry and frustrated about all the questions about us or even at the way he treated Steven, and then *poof*, it's gone. He's the opposite of so much that's inside my head . . . an escape for me. A drug.

"How will I know when I can do this?" He holds my hand. "Or this?" He kisses my shoulder before I pull away again, despite how good it feels. "Do you want to come over?" he asks me, in between more kisses.

My body tenses. I know what it means when a boy—let alone a celebrity—asks if I want to go to his apartment. My brain is telling me no. But then he kisses my neck so slowly and tenderly that I need more.

I whisper an "okay," so Alan hurriedly asks for the check and we get out of there. Seven minutes later, we're inside the lobby of a building I know only rich people live in. It has doormen in uniforms greeting people by name, one outside the door, one inside, and then another at the desk. There's one of those intense waterfalls and artwork that looks like a kid threw paint on a canvas and blindly spread it around that probably sold for a million dollars.

"You live here?"

"It would be pretty weird to be taking the elevator right now if I didn't," he jokes.

Alan's apartment is just what I'd imagine a young male celebrity's place would look like. High ceilings, the Manhattan skyline, the insane floor-to-ceiling windows, the pristine kitchen island because he probably never cooks. I walk around on a quick, self-guided tour, my socked feet padding through the apartment. There are stairs that lead to an open lofted area where I can see his bed and a nightstand. I'm tempted to see what books he keeps by his bedside. It tells so much of someone's personality.

Alan's in the kitchen pulling out glass bottles of Perrier. He hands one to me then brings me to the massive window, with most of Manhattan laid out in front of us.

"Wild." My voice comes out quietly. "You live alone?"

"Yeah. My parents live close by, though. Tribeca's pretty small."

"Why don't you guys live together?"

He shrugs. "I like my privacy."

"Which reminds me," he says. "Want to come to my birthday party? We're going to have it here, but I hired a company to set it all up. It'll be pretty cool. I want you to be there." I already know this is going to be a party unlike any other and I'm dazed to be invited by the birthday boy himself.

Then in one swift motion, he pulls me in and kisses the crook of my neck as I murmur a *yes* and he teases that we're no longer in an Asian restaurant. The kisses get slower, more intentional, more longing. He pulls away for a second and I immediately want him to continue.

This doesn't feel like my life. A guy like Alan asking me to come to his party, making me feel confused and giddy and horny all in one evening. But there's an uneasiness to everything. A question gnawing at me. About choices, about people, about who we're destined to be with. But I keep my mind focused on kissing Alan and not overthinking all of *this*.

He carries me to the sofa and pulls me onto his lap. My legs are straddled over his hips and we're making out hungrily and I can feel him get harder against me. His hands slide under my shirt and it sends a jolt throughout my entire body. They find the clasp of my bra and in half a second, it comes undone. I feel exposed, bare, and too horny for my own good. And I suddenly wonder if Steven's mad at me.

His fingers are lightly on the underside of my boobs. I freeze and grip his wrists, preventing his hands from going higher.

"Something wrong?" he asks, slightly breathless.

"No, sorry. Let's just . . ." I climb off his lap and sit down next to him, angry at myself for stopping. If there's ever a time for this kind of thing, being with Alan is it. He's clearly experienced, I'm attracted to him, and he wants me. But I can't bring myself to give in to it.

He sighs, and even though it's subtle, I hear it. And it makes me resent myself even more.

"Sorry, I just got distracted." I sweetly plant a kiss on his cheek and his head turns to me, forgiving me. I kiss his neck like he does mine and let my hands explore under his shirt. Just like that, the rhythm is back and he pulls me onto him once more, letting his mouth meet mine. His arms are around my waist, pressing me against him. As if wanting to steer clear of my upper half, he rests his fingers on my jeans. I focus on the kissing, on how good it feels, how exciting it is. Things start heating up again and there's a burning between my legs. The pleasure and the desire for more feels overwhelming.

His hands find their way to the button on my jeans and he undoes it and pulls down the zipper slowly. It's sexy. It feels like we're in a movie and this is what I've been waiting for my entire teenage life. If it ever happened with anyone, I thought it'd be Steven, but it's a hot celebrity. I'll take it. Then he begins pulling down my pants and I grab his arm and pull away. Again. I hate myself. My body and brain are not agreeing.

He looks at me, trying to hide his frustration. "Is everything okay?"

I nod. "It's just, I don't think I can do this tonight."

He runs his hand through his hair and nods, clearly disappointed. "Did I do something wrong?"

I shake my head. "No. Just . . . it's a me thing," I tell him.

"Gotcha. Yeah, no worries. We're good," he says, but it doesn't feel good. The vibes are suddenly awkward. I know what he wants now, and I'm not ready to give it to him.

I make an excuse and mention Jojo and how I haven't spent time with her lately, which isn't entirely untrue, and fasten my bra. Alan offers to send me home in a car but I assure him that the subway is faster.

On the ride home I feel hollow and angry. Steven got inside my head with all that stuff he said about how I can't trust Alan. It's not like Alan forced me to do anything. At one point I wanted it as much as he did. So why do I feel like shit?

When I get to my apartment, the tension feels palpable. It's so dark and depressing that I have half a mind to just go back to Alan's. The only light is wherever Jojo is and she run-jumps into me before I finish closing the door.

"Sharty!" Jojo grabs my arm with her chubby hands and holds it against her face. So sweetly, she nuzzles my arm, and the anger I have toward myself feels momentarily distant. My dad is reading a book in the living room and my mom is nowhere to be seen.

I escape to my room when Jojo returns to my dad. My phone buzzes and I wonder if it's Alan, telling me he's moving on. I consider turning it off. I open my phone, and as if the universe knew I needed a break, I sit up too fast when I see who it's from.

Finally, I'm being acknowledged.

✦✦✦

I make myself a cup of yuzu tea and sit on my bed cross-legged, ready to dive into the details. I read on with a knot forming in my stomach. I know I shouldn't even spend time reading it, based on what the other girls said about Lavish & Pearly. I know I'm just another POC influencer they're trying to tokenize, but my eyes keep going.

. . . Creating a diverse portfolio . . . took time to hear from our fellow social media family . . . value and respect the work you're doing . . . ongoing sponsorship opportunity . . . $10,000 per post. Minimum of two posts, more pending the performance of the initial two . . .

I close my phone screen to take it all in. This is more money than I've ever dreamed of. In my head, I see my parents: they're proud of me and smiling at each other, and we're in Aruba, carefree and spending perfect family time. Like a poster of an American family vacation. I think about how one post could pay for the whole trip and then some. It could probably pay for rent and give my dad some time to find a job he can do easily without further jeopardizing his body. Jojo could take even more dance lessons and my mom wouldn't have to work double shifts.

But then I think about what Audrey said, about how Lavish & Pearly doesn't value POCs, about how they stole our designs, and how the Asian American online community has been shunning them, like they shunned us. How frustrated Swan was.

My fingers fidget with a stone on my nightstand that's been softened from years of turning it over in my hand. I got it when I went to Coney Island with Steven on a boring summer Saturday. It was hot and we had no money, so we hopped on the subway and sat in our tanks and shorts until we were freezing from the subway

AC, and then we lay out on the rocky beach. I remember the very moment I stepped on the stone at just the wrong angle, when a shooting pain went up from my ankle to my calf. I remember Steven asking why I was bringing it home with me and I told him I was determined to make it soft, to conquer it. *You're ambitious about the strangest things*, he told me. *It's my favorite thing about you.*

I take a few deep breaths. Lavish & Pearly is making genuine attempts to diversify their portfolio. To be the first Asian influencer for them would be a big deal. This was the whole point of starting this career. I've been building my profile for years to get here. I have to choose my family, even if that means I lose everyone else. All of this was for them.

Ten thousand dollars.

Before I can change my mind, I open my inbox to respond.

CHAPTER FIFTEEN

I don't know how many days go by in this haze. And being in school never helps. It's just a sadistic bubble of emotional volatility waiting to burst.

Steven and I still haven't spoken and the silence feels deafening. Sunday dinner at Carol-eemo's was barely manageable. I didn't last more than an hour before I pretended to be nauseous. Steven glared at me from across the table and I knew I fooled everyone but him. His mom spent most of the dinner trying to convince my mom to take the vacation, claiming we all needed one. Right now though, a week trapped with Steven sounds like a nightmare.

My only upside lately is getting another partnership, this time with a large coffee company. It wasn't as much as Lavish & Pearly, with seven hundred dollars per post, but it's an ongoing sponsorship where they request I post regularly over the next three months, with the goal of integrating their coffee into my stories consistently. I already posted the story from Sunday morning before church where I filmed myself pouring water from the kettle into the mesh filter filled with grinds. Creating reels has been fun for me lately, so I spent most of the church service guiltily putting together a reel of the coffee-making process.

Steven and I ignored each other throughout and after the service. It's our second week not speaking and the silence has been taking its toll on me. I didn't realize how little I spoke to anyone else in my life. I've been largely avoiding Audrey, too, thanks to the guilt that's slowly eating me from the inside out. I miss her and the urge to spill everything to her comes over me a few times, but I know she won't understand. And she's been busy with events and other friends. Unlike me, she has a lot of other people in her immediate circle.

Same goes for Alan. He told me he was busy with work lately, but it can't be coincidence that after that night at his apartment, we've barely talked. It wasn't until my fight with Steven that I realized I could go days without interacting with anyone in person besides brief moments with my family.

Wednesday morning, I wake up early to take a few pictures of my outfit—the one for Lavish & Pearly. It's luxury athleisure and the bright pink cropped sweater is trendy. If it weren't for this specific brand, I'd be proud of my outfit today. It's going up later this afternoon and there's a tightness in my stomach. I push all sense of morals to the back of my mind as I draft up my post to upload after school today. All that matters is my family.

After second period, Steven and I run into each other by our lockers, and we wordlessly stare at each other, both of us waiting for the other to break the ice. I grip the paper I received from my teacher tightly, irrationally terrified he'll see the bright red C at the top. He must notice my clenching because his eyes slowly drop to the paper in my hands.

"AP World?" he finally asks.

I nod.

"You rolled it up," he points out.

We both know what he's getting at, because Steven knows everything there is to know about me. He knows that I roll up tests and assignments whenever I get a bad grade. He also knows AP World is an easy subject for me, easy enough to be a big deal if I don't get a good mark. And in this particular moment, I hate that sometimes the impulse to cry, to sob, is something that I can't suppress. I hate even more that in this moment, everything going wrong—the C on my paper, the shame that Steven senses it, that we're ignoring each other after everything that was said or unsaid—builds up to right now where my eyes begin to fill up. I look to the side to try and keep the tears from falling.

Steven fidgets uncomfortably, fighting his instinct to ask if I'm okay.

"Sorry Alan was an asshole the other week." I blurt it out before I change my mind.

He shrugs. "I don't get offended by strangers."

My lips thin into a line. "Good, I guess."

Steven rubs the back of his neck and looks down the hallway. "I'll see you," he says and walks away before I have a chance to respond. I slouch to the ground as my backpack lands on the vinyl floor with a thud.

I open my phone to review my drafted post for Lavish & Pearly. For a while I hang my head between my knees, unsure.

"Don't do it, Charlotte," I tell myself quietly.

I think of my parents, the way they hurl harsh words at each other. I think of the subtle relief I saw on their faces when I handed them the two grand. The way my dad beamed, the peace during that dinner. How the tiniest bit of weight lifted off my shoulders. *Deep breaths.* I turn my phone over and tap Post before shoving my phone into my bag.

That evening, I get a lot of new followers, the majority of them non-Asian. I try to not feel good about this, but it's hard. We still live in this world dominated by whiteness, so I know the larger demographic of white people that I'm gaining will help with future sponsorships.

I get a few unfollows, too. As I reply to comments, I'm filled with hatred for myself, too aware of how easily I've been bought. There's one more thing I notice from this post. A friend who's liked every single post and Story of mine has remained silent on this one: @AudreySena. But she hasn't texted about this either, so it's hard to gauge how annoyed or upset she might be.

A knock on my door jolts me out of my thoughts.

"Come in."

"Sharty?"

"Hi, Jojo."

Her little feet pad over to my bed and she climbs into it with me. "Will you play with me?"

I snuggle her, smoothing her soft hair that unfortunately looks like a long mullet. It feels like the last sign of her babyhood. "Of course."

In the living room, we play with her dolls until it's time for dinner. My dad picked up some dumplings a few weeks ago that we defrost for quick meals. That's the great thing about Chinatown—fifty delicious dumplings for twelve bucks! Jojo gleefully peels the skin off the pork and chive dumplings and piles the meat into a corner, refusing to take a bite of it. My parents, like classic Asian immigrant families, never actually make up after a fight. If enough time has passed, my mom begins to acknowledge him again and then eventually, everything returns to normal: my dad his jovial self and my mom, colder to him and average with me, and most expressive with Jo. I know my mom's feeling better by now because she plates some of the dumplings onto my dad's plate, an expression of acceptance.

I excuse myself for a moment to grab the envelope in my room. The coffee brand's ongoing structure is to pay twice a month, once at the start and once at the end, for a total of four posts a month.

My parents look up from their plates at the envelope I place in front of them when I return. "*Another* competition you won?" my dad asks.

I shake my head, trying not to feel offended by his disbelieving tone. "Don't get mad, okay?" I close my eyes, remembering the story I carefully concocted for this very moment. I needed a consistent cover for the growing sponsorships I was getting. "During my free period at school, and only on the days I'm done with all my work, I've been tutoring some of the other students. I help them with their schoolwork and get paid. It's all approved by their parents and everything." I've decided to start giving them a few hundred dollars at a time to not bring in questions of having *too* much income from tutoring. It's the only way to consistently give them my influencer income without suspicion.

"Seoyoung-ah," my mom says, but I cut her off.

"Umma. It's *really* not a big deal. I have literally nothing better to do than sit there if I'm all done with my work and there are no exams to prepare for. It's only when I know I have the time, okay? Trust me? Just this once?"

My dad exhales slowly then nods at me. "She's right. She's a junior now, yeobo," he says in Korean. "She old enough to know what she's doing."

I bite my lip as I wait for my mom's approval. I eat two dumplings in the time I'm waiting for her decision. Even Jojo looks at her and the world stops for a second as we all wait.

Finally, she looks at me. "*Only* when you're really free, and *only* when you're completely done with *everything* you need to do. Deal?"

I smile, nodding multiple times. "Deal."

It's better this time, when I see them take the envelope. Less awkward for me, less awkward for them. They beam at each other, as if they're sharing a moment of pride for raising me right, and I thank the gods for Instagram. For this one dinner, things feel manageable, peaceful, even.

Once I'm back in my room, I text Audrey.

hi. are you pissed at me?

audrey
Honestly? A little, yeah

I'm not sure how to continue the conversation. Maybe it'd be better to talk in person.

can u meet tmr

Yeah. You can come over
after school if you're free.

I confirm for tomorrow, frustrated by her coldness. She shouldn't treat me differently when she doesn't even know the full context. Just because others are boycotting this brand doesn't mean I need to. I know I'll need to explain everything tomorrow. Maybe she'll stop being angry then.

I end up in a rabbit hole, looking at posts from Audrey's account dating back to almost a year ago. Her online persona is consistent, and even then, her focus has been on supporting the Asian American community with her platform and partnering with mostly Asian brands. It makes me wonder how many times she turned down a good opportunity with a brand that she felt wasn't inclusive enough.

Compared to how I jumped at the first chance of a big payout.

◆◆◆

The next day, I'm not sure what period I'm in when there's a loud knock on my desk and I look up in surprise.

"Ms. Goh?" Mr. Anderson says sarcastically, and I know I'm in trouble. All the teachers call us by our first name, except when we don't listen.

"Sorry," I mumble, putting my phone away.

"What could be so important that you're ignoring your trigonometry teacher, hmm?"

He walks away before I have a chance to answer and goes back to his lecture. At the end of class, he asks me to come to his desk.

"Sorry again, about that," I tell him, hoping to get off on a warning and not detention.

Mr. Anderson peers at me through his gold-rimmed glasses before handing me a paper face down. "Charlotte, I know trigonometry isn't always easy, but your lack of focus is getting concerning. This is not the first time I've seen you distracted in the last few weeks."

I flip the paper over to see a C+ on the pop quiz from last week. It's my second C in the last two days. My stomach drops. I didn't realize I did so poorly.

"Is something going on?" His voice is kind and it makes me feel even worse for ignoring his lectures these last few days.

I shake my head. "Just a little busy."

"Okay, but midterms are around the corner and you'll need to focus if you want to bring your grades back up," he says with a mild tone of urgency.

I've been ignoring some of the lower marks I've been getting on assignments lately because they're not a big deal, but bad marks on quizzes and papers will take their toll. I nod. "Will do. Sorry. Again."

He nods encouragingly back at me, like he knows something is up but is respecting my privacy. I wonder if this is what it's like to have white parents who are mostly supportive while minding their own business. What freedom.

I roll up my pop quiz and slip it inside my textbook before shoving them into my locker. As I leave school, I'm thinking about how Steven and I still haven't really made up when I spot him alone a half block ahead of me. I contemplate going up to him, but I don't know what to say, so I trail him from farther away, waiting for the words to come to me. We walk slowly for some time until he finally sits down on a bench outside a park. Sitting a few benches away, I can see that he's in his own head. He probably wouldn't even notice if I was sitting next to him. He doesn't look at his phone or a book or anything. He stares at the cement under his feet, shifting positions every so often. I can tell something is really bothering him, something bigger than he thinks he can handle. An hour goes by like that: him on that bench, me on mine. Eventually, he stands up and starts walking and I follow, all the way into the subway, where I get off shortly after to start the longer walk to Audrey's apartment.

In her lobby I sit on a chair and take a few slow breaths. Something's going on with Steven, but right now, I need to fix things with Audrey.

She lets me in and we make our way to the kitchen where she offers me water.

I politely decline and avert my gaze. "Listen, I know you're mad . . ."

Audrey seems unsurprised by my comment. She stands on the other side of the kitchen island and looks at me. "Mmm. Wouldn't you be?"

"But it's not really about you . . ."

Audrey looks at me like I've offended her. "What do you *mean*? I feel like we all talked about this together. We were being honest with you and you totally backstabbed us."

"Just because I make decisions that you wouldn't have doesn't mean I backstabbed you, Audrey."

"You knew that we all weren't going to take them up on their offer."

I don't respond. I can tell that Audrey's upset, that maybe she thinks we don't know each other enough to get fully mad, but if we were closer, perhaps she'd be livid with me right now.

"I mean, it's not like they didn't give us great offers, too, Charlotte. It's a solidarity thing that you chose to skip out on." A beat later. "Even when I gave you the memo."

"It's not like I *wanted* to do this, Audrey. But some of us don't have as many options as others."

Audrey shakes her head. "No, you had a choice, Char. No one forced you to be a sellout."

I flinch at that but stand my ground. "That's a strong accusation, Audrey."

"Am I wrong?"

"Yeah, you are. And you don't even fully know my situation or where I'm coming from. And you jump to these stupid conclusions that are completely out of line." I can feel the heat rising to my cheeks.

"Then tell me." Her stare is cold but there's a bit of sincerity to it, like she's waiting for a better explanation. A way for me to prove her wrong so she can like me again. "It's not like I've never gotten roles for movies, Charlotte. I've gotten a good amount, actually. But they were for roles that were stereotyping Asians, with no respect for the character, no true storytelling. So I turned them down. You can't just give in to everything because you want to be known. That's not how it works."

She doesn't get it. Not even a bit of it. It's not for her to know why I'm trying to desperately make money, that I need to please my parents, keep our family together, make sure Jojo never faces these burdens. She doesn't live with that kind of pressure, in her pretty two-bedroom apartment that her parents pay for. She doesn't understand that ten thousand dollars is life-changing for our family. I won't shame my parents like that.

"Well?" she persists.

I pause. I know my response could kill our friendship, but my family comes first. "It's none of your business, Audrey."

The last bit of sincerity goes cold and her stare turns darker as she glares at me. "Get out of my apartment."

I grab my backpack from the table behind me and storm out. The door slams shut behind me as I press repeatedly on the elevator button, silently begging for it to come quickly so I can escape this place.

CHAPTER SIXTEEN

I sit in a local playground until my racing mind and pulse calm down before going home. Is this what it feels like to have no one on my side? If I don't give people what they want, what they want to hear, they just drop me. At least that's what it feels like.

When I get home, my parents are seated around the dining table together, huddling over a phone.

"Hey," I say, dropping my bag to the floor. I dig around the fridge for a snack and automatically make a plate for Jojo as well. It's unusual to see them together like this and I keep my eyes on them, trying to decipher the vibe. "What's going on?"

"Oh, it's *nice*," my mom comments, using her fingers to zoom in on a photo of something.

"I told you, yeobo," my dad replies. "You never believe me!" His Korean sounds lighthearted, relaxed almost.

"What's nice?"

They both look up at me, finally acknowledging my presence.

"Jojo," my dad calls out. Little feet come running into the kitchen and my dad tells her to tell me the Big News.

"Trip with Steven!" she screams.

I look at my parents, unsure what to make of Jojo's reveal. "Huh?"

"We're going on that trip with Steven and his mom," my mom says.

I can't figure out how I feel upon hearing this news. Instantly, I feel happy, mostly for my parents. Seeing them huddled over these resort photos, even though my mom was appalled at the idea initially. But Steven and I won't be able to avoid each other there, and if we do, our parents will definitely pick up on it.

"What changed?" I ask.

"We could all use a vacation," my mom says. "But you and Steven will be missing three days of school for this. We're making an exception this one time." She takes Jojo by the hand and heads over to the living room.

I shrug. "Fine by me," I lie. I'm acutely aware that I'll fall behind on schoolwork and that my parents don't know how poorly I've been doing.

I'm about to turn to go to my room when my dad grabs my hand and holds it in his. "Seoyoung-ah," he says, wrinkles forming by his eyes, "it's all because of you." In English, the literal translation is more like *it's our luck, thanks to you.* "We're so proud of you."

I give him a small smile and head to my room, thinking about my fight with Audrey. I don't regret it, working with the brand. Even if it taints my reputation among other Asian influencers and drives my best friend away, no one knows the full picture but me. This moment, seeing the pride on my dad's face, the relaxed shoulders on my mom, makes it completely worth it.

◆◆◆

The next few days are hectic as everyone gets ready for the trip and digs through closets to find appropriate resort wear. I can't even remember the last time we went on a family vacation that wasn't on the East Coast. Each night, I sit in my bed with a tightness in my chest when I check Instagram. A lot of Asian American influencers have unfollowed me. And even though I haven't met the bulk of them in person, it still stings. I didn't know strangers could have so much power over me. I'd welcome the distraction that Alan brings, but he still hasn't texted me since that night. Maybe whatever our situationship was ran its course. Or maybe I'm overthinking it. His social tells me he's traveling again for work. Probably hanging out with a bunch of other girls and doing god knows what.

It's late and I'm washing up in the bathroom, trying to forget the sigh in Alan's voice and my fights with Audrey and Steven when the door opens slightly and my mom's face pokes in.

"Seoyoung-ah," she says, with a tired resignation, "are you busy?"

I shake my head as we look at each other through the bathroom mirror.

"Can you come to the living room after you're done?" she asks in Korean.

I stop moving my toothbrush in rhythmic motions, letting the foam drip down the sides of my mouth. I spit some of it into the sink. "Everything okay?"

She nods. "I just want to talk to my firstborn."

I hold it together just long enough for her to close the door behind her before I fall to the floor and press my forehead on my knees. I fight it but my eyes and nose sting, and a few moments later, I let tears drop to the bathroom floor. I wipe them away with my feet, hiding the evidence with every smear. I know my mom needs another release, another conversation where I pretend to be a sounding board, but what she wants is just a hole for her to shout her woes into. I fight the urge to scream at her, to tell her to go find a therapist, to stop burdening me with her trauma and useless dreams. Instead, I finish washing up, dab my face with a wet towel, and make myself a mug of Korean instant coffee before joining her in the living room.

"Seoyoung-ah, it's so hard sometimes," she says when I sit next to her.

"What's hard, Umma?" I look at our feet, almost touching from the opposite sides of the sofa. Her toes are long and her feet are slimmer than mine.

"Your appa tried his best, I know he did. But his injury went beyond his physical body."

I wait, letting her continue.

"He couldn't get back into the mindset to work again. He lost that fire. You remember when he used to come home and tell me all the weekend plans that he lined up for you and Jojo?"

I do, vaguely. I almost forgot about those days. I remember my dad coming back from his construction work, still dusty from being on site all day, but excited, like you could see the adrenaline behind the whites of his eyes. He'd come back with all these plans for new parks in different parts of New York and we'd explore them all, one by one, weekend by weekend. Or we'd go to free events he heard about through his co-workers. He was the king of finding affordable and fun activities to do. It was fun for me, too, seeing my parents light up under the warm summer sun. I'm brought back to the present when I feel my mom's hand on me.

"Seoyoung-ah, are you okay?" she asks.

I was zoning out. "Yeah, I remember, Umma."

"Remember he used to go visit multiple construction sites, making sure everything was running smoothly? He'd feel so proud, pointing at finished buildings and how he helped make them."

I nod again.

"The doctor said his knee will never be fully back to how it used to be. He broke after that," she says quietly. "Even with physical therapy, he warned him not to walk around too much." She shakes her head. "I hated that doctor. Hated him for breaking your dad." My mom smiles a sad smile and takes my hand in hers, patting it a few times. "Maybe this trip will bring him back."

An hour later, I feel relieved to be back in my room, and that this talk was different. Less emotionally draining. It's like being excited for this trip brought back memories of the better days for my mom. We recalled how much my dad enjoyed walking trails from one end of a park to the other as we all complained about how tired we were. He'd then pull out secret snacks he had been stashing as bribes to keep us going. It always worked.

I automatically open Instagram to see how I'm doing on metrics and devour all the content it offers until my mind feels clouded enough to sleep.

◆◆◆

It's the end of the school week and Steven and I and I are still barely speaking, but something's shifted. We're not completely cold toward the other anymore. When we meet eyes in the school hallway, it's not an immediate look-away moment, which is enough to give me a bit of peace. At least he doesn't hate me completely. There was a small part of me that thought maybe our fight would be irreparable, that Sunday dinners would forever be faked until our parents caught on and we stopped them altogether eventually.

Today, Steven's up ahead of me again, right outside school grounds. It's funny that despite not talking, we run into each other so frequently, in a school as large as ours. It makes me wonder if we're so synchronized from years of being inseparable that our bodies naturally gravitate toward the other person at the same time, down to the minute. What are the chances that we'd both be exiting the school at precisely 3:07? Pretty small, in a building of five hundred kids.

We head to the same subway station but we don't take the same train. At the top of the stairs, he turns around, as if knowing I'm there, and gives me a slight nod. I lift my hand in a half wave before he descends out of sight. I stop near my apartment to take a few photos in a discreet area, though the benefit of Long Island City is its prevalence of Asians doing somewhat similar things.

◆◆◆

On Saturday, I lie around and scroll through my photos, digging through pictures taken that I can use and post for upcoming stories or my feed. Two hours go by like that and a knock at my door jolts me out of my digital stupor. Jojo's tiny head pops into my room. She's back from ballet practice and still in her pink leotard and white tights.

"Sharty, I miss you." Her voice is sweet, like caramel melting off a summer apple. "You don't play with me anymore."

My insides twist with guilt as I manage a smile and propel myself off the bed. "You're right. Let's go. What do you want to play?" I ruffle her hair as she giggles and drags me into the living room where *Bluey* plays on our TV. She asks me to restart the episode and, when the theme song plays, Jojo starts yelping with glee, running around and jumping when Bluey jumps.

I sit there next to her, but I can't help but reach for my phone again. Three times I open my texts to message Audrey, but I don't know what to say. *Hey, Alan wanted more than kissing and I wasn't ready. Also, my family's financially irresponsible so I'm trying to help them, sorry I took the partnership?*

Instead I browse Instagram, viewing stories, looking into the curated lives of other people awash with a sense of envy. Why are there always so many people on vacation? I check my DMs to see if Alan messaged me. Of course he hasn't and I hate that I'm waiting, wishing. I feel so pathetic.

When Jojo's focused on Bluey, I sneak away to my room and

spend too much time trying on twenty outfits for our upcoming trip, looking at my phone then throwing it on my bed, looking at it again, then trying on more clothes.

Exasperated, I head to Brooklyn, determined to turn this day around. There's a small store in Williamsburg that I like to go to. It's owned by a Korean ahjumma and she brings clothes from shopping districts in Korea and sells them here. And they always have a 50 percent sales rack in the back that I love. I'm lost in the beautiful sea of clothes and accessories. Trying on dresses here in their single fitting booth with a curtain for a door feels still more glamorous and special than in my room. And for two hours, I dream of the outfits I can wear and finally narrow my selection down to two dresses that I purchase on sale.

When I'm back home, I feel loads better than I did this morning and even Jojo's fussing sounds endearing. She's screaming for food.

"Soon, soon!" I hear my dad telling her. Steven and Carol-eemo are coming to our place tonight and we'll order pizza. We've decided on a family sleepover so we can all head to the airport together first thing tomorrow morning.

Half an hour later, I hear the buzz from the intercom and I tense, wondering how tonight will go. School's easy enough to avoid each other, but we're about to embark on a four-night trip together, five if you include tonight, and it won't be easy to keep going like this. I stay in my room, even as I hear the door opening and Carol-eemo's familiar voice filling up our home.

"Seoyoung-ah! Come out!" my mom shouts out into the hall.

Deep breaths, then I join them in the kitchen where three pies from Slice sit side by side on our countertop. My mom's cutting thin slices for Jojo and my dad gets the plates.

"Hi, eemo," I say, giving her a hug. Steven's holding Jojo already and it makes it easy to not hug him with his hands full. Like divorced parents, we both focus all our attention on Jojo throughout dinner, instead of making eye contact and talking to each other. Fortunately it's easy enough to avoid Steven with all the buzzing excitement everyone feels about tomorrow. Carol-eemo outlines all the activities offered at the resort, asking a million questions about what we should do, what we want to do, what Jojo can do.

"Jet-skiing for me," Steven answers.

"Maybe yoga?" I offer, sending the parents back into a frenzied discussion.

Our apartment is small so the sleeping arrangements are a little wacky. My mom and Carol-eemo take the master at my dad's insistence, and he and Steven sleep in the living room. Jojo's room is more of a glorified closet and her bed is way too small for Steven so she and I get to keep our spaces. But after I see my dad rubbing his knee all throughout dinner, I bring my pillow and blanket into the living room when it's time for bed.

"Appa, go to my room," I say as he settles himself on the couch.

"Aniya, aniya, dwaesseo," he says, waving me away. I pull him up and practically drag him into my room.

"You're going to need to be comfortable for the flight tomorrow and for the trip."

He sighs, looking at me with sad eyes. "Seoyoung-ah, I don't want you to look after me." His quietness makes me overcompensate.

"I'm not, Appa. I just want you to be comfortable. You're not young like me," I tease him.

In the living room, the lights are dimmed and Steven is sitting on the ground, reading a book. His mattress is Jojo's playmat, padded with layers of thin blankets.

I force myself to break the ice. "I know you're not actually reading," I say, holding my breath, waiting for him to say something. Anything.

Finally, finally, he puts the book down. "Yeah? How?"

"You haven't turned a page in a really long time."

He nods a few times, slowly.

I want to ask him if he's still angry at me. If we're okay. If he's even excited about this trip.

If he hates me.

I want him to talk, to say something, not just to respond to me. I miss my friend. So much more than I realized. I wish I could tell him, but it's like a lemon wedge is stuck in my throat every time I try to get the words out.

He stretches and I know it's fake. I know what he's doing.

"Good night," I mumble.

"Night," he says back.

I watch as he lies down and covers himself with a blanket before settling down on the couch, wondering how things went so wrong. Maybe it was always destined to go sideways once one of us found someone else. Maybe our friendship can only exist when no one else is a part of it. Like it was always meant to be just us two, or not at all.

I think about the things I said to Steven that night at Chuseok, wishing I could take it all back.

CHAPTER SEVENTEEN

"STEEEEEBEN!" Jojo's squeals reverberate through the entire apartment.

My mom is running around the apartment trying to pack last-minute things while my dad dodges her and does the same thing. Steven and I are barely awake and Carol-eemo is making coffee.

"Why is this house always so chaotic?" I say, groaning and rubbing the crust out of my eyes.

"SHARRRRRTY!" Another squeal. Before I have a chance to run away, Jojo jumps onto the couch and lands on my body with a thud.

I groan again and roll Jojo off the sofa. She loses her balance and falls backward instead of sideways, thumping her head on Steven's blankets. She screams and runs out of the living room, little footsteps rushing away to find comfort.

Three . . . Two . . . One . . .

"Charlotte!" my mom shouts. "I don't need Jojo crying right now!"

I put a pillow over my face to drown out the noise. Two more minutes and I'll wake up. It's not even seven in the morning yet.

From the corner, I can hear Steven rustling his blankets, layer by layer, folding it neatly into thirds. As if reading my mind, he talks first.

"Morning," he says. His voice is calm, almost pleasant.

I sit up and peer at him from the sofa. "Are you talking to me?" I ask, half in jest.

He rolls his eyes. "Ha ha. Yes, you. Charlotte Seoyoung Goh."

I give him a small smile. I like hearing my name like that, in a tone that's not a shout or a demand. Steven talking to me is the opening I've been waiting for. Hope rises in me that the trip won't be four days of intense discomfort and avoidance. Excited, I swing my legs off the couch to grab my things.

Thirty minutes of shoving last-minute things into suitcases and Jojo throwing a tantrum to bring all three of her stuffies, one hour of being squished in an Uber and begging the driver to make it to the airport stat, and fifteen minutes of running through security and the terminal *Home Alone*–style later, we finally board the plane and collectively sigh in relief. Before putting my phone on airplane mode, I post a view of the city through the window, reveling in the joy of finally sharing vacation content.

"Can't believe we made it," my mom says in a loud whisper, squeezing my arm. "Get some rest, sweetie." She gently rubs the back of my head.

I smile, studying her profile. The lines on her face have settled in, making their permanent homes, but she looks so at peace. I lean my head on her shoulder and close my eyes. A wave of pride rushes through my body and I smile again as I slouch lower in my seat, dreaming of many more trips in our family's future.

When I wake up, it's because we've landed. Jojo is passed out on my dad and Steven's asleep, too. My eyes trail down to his right hand. It's holding Jojo's small fingers and warmth spreads across my chest. I will this trip to be good, to repair us.

A van from the resort picks us up and the parents chatter in Korean about the gogeup (elevated) service of this hotel, how it's definitely a steal that Carol-eemo found, and how lucky we are. Steven and I exchange eye contact and the corner of his lips twitch up in a smirk. Nothing like the delight of immigrant parents feeling confident that their bargain was the best one possible.

It's almost ninety degrees in Aruba and, when we get to the resort, we're greeted with virgin piña coladas for the kids and rum and cokes for the parents. As our parents get us all checked in, I use this moment to immediately connect to the resort's complimentary Wi-Fi. My fingers are itching to scroll through Instagram, but within minutes, the bellhop takes our things and shows us in the direction of our room. We split into our respective families, agreeing to meet by the pool once we're ready.

We open the door to our room and gasp. It is gorgeous.

"Wait, wait, leave your bags outside!" I say urgently, and they shoot me surprised looks. "Just for a sec. I want to take a few photos."

Jojo runs around the room and it makes for some cute pictures, the back of her dress bouncing behind her, the Caribbean sun streaking in through the windows.

"Umma, can you take a picture of me?" I show her exactly how to angle it and I lay down on the bed, pretending to relax on the soft sheets. Sunglasses on, pin-striped dress spread casually around me.

They're not perfect but it's just the first hour, so I'm about to put my phone away when an unexpected text pops up.

> **ATS**
> You're going somewhere?!

I stare at my phone until it feels like my pupils are dilating. Did Alan really just text me? After almost two weeks of not speaking?

> Yeah aruba

> Ah so far from me ☹
> I wanted to see you

I draft a few messages and keep deleting them. *He wanted to see me?* He could've seen me this whole time. What was stopping him? Finally I settle on a message that hopefully comes off a little cold but not ice queen.

> Haha ive been here
> where were you

> I've been so busy with work
> But still want to see you
> Soon ☺

As my mom wrangles Jojo into her swimsuit, we text for a while, back and forth, back and forth. He doesn't bring up *that* night and neither do I. If there was any ice on my end, it's thawed. After all, it makes sense that he had work. Most of all, he feels familiar again, easy. A distraction from real life.

◆◆◆

"*Look* at this sun!" Carol-eemo says, stretching out on a beach chair. There's even a smaller one for toddlers that Jojo claims and covers in her snacks and water toys. Steven and I sit next to each other and cheers with our plastic cups. For a few hours, all anyone does is sit, lounge, jump into the water, and read, while I take selfies when I feel like people aren't paying attention.

"Steben?" Jojo lifts up her head from filling her pail with water at the shallow end of the pool. She uses her baby voice and I know she's going to ask for something.

"Hmm?"

"Will you make a sandcastle with me?"

"What about me?" I pretend to look offended.

"You tomorrow. Steben today!"

"Jojo, it's Ste*ven*, okay?"

"Steee*even*," she repeats.

My mom throws me a reproachful glance and I shrug. "She can't use baby words all the time, Umma."

"Char, come on, we're on vacation."

I fight the urge to say something back at her, that Jojo will be turning four in six months and we can't treat her like a baby. But I don't, because she's right. We're on vacation. And that is *rare*.

"Let's do it, kiddo," Steven says, rising from his chair. I avert my eyes as he rubs a layer of sunblock over his chest and face and neck. I feel weirdly shy being next to him in a bikini. It's such a weird concept to me that, at a beach or a pool, people walk around in glorified underwear, but if you do that anywhere else, it's suddenly inappropriate. It's like the beach is the one place where people are so casual being half naked.

Come to think of it, I've never really been around Steven in pool settings. The public pools were always so crowded, so we spent most of our summers sweating through free park concerts or spent evenings at night markets in Queens and Flushing. I grab the bottle of sunblock after he and Jojo dash off to the beach. Halfway through their sandcastle making, I get my phone and snap a few photos of them. It's super picturesque, the way she keeps giggling when he splashes water on her tummy or how he buries her little fingers in the soft white sand. I also use this opportunity to force my mom to take more pictures of me, before Steven comes back to make any judgy remarks.

I open Instagram and spend a few minutes scrolling. Alan's stories pop up in my feed. It's a video someone else is taking with Alan and a girl waving at the camera. He has his hand around her bare waist. She's wearing a super-high crop top with baggy neon green pants. Her hair is pulled tight into two braids. A level of trendy I'll never reach. She has a drink in her hand and an arm wrapped around his neck as she kisses his cheek, laughing like it's the funniest thing in the world. He grins back and I swipe to the next story before it ends.

I shove my phone into my tote and try to control my breathing. We weren't official. He never even said we were exclusive. I shouldn't be bothered. I know Alan wants more than just kissing and I don't. At least not right now. One hour ago I felt special from his texts. Now I feel stupid.

"You okay?"

I jump a little, suddenly seeing Steven right in front of me. Water drips from his wet black hair and from his swim shorts.

"Yeah, fine."

"Jojo wants chicken tenders," he says. "And so do I. Want to join?"

I take a beat to observe my situation. I'm at a beach, on vacation, with my hopefully still best friend. I don't need to be thinking about a guy who's too cool for me, probably too open to ever be committed, and who has desires I'm not willing to meet.

I nod. "Definitely."

Our parents are all still in the same spot they were three hours ago. We promise to bring back food for them as well and make our way to one of the buffets. We load our plates and grab virgin daiquiris for ourselves. Jojo happily munches on a chicken tender as she trails us back to the pool.

"Hey, kids, there's a movie and pizza night at the teen club tonight," my dad calls out in Korean.

I shoot him a thumbs-up.

"You and Charlotte should go to that, okay?" Carol-eemo says, looking at Steven meaningfully. "It's a super-fun movie. *Lego*-something. We're using the hotel's babysitter once Jojo's down." She lowers her voice so my sister doesn't hear.

Steven and I exchange glances. "You know you guys don't need to hide the fact that you want to drink your brains out tonight, right?" Steven says, smirking at the three guilty faces.

"That's not what we're doing!" his mom says defensively in Korean.

He shrugs. "Sure, we'll go to the teen club. You down, Char?"

I raise my eyebrows. "Mm-hmm."

We both know we're definitely not going to that. We're the oldest possible age to be admitted before being legal adults in two years.

They look so satisfied, like they think their plans for getting rid of us actually worked, that we just shake our heads and start to eat the food we brought back. It's then that I discover the beautiful combination of chicken tenders and pizza poolside.

The rest of our day is spent relaxing until evening. Steven and I volunteer to put Jojo down so our parents can go straight to the adults-only section of the resort. After an hour of endless story time (Steven), wrangling a hyperactive three-and-a-half-year-old into pajamas (me), asking twenty times if she wants to use the potty (both), she's finally down for the night. Relieved, we give the sitter our numbers and where our parents are before we step out as well.

At the lobby of our hotel, I turn to Steven. "Well . . . what should we do?"

"Wanna go watch *Lego*-something?" he jokes.

I give him a look.

"Let's go for a walk," he says.

It's the perfect weather for a stroll down the beach with a light cardigan. The wind from the waves feels so freeing. I kick the white sand in front of me, feeling the softness between my toes. We walk in silence until I muster up the courage to say what I've been meaning to for days.

"Steven?"

He turns to look at me. His hands are in his pockets and he looks a little distracted, like his mind is on something else.

"I'm sorry."

"For what?"

"For being shitty."

He gives me the smallest smirk. "Care to elaborate?"

A small smile escapes me, too. He's going to make me work for his forgiveness. I guess I deserve that. I stop him and we stand there on the beach, face-to-face.

"I'm sorry I said it was obvious you quit therapy. I'm sorry I used that against you. I'm sorry Alan was a dick to you. I'm sorry I didn't defend you then and there. I was just . . ."

"Shocked, I know. I'm sorry I didn't tell you about the job," he finishes. "I was going to, but we got into it that night at Chuseok," he says.

I realize I'm holding his arm as I talk, so I drop it awkwardly. The sun has set, and the light from the moon is hitting his face in a way that makes him look mysterious almost. But then he smiles and the light highlights his right dimple and he looks like the little boy I've always known. It's a small smile, not his usual jokey grin, but everything feels a little better now.

"I'm sorry, too," he says sincerely. "I didn't mean anything I said. I'm sorry," he says again. He puts his arm around me casually and that's when I feel it—a flutter in my stomach. The kind reserved for people you might . . . like.

"Man," I say, "I missed you." I try to sound like a best friend and not like I've just felt an explosion of caterpillars all becoming butterflies in one singular moment.

He nudges me lightly, like he's done many times before. "It's been lonely without you, if I'm being honest." We walk a few steps before he breaks our silence. "I have to tell you something, too," he says. He doesn't stop to face me. A part of me wonders if maybe he felt it too—the flutter. But then he continues. "My dad wants to see me again." His voice is so quiet, it's almost a whisper.

I stop in the sand, looking at him with concern. I remember seeing him on the bench that afternoon, his head in his hands. I know in my gut that's the day his dad contacted him. I scramble for the right words to say, wishing so desperately to help him.

I recall the day he found out his dad was cheating on his mom like it was yesterday. It was one and a half years ago, when Steven ran nine miles without stopping, when I tried to call him over and over again until I found him, sprawled out on the grass at Queensbridge Park with tears spilling from his eyes. I was tracking him on our shared location app and waited until his icon had stopped moving. I remember his face when I joined him: splotchy, red, puffy eyes, dried skin from all the tears soaking his cheeks. He didn't want to talk about it. So we lay down together on the blanket I brought and cried until my face matched his. I don't know how long we sat there like that. I turned my phone off and trusted my dad's instincts would be good enough to know I would be with Steven, being present with him.

"I need you, Char," he says now, barely loud enough to hear.

"I'm here," I whisper back.

"Can you be here, with me?"

"Anything you need."

"No, Char. *Really* here." He looks down at my hand, the one that's clutching onto my phone. "No Instagram. No phone?"

Understanding dawns on me. I'm more selfish than I ever thought I was, because I don't want to agree to this. It's my one vacation in years, and I want nothing more than to share the overload of content that I can film while here.

He must sense my hesitation and it makes me feel like the world's most horrible person. "I know it's asking for a lot," he says, "but can we just keep this trip for ourselves?"

I snap out of being a shithead and escape the pits of hell that would wait for me for choosing social media over my best friend, and smile confidently. Before I can think twice, I grab his shoulders and nod. "Of course. Yes. Absolutely. Just for us," I say, pressing my forehead into his. I can feel him relaxing a little, the tension in his shoulders easing just a bit.

"Thank you," he whispers, closing his eyes. My eyes are open and I see a tear trickle down his cheek and fall on the soft white sand, turning it into a spot of dark brown. I can feel his breath on my lips and again I feel it, for the second time—butterflies. I quell the panic rising in me and focus on being present for my best friend.

Even as I'm thinking about kissing him.

CHAPTER EIGHTEEN

When I wake up, I can still feel Steven's breath on my lips and I bury my face under my sheets. What is going on? I can't possibly be falling for my best friend when things are finally getting back to normal between us. We didn't speak for two weeks (though it felt much longer), so maybe I just *really* missed him. *Yes, I tell myself, I just really missed him. As a friend.* I throw off my covers and go to the bathroom sink to splash cold water on my face and start my day. I'm committed to keeping my promise to Steven. Even when we're not together physically, I told him I would stay off Instagram. It's a mental exercise to be fully present, whether he's around or not. But the morning crawls by without mindless scrolling and I feel like I'm going through withdrawal.

"Char, why don't you take your sister down to the buffet and we'll meet you there?"

I glare at my mom. It's a command more than a suggestion. "Why? We can wait for you guys."

My mom is waiting for my dad to get out of the shower so she can go in after. She's holding a book that's bookmarked very close to the beginning and she looks at me pleadingly. "Thirty minutes of alone time, okay?"

I roll my eyes and smile. "Fine. Come on, Jo, let's go make some ice cream sundaes."

"ISCREAM!"

Everything with Jojo is a shout or a wail. I scrunch up my face and tell her to use her indoor voice.

"She needs a real breakfast, Char!"

I shrug as we exit the room with our beach bags and swimsuits. "You put me in charge, I choose what we eat. See you downstairs," I say, closing the door behind me.

Hours later, everyone's lounging poolside. I could get used to this. I hear Carol-eemo and my mom giggling like schoolgirls, and Steven and I exchange a look.

"What's so funny?" we ask them.

My mom looks at me, hands clasped together like a kid wanting candy. "Honey, do you and Steven want to spend the day with Jojo so we can go somewhere real quick?"

I raise my eyebrows. "Where real quick?"

"The casino next door at the adults-only resort," Carol-eemo blurts out. My mom tuts and smacks her knee lightly.

I make a face, but I don't want to say no, not when Jojo is right next to me. Her eyes are gleaming. It's probably her dream day, to spend it with me and Steven and no adults. I hold in my sigh and look at Steven. "If Steven's okay with it?"

He gives a thumbs-up. "Sounds great to me."

Our moms shout loud thank-yous and run off so fast they don't even say goodbye. My dad gives us more detailed information of how to find them in case of an emergency and trails behind them.

When Jojo is out of earshot, I groan. "Babysitting wasn't on my agenda today."

Steven laughs. "It's all good. It'll be fun. A friend-date-slash-fake-parents day."

I will myself not to overthink at the word "date" that he just threw out. What would a date with Steven look like? Would it be everything we do as friends but with more? Or would it be completely different? I feel like we've done so much together since we were kids. But there are still so many things we've never done. Things like ice skating at Rockefeller Center or eating at a fancy restaurant. Maybe those things are reserved for dates.

"Hey," Steven says, nudging my thigh. I snap out of my delusion. "You okay? Come on, I'll make it extra fun."

I smile at him. "I'm fine. *You* should not be the one asking *me* how I'm doing. Sorry."

"Are you annoyed your mom asked you to watch Jo all day?"

I shake my head. "It's fine," I say, waving my hand away. "How about you? Do you want to talk about it?"

"Not yet. And not with Jojo here."

I nod. 'Kay. I'm here, though." I shoot him an awkward thumbs-up. "And present," I quip. But my fingers are already itching to post pictures of the beautiful white sand beach in front of us.

He squeezes my knee and Jojo interrupts our moment by tugging on my arm. "Ava said kids club is showing *Trolls*!" Sure enough, a slightly older girl repeats what Jojo just told us.

"You want to go to the kids club instead of hanging out with Steven?"

She nods shyly. "With my friend Ava."

Steven pretends to look hurt but laughs. "Let's go drop her off."

After, Steven and I wander toward the spot on the beach we were at last night.

"I have an idea," he says, pointing at something far away. "It'll help get over your annoyance."

"I'm not annoyed!"

"Liar. You're totally annoyed at your mom."

I roll my eyes. "Well, I'll get over it."

"Yeah, and this will help."

He drags my hand and starts running on the stretch of sand in front of us. I'm out of breath trying to keep up, and I yell at him to slow down, but he doesn't. He's grinning at me, running backward, telling me to hurry up. The sun is high above us and we're already sweating. Steven looks so carefree, like he's not constantly probably thinking about his dad and what this means. The tide is low and a lot of kids are in the water or playing on the sand. We dodge them and slow our pace as we reach a hut with life vests and surfboards. Parked along the sides of the huts are kayaks, Jet Skis, and banana boats.

"This," he says, pointing, out of breath and excited.

"A Jet Ski?"

"Have you ever tried it?"

I shake my head. "*When* would I have ever tried riding a Jet Ski?"

"Good point." He pulls out his phone and shows a voucher from his emails to a staff member. "Can we rent one, please?" he asks.

We fill out a couple of forms, then the instructor shows us how to work the Jet Ski and we head out together onto the beach. We each ride briefly with the instructor to understand what it should feel like, and how to turn and stop before hopping onto one together.

I didn't think it through until now, until this very moment where Steven's seated directly in front of me, my bare legs wrapped around his hips. The waves create a bobbing movement on the Jet Ski, and I lightly put my hands on his shoulders.

"You're going to have to hold on to me if you don't want to fall off," he says loudly, turning his head slightly toward me.

"Don't go too fast, then!"

"It's not fun unless you go fast. Trust me! Ready?"

At first, I *very* loosely wrap my arms around his waist. But when the motor reverberates the Jet Ski and he takes off, I clutch my hands together around his stomach. My chest is pressed into his back, and I can smell the salt on his wet black hair, blowing wildly in the ocean air.

The first few minutes are terrifying. I worry about tipping over or falling off if I let go even a bit. But slowly, I relax my shoulders, loosen my clasped hands on Steven's abs (he has abs!), and sit up more to feel the sea breeze on my body. I breathe it in deep and close my eyes.

"This is amazing," I say loudly so Steven can hear me through the waves.

"Try shouting as loud as you can!" he says.

"What?"

"I've always wanted to try it. Out here, where no one can hear you in the middle of the ocean."

"Do it, then!" I encourage him.

"You first!"

I let out a yell, but it doesn't feel as good as I want it to. "Wait, once more!"

He nods, and from his profile, I see his smile. And I notice how handsome he is. I'm not sure how I never really saw it. And being this close, the desire to kiss him grows in me again. Just one small kiss. But I pull myself out of it and instead let out a deep shout from my gut.

I yell at the top of my lungs, and the anger from feeling like one of many girls to Alan, of feeling misunderstood by Audrey, the burdens my mom puts on me—they all burst out of me. It feels incredible, so I do it again. I try to let go of everything: of knowing too much at a young age, of having too much on my plate, of choosing Jojo time and again instead of myself, of having Jojo chosen over and over again by my mom and never me, of what my dad's injury did to our family. I shout and shout until I'm out of breath and it's the greatest catharsis of my life.

And I have Steven to thank for it.

Steven, my rock for every year of my life. Steven, my best friend and confidant. Steven, who made me feel like I never needed anyone else because he was more than enough. Steven, who I am realizing I might be in love with.

I rest my head on his shoulder, eyes closed, smiling. I lift my head back up once I catch my breath. "That was everything," I tell him.

"Right?"

"Okay," I say, grinning, "*your* turn!" I poke his stomach with my index finger and he squirms and instinctively grabs my hand to stop me from poking him again.

I might be imagining it, but he turns his head, enough for me to see, and a warm smile spreads across his face, one that feels different from the ones we've shared. And then, after a big deep breath, mouth open wide, he lets it all out, too. As he screams into the wind, I hug him tightly from the back, shoving aside my shyness for this moment. I clutch him desperately, trying to tell him I understand. In my mind, I tell him what I don't say aloud. *You don't owe your dad anything. You can be selfish. You have nothing to worry about, because you're already so much better than your dad ever was.*

I can't explain what comes over me next. I lift my head from burrowing it into his back and I gently kiss the nape of his neck. It's soft and slippery from the water splashing onto us with every bob in the ocean. This time, he doesn't turn his head, he doesn't react at all, and for a moment I wonder if he didn't feel it.

But then his hand covers mine briefly. It's for maybe less than two seconds, but it lingers, before it goes back to holding the handle. The lingering is all I need to know that he definitely felt my kiss.

The rest of our ride we spend being stupid and silly, shouting into the void and trying to poke each other while staying on the Jet Ski. Multiple times, the instructor yells at us to stop fooling around.

We exchange grins and let the salt water dry out our faces and tangle our hair.

When we get back to the shore, we're exhausted and collapse on the wet sand, letting the shallow water cover our bodies with every ebb and flow. I don't know if it's the adrenaline from the ride or the freedom of shouting endlessly and not hearing our own voices, but the high of coasting over the ocean overrides it all and we burst into an uncontrollable fit of laughter. The instructor tries to get our attention but we can't control it. We're rolling around, fresh sand sticking to us after each wave that cleans us off. We're pulled in deeper into the tide and we regain our composure so we don't get swallowed by the sea. In the water, we stand up and the waves splash just above our hips.

Then he looks at me, *really* looks at me, before pushing a strand of hair away from my face. It's the sweetest and gentlest gesture.

"We *needed* that," Steven says, now running his fingers through his hair to tame it. I do the same, throwing the rest of my hair into a high bun with my scrunchie. And just as quickly as the tender moment came, it's gone. I can tell by the way he boyishly grins.

"I'll race ya," he says. He takes off before I have a chance to say anything back and I watch him for half a second, wanting to pull him back to the second right before. Then I wade through the water to catch up to him and race back to shore.

◆◆◆

Our parents are still at the casino, so we head to the kids club to see if Jojo wants to be picked up. It's not quite sunset yet, so after we get her, we order food on the beach and eat on our chairs. After consuming two platefuls of jerk chicken, the three of us make sandcastles, not far from the water where Jojo keeps going back to get more wet sand for us. Together we're building a giant mound before Steven clutches his stomach.

"Ugh. I think I overate," he says, as a wispy little fart exits his body.

Jojo and I burst into laughter and before we can make fun of him, Steven, cheeks red and mortified, runs toward the restrooms. When five minutes go by and he's still not back, I grab my phone from my tote in a moment of weakness. As I scroll, I try to keep an eye on Jojo, who's still adding wet sand to the mound.

So many people are asking me to post vacation content since my story through the airplane window. I desperately want to share. After all, this is my job, and my family is depending on me. I need to keep followers engaged and interested. Plus, Steven deleted his Instagram. There's no way he would know.

I glance up again to see if there's any sign of Steven. I quickly snap a picture of the waves and share it to my stories and tag the hotel location. Then, scrolling to earlier photos, I upload a carousel of some of the pictures my mom took of me in the hotel room, the white sand beach and perfect clear waters, of Jojo and Steven playing together, of Jojo running around. All the while, I look up from my phone every few minutes to make sure Jojo's still there. Eventually, as I get sucked back into the social media vortex, I stay on my phone a little longer and just scroll. Audrey hasn't posted in a while. I check to see if she's still following me, and I'm relieved to see that she is.

I don't know how much time passes before I check on Jojo again, but when I do, the mound of sand is there but Jojo is not. I drop my phone and look to my left and right, calling her name loudly. Assuming she's hiding from me, I beg her to come out. I still don't see her, and she doesn't respond. My head starts spinning and I feel dizzy, like I can't seem to stand still as I search for her desperately.

Then I hear a distant scream and I look out toward the ocean. That's when I see someone in the water. Someone little. Someone whose chubby arms and stubby fingers look eerily familiar. I see Jojo walking into the waves with her bucket, but in the next instant, I see only half of her. Everything feels like it's happening to someone else, but I know I'm screaming as I run toward my baby sister. The sand is slowing me down. I can't see in front of me but I know I'm running. Someone is screaming behind me, too. The screaming gets louder and an arm shoves me aside so hard I lose my balance on the shifting sand. It's my mom. When did she get here? I can taste grit in my mouth from falling. But before my mom can even reach Jojo in the water, the lifeguard runs in, and with one precise motion, swiftly pulls her out and has my sister over his shoulders. She's wailing.

When I'm able to stand up again, I keep running. *Jojo is breathing.* My brain processes that much. I know at some point Steven shows up and is trying to calm me down.

"*Char, Char, she's okay, she's okay,*" I hear him saying. But it's all muffled. I think I'm sobbing. I'm hugging Jojo even as my mom pulls me off her. I can't really begin to explain what I'm feeling. Only that I'm vaguely aware that Steven is talking to the lifeguard and the hotel staff as my mom cradles Jojo. I'm sitting with sand stuck all over me, staring at the spot in the water where I saw my little sister gasping for air before the lifeguard brought her out.

Time stops. I try to breathe while counting to five in my head; then I start all over. Again and again and again, until it feels easier. Eventually, I can hear loud and worried voices around me more clearly. Voices that belong to three adults I know. My mom is shaking me by the shoulders and I can't focus on her even though I'm trying to. I still feel out of my body, and my mind is in the darkest places of what could have happened. How this could have ended.

Finally, my eyes focus and I look at her. My vision is blurry and I realize I haven't stopped crying. My mom's face is blotchy as well. She's sobbing and my dad and Carol-eemo are trying to calm her while she screams at me. *"You almost lost her forever!"* Does she think I don't realize that?

I finally open my mouth. "I'm . . . I'm sorry." The words feel so futile. I look up and see Jojo, now snuggled against Carol-eemo, while my mom looks at me like I'm her biggest disappointment.

She's talking to me in rapid-fire Korean. "Sorry? You think 'sorry' is enough right now? What could possibly have been so important that you let your sister almost drown? Don't you know how common this is for kids, especially at a beach? What were you thinking? You weren't thinking, obviously. Have you lost your mind? You can't be trusted with anything. What kind of older sister are you?

"Answer me!" she shouts. Carol-eemo is pulling my mom toward her and telling her to stop being so harsh; it was an accident and Jojo is okay.

It's the wrong thing to be focused on right now, but I feel so humiliated. Being yelled at like this, in public, in front of Steven and our families. In front of strangers, in front of the hotel staff, in front of Jojo. A lump forms in my throat. I meet my mom's eyes and my vision is still blurry from fighting tears that want to spill over. I know I almost lost my sister. I know my mom's never going to forgive me for this. But the same thing keeps coming to mind and it's not about Jojo.

"Well?" she demands, anger exuding from her like heat.

Tears streak my cheeks. "If I was the one that drowned, you wouldn't even care, would you?" My voice is hoarse and heavy with bitterness. "Would you even look for me?"

My mom's face changes, like I just slapped her. She looks shocked and speechless, for once. Before she can say anything else, before anyone can stop me, I get up and start running.

CHAPTER NINETEEN

I don't stop. I run along the beach as fast as my legs will carry me, on the sand, just firm enough to leave traces of my footprints. A few steps behind, I can hear Steven's breath, rhythmic exhales, like he's jogging. I know he's letting me run ahead of him, letting me quiet my mind until I'm so exhausted that all I can focus on is how out of breath I am. I shut my eyes tightly, knowing nothing is in front of me, trying to will this past hour to never have existed. However much later, my legs buckle, my lungs give out, and I let myself fall to the ground and lie on my back. My eyes are closed and I think about nothing until my breathing evens.

Steven reaches for my fingers and laces them slowly with his and we lie like that, fingers loosely intertwined, resting on the sand.

"You're everything to her, Char," he says.

We're not looking at each other, but I finally open my eyes and stare up at the infinite night sky. "You can't possibly think that. Look at the way she treats me," I say. "Jojo's the world to her."

"She relies on you so much because she trusts you."

"Relying on me isn't the same as loving me." Anger wells up in me, slowly at first, then all at once. I can feel the familiar sting in my nose. "She trusts me to take Jojo to lessons because my dad is always depressed, trusts me to keep Jojo entertained, to discipline her. All so she can keep spoiling her in a way she's never spoiled me." I pause. "I'm so happy Jojo can grow up with that version of her. But I wish I got even an ounce of that and less of . . . everything else." My voice quiets at the end.

Steven turns on his side and looks at me. "Is this something you think about a lot?"

"She's just such a different mom with Jojo. A mom I don't recognize. Maybe all this time I've been doing everything for Jojo, hoping she'd do something more for me." As I say it, my blurry vision clears and tears slip past the edges of my eyes. "But instead she just sees me as a second her, as the help."

Steven brings his hand up to my face and gingerly wipes my tears before they fall.

"I'm sorry," I whisper.

"For what?" he asks, sitting up.

"For making this about me. You're going through so much more and—"

He cuts me off by pulling me up and wrapping his arms around me. "I had no idea you felt this way."

When I pull myself away, I see the wet patch on his light gray hoodie. "She puts so much on me and has no idea how it affects me, you know?"

"Like what?" Steven's question is inviting.

I think about everything I told Alan. Things I never told Steven after all these years. There's something about being closer to someone, someone who knows your family so intimately that prevents you from lowering this mask to reveal things they never knew. So I finally tell Steven everything. About how I cry in the bathroom alone, about how I make instant coffee before I know she's about to go into her god-knows-how-long monologue about a better future or a bitter past or a more prosperous plan. About how I'm a sixteen-year-old confidante to a woman in her late forties. About how it cripples me in ways where I've never been rebellious because that's a leisure I can't have if I'm carrying the mental and emotional burden of my parents.

We sit facing each other, me in the hoodie he took off so I'd be warmer, him with a loose tee and swim shorts. He listens intently as I walk through some of these moments, recalling conversations that feel triggering to me now, so much so that I have to take a few deep breaths as I continue. He places a gentle and encouraging hand on my knee, letting me go at my pace. Finally, I finish and he sits there, looking at me. I can't make out what his expression says.

"You're . . . like the perfect daughter."

I laugh at this, because it's the most unexpected thing to hear. "Low-key, I think so, too."

"No, but really." He says it lightly, but with sincerity.

"Right? I could be rebelling. Smoking weed."

"Drinking a ton."

"Cheating."

"Lying."

"Well . . . I am doing that one," I say.

Steven shrugs and stands, dusting the sand off his shorts, then extends his hand, which I take. We walk slowly back to the hotel. The sky is completely black and all the stars are out. "Do you think you'd ever talk to her about this?"

I shrug. "Probably not."

"Yeah, I figured."

"She wouldn't get it."

"Might be worth a shot, though," he offers kindly.

I feel more relaxed knowing that Steven knows everything there is to know about me now. I wonder why I never really told him. I always thought we told each other everything, but I think about his side gig, his dad, about my mom and how I've felt all these years.

Maybe even with best friends, we all hide a lot more in our hearts than we think.

I'm dreading going back to our hotel room. I don't want to be reminded of my idiocy, of my mom's fury, of my perfect little sister I almost lost. As if sensing my soul, Steven turns to me and holds my shoulders. "Char. You know Jojo's okay, right? She's safe now. Kids are so fast. Anyone would've missed her." He says it with so much assurance, but it's not true.

I shake my head. "You wouldn't have missed seeing her run off like that."

"Things can change in an instant. You learned, we learned, she's okay. That's all that matters."

Guilt stabs me from every angle. If Steven knew I missed my sister running off because I was scrolling through Instagram and breaking my promise to him, I doubt he'd be comforting me right now. I muster a smile. "Okay. Thanks."

I open the door to our room quietly, knowing Jojo is asleep. Only the dim bedside lamps are on and my dad is reading a book. My mom is just sitting upright, as if she was waiting for me. But not in a caring way. She looks livid.

"Where were you?" she hisses in a loud whisper. She talks in Korean and it's obvious she isn't actually curious where I was. Just angry that I'm back so late.

I feel like there's an IV of pain and anger coursing through my bloodstream. Why isn't my mom worried at all about me?

"Aren't you going to answer me?"

My dad tries to calm her by holding her arm lightly but she jerks it away. He never knows what to do to actually get her to calm down.

"As if you care," I respond. I climb into bed and shove my earphones in so they know I can't hear them anymore.

When I wake, everyone is still asleep. I reach down and hold Jojo's hand gently, careful not to wake her. She looks so at peace, thankfully, and I silently apologize to her again and again in my mind. Eventually, even when everyone is up, it's quiet because no one tells me to do anything for Jojo or asks anything of me. My goal for the remaining two days is to avoid my mom as much as possible. Last night, Steven and I agreed to meet in the lobby by nine in the morning. He said that the resort is holding a water aerobics class in the pool that kids aren't allowed to attend, so I could steer clear of my parents.

I put my swimsuit on and get ready in the bathroom. I can hear my mom trying to wrangle Jojo into getting ready. I can also hear her refusing my mom in her usual shriek.

My dad comes in and closes the door. I give him a *Don't tell me to apologize to Mom* look.

"My Charlotte." He greets me warmly.

"Hi, Appa." I squeeze the toothpaste onto my toothbrush and avoid his gaze.

"Seoyoung-ah, your mom loves you. You know, right? *We* love you."

"Really? Are you sure I'm not just the family nanny?"

"Aigo, Charlotte. Your mom just really scared. She didn't mean those things. You hurt her too with what you say. That she not care if you drown."

I put the toothbrush down with a frustrated slam on the sink. "I *don't* think she'd care. She'd probably be sad that she lost her baby-sitter. Stop making so many excuses for her. You always take her side."

I hear the hotel door open then close and feel so much relief knowing she's out of the room.

"You don't see full picture. That's why Appa trying to help."

"Fine. What's the full picture? What am I missing here?" My voice is aggressive, fighting.

"It wasn't easy for her to pick up pieces after my injury. It's Appa's fault and Appa always feel so mianhae to Umma. That's why maybe I make excuse for her." His voice is so soft, so full of ache.

It fills me with the same feeling again, the familiarity of me trying to bottle up my own emotions to make room for everyone else. It kills me that my dad feels so sorry to my mom because of an injury that was out of his control. But I hate this feeling: the repression I do to myself because I feel bad for others. For once, I want to choose myself.

I look at my dad sternly through the mirror. "She shouldn't make you feel bad about that, Appa. It's not your fault some idiot dropped equipment on you. She should just be thankful you're alive."

"Aigo." He switches to Korean. "It's not that easy, Charlotte. When you're a parent, there are many layers to making a marriage and a family work. Yes, of course your mom is happy I'm alive, but it's not so black and white. She's had to do so much more since then to make up for what I lost, and it makes her angry sometimes. She can't help it. And it's not her fault. Anyone would be angry."

I shake my head. "I wouldn't be. I'm just glad you're here. But don't tell me how to feel toward Mom. I lived my whole life feeling guilty and trying to do everything she asks of me."

"We only have two more days," he says. But my dad already knows I've made up my mind.

"Appa. Why don't you try talking to *her* for once?"

"Of course I will, Charlotte. I always do."

"Yeah? Then why does she never change?"

He sighs and, for a moment, I reconsider giving in. But I remember that I want to be selfish, and I know what I want: I want to be alone with Steven and be a kid with my best friend. I want my mom to think about how I felt, too.

"I'm sorry, Appa," I add. "But I don't want to spend time with Umma until we're back in New York. I'm not going to apologize for what I said. I meant it." My voice is firm and I pick up my toothbrush to start my day. Why should I say sorry for saying one thing that feels true when she says all sorts of things to me anytime she wants?

He watches me through the mirror and nods in defeat before closing the door behind him. After a moment, I hear the front door open and close.

The water aerobics class is the ideal way to spend the morning. My family is nowhere in sight and I know Carol-eemo is keeping my mom away from us. Steven and Carol-eemo both have so much sense like that, and I'm ready for my mom-free, aka *care*free, day.

I'm sweating as we do leg shoots and I squint to keep the sun from blinding me. After arm exercises, jumping jacks, and leg kicks, the class comes to an end and the music quiets down. We dry off with our towels and Steven pulls out a pamphlet from his bag.

"What's that?"

"A list of activities happening today around the resort," he says, grinning. We study it together.

His thoughtfulness warms me. My bare shoulder presses into his arm as we sit close, reading through the descriptions and I wonder if he too feels the sensation shooting through me. "Ooh, snorkeling?"

"Yeah, that's in . . . oh, one hour. Perfect. Can we eat first?" he asks. "I'm starving. That class kind of wrecked me."

"Same. I could go for some breakfast tacos." I throw on my cover-up and we head to the breakfast area, sure that my mom is long gone by now. I don't know where she is, but I know she won't be snorkeling.

We find our instructor and eleven others at the meeting spot. Some are younger kids, like middle schoolers, and their parents, but most look like married couples. I wonder if adults look at us as siblings or as a couple, just like them. The instructor is super friendly and eager to get started. He spends a good ten minutes talking about how to respect the coral out at sea and keep our fins close to the surface so we don't kill reef life. Once we settle into the small boat that takes us out deeper into the ocean, he continues talking about the "fantastic sea creatures and extraordinarily colored fish" we will see and how to "send our love vibes" to them while snorkeling.

"He's a fish hippie," I whisper to Steven, who grins at me.

The waters are still shallow even though we're farther out, and because of the warm weather and part of the reef we're in, there are no waves to be found. The sound of the water is so relaxing. We line up as each person descends into the beautifully clear turquoise water to be one with the fish and coral. With the instructor's warning to be careful, Steven and I decide to use the boat's mini slide that lands us into the ocean. It's not high at all but it's fast and I land in the water with an aggressive slap. With no shame, I know that this is what I want to spend the next two hours doing. It's levels better than anything I would've otherwise been doing with my family.

Under the surface, there's a big school of fish swimming past us, a deep rich blue with yellow stripes, in a rush to get somewhere. They remind me of the energy of New Yorkers back home. There are a few starfish lying around, too, scattered throughout the reef and the ocean floor. A short time later, the instructor hurriedly waves all of us over and, as we go underneath the current, two beautiful sea turtles are swimming near us. Steven and I exchange looks, knowing this is both our first times ever seeing a sea turtle. They're so much bigger in real life than you could imagine. I watch in awe as they move past us, flapping their front flippers up and down like birds soaring through the water.

There's a calm in these waters I've never known, as I float in the middle of the ocean, surrounded by beautiful creatures. Me, just one of so many. I feel so small in the best way.

Even through goggles and mouthpieces, Steven and I can see each other smiling. And I wouldn't give up this moment for anything. Back on the boat, Steven hands me something wrapped in a napkin.

"No way," I say, gratefully unwrapping the sandwich he packed.

"Genius, right?"

"A miracle worker."

"The king."

"The love of my life." A beat and then all the regret. I hope it doesn't scare him off. "I didn't mean—"

Steven grins casually. "Yeah, I know," he says, cutting me off.

I close my eyes, mortified, as I take another enormous bite of my ham and cheese so I don't need to talk.

"You know how people are always starving after swimming?" he says.

"I'm starving right now. I'm starving *while* I'm eating this."

"Exactly. So," he says, pulling out his bag, "I brought more." His smile is so proud I fight the urge to bear-hug him.

"What other treasures are in there?" I ask, peeking into his bag.

He opens it up with the pride of an Asian man after a success-ful bargain, like getting a pound of cherries for five bucks instead of seventeen. "I took extra food from the breakfast buffet."

"A rule breaker! You're not allowed to take food from the buffet," I tease.

"Yeah, but desperate times and all."

He hands me his haul of rolls, mini boxes of cereal (Frosted Flakes—my favorite, and Honey Bunches of Oats—his favorite), two apples, and a cranberry muffin. "Take your pick."

"I feel like this needs a sign that says 'All-American breakfast.' "

"In Aruba," he adds.

"It's weird how American this place is, though."

"Does it make you sad?" he asks, knowing me too well.

"More annoyed than anything. It should be only Caribbean food, and as specific to Aruba as possible. But you just *know* people will flip their shit if they can't get hot dogs and fries anywhere they go."

He nods. We've talked this subject to death. Picked it apart and all, how catering to generic whiteness ruins cultures and the beauty of acclimating to new settings.

"I don't want Jojo growing up and being like, 'Why doesn't this non-US country have Taco Bell?'"

"Yeah," Steven says, sighing, "people just need to deal if they don't like another culture's food."

"*Exactly.* But I'm hungry. So pass me the Frosted Flakes?" I say sheepishly.

He busts out a laugh and I join him. I hope when I'm a full-grown adult with a family of my own, I'll actually follow my own high-minded principles. I wonder if Steven and I got married one day, if we had kids together, would we lead the kind of family life where our children aren't burdened or left behind? Would it be a household full of easy love?

The instructor asks if all of us are free for an additional thirty minutes, because there's a special school of fish we might be able to see if we go to a different part of the beach. Since it's an all-inclusive resort, all of us are down and chill.

"This is amazing," I tell Steven over the rhythmic bobbing of the boat. Our faces are getting splashed lightly with the salt water from the waves.

"What is?"

"That we're not needed."

Steven throws a carefree arm around my shoulder and leans back with his other arm. "Bask in the freedom!"

"To freedom!" I shout into the breeze. "What should we do next?"

"Absolutely nothing," he answers. Steven dips his head back and the light drenches his face. It makes me happy to see how relaxed he looks.

"Perfect."

◆◆◆

The other part of the beach turns out to be even more beautiful than the first snorkeling site. The instructor definitely knows his way around. But by the time we're back at the resort, I'm ready to sunbathe and think about nothing.

"I need to lie down. I feel like we're still on a boat," I tell him.

We grab towels from the pool area and lie out on the beach and let the sun crisp our skin. Someone plays music nearby and the song is Korean. It's upbeat and fun. I turn my head to get a better look and the person playing it is definitely not Korean. It's a good feeling. I listen carefully and understand some of the lyrics: *I can feel it in my heart. Things in the past are just that, the past. Leave the regrets buried. Just look to the future and run.* I feel these lyrics in my bones.

I'm running to what's ahead.

CHAPTER TWENTY

I open my eyes and I realize I was asleep.

"How long was I passed out for?" I turn to my side to face Steven, whose eyes are hidden behind his sunglasses.

"Thirty minutes? Not long, but you passed out. I was talking and was wondering why you weren't interrupting me," he jokes. "Do you feel better from the motion sickness?"

I nod and force myself to sit up. "Yeah. I need to take a dip, though." It's only when the sun is almost at its peak that I realize I completely failed to put on sunblock this morning. I feel so burned already. All I want to do is soak in the cold seawater.

"Wait up!" Steven jogs behind me and we race into the water. I beat him to it. We dive in and swim out, letting the waves slowly carry us.

I watch Steven dunk his head and come back out, wiping the salt water out of his face. He looks so good with his wet hair, the light glistening in the water, his goofy grin looking back at me, that I want to take a picture.

"Wow."

"What?"

"You looked so picturesque I wanted to take a photo of you, but

I just realized that I barely thought to take pictures on the boat."

He wiggles his eyebrows. "Freeing, huh?"

I splash water at him. "Yes," I admit. Everything looks stunning and not taking a picture of any of it makes it all shine even brighter. I take it in slowly when Steven breaks into my thoughts.

"I'm ready," he says.

"For . . . ?"

"To talk."

"Right now? In the ocean?"

He nods. "Feels less official, you know? Like it's not as intense."

We make our way toward the shore until our feet can comfortably touch the soft sand.

"Does it make me a shitty person that I kind of want to see my dad?" Steven asks.

"What? No, of course not."

"It's just . . . he really left us. He left our family for someone else. Someone who should be nothing to him. He left people who are supposed to be everything, for someone who is supposed to be nothing." He dunks his head in again and I wait patiently. "I had to talk about it in therapy, how I felt like I had become nothing to him. And he keeps insisting that that's not the case, but I mean, what did he do? He literally left us. How can I *not* think that, you know?"

I nod along. "Anyone would feel that way."

"But even after all that, after seeing my mom fall apart then barely get back up . . . he wants to see me and . . . I kind of want to see him, too?" Steven starts shaking his head so much that I take his arm under the water and hold it lightly.

"Do you miss him?"

"Yeah. I guess I do. And I feel like the worst son in the world for it."

"Well, depending on the perspective, maybe the best son, for your dad . . ." I trail off.

Steven hesitates. "I want to tell you something, but I don't want you to hate my mom for it."

"I'm obsessed with your mom, Steven. I could never hate her."

Steven looks away, instead focusing on a spot in the water. Underneath the surface, we can see the sand dancing around with the ebb and flow of the waves. "The first few months after my dad left, my mom would lash out at me. She would tell me to stay in my room and close the door because I looked too much like him. She found me repulsive."

My mouth opens slightly, no words coming out, just utter shock. Precious and kind Carol-eemo, telling her one and only son to get out of her face is something that doesn't compute to me.

"Anything I did was like a trigger to her. She's really the reason I started therapy, more than when I first saw him on social media cheating on her with his new girlfriend," he admits. "But I don't want you to hate her, Char. She wasn't herself, you know?"

I scour my mind looking for something to say, anything. A moment passes and I look up at him. "You know what? You really are the best son in the world."

He gives me a small smile. "So, what do I do?"

I look at him helplessly. "Are you going to start therapy again?"

"I'm thinking I probably should. I hate that I miss him. I wish I didn't. That's what I want. I want to not miss him."

"He's your *dad*, Steven. Your DNA is his DNA. I'm sure there's some connection you can't fully break free from. Like an invisible umbilical cord to both parents," I tell him.

We sway back and forth in the water, sometimes wading, sometimes standing. "Does your mom know he's reached out to you?"

Steven shakes his head. "No. I don't think I could see him even if I wanted to. She'd never let me."

"Maybe just talk to your therapist and ask her for some advice? Is he coming to New York?"

"No, he wants me to visit him and his girlfriend in Panama."

My jaw drops at this. "Wait. *What?*"

"Yep. No chance my mom is letting me go, right?"

"I have no idea. I don't know. Maybe?"

"I can't wait to be an adult." Steven says this bitterly and it almost hurts how much I feel that. "To make any decision you want when you want to."

I sigh. "Me neither."

"Do you think it'll be everything we wanted?"

"Probably not," I joke.

"But better than this."

"Definitely better."

Steven looks at his hands. "Can we get out? I'm becoming too pruney."

I know he doesn't want to talk about this anymore. I nod. "Sure."

As we turn to leave, he grabs my hand under the water. I stop and hold my breath. But it's not the fingers interlaced sort of hand-holding; it's like the "hold the hand of your neighbor and pray for him" hand-holding. The neutral kind, reserved for friends. My heart sinks, wanting more.

"Thanks, Char," he says.

He needs his best friend right now. I smile and squeeze his hand back. Then I pull away and challenge him to beat me back to shore. We take turns spending the next few hours wolfing down all kinds of food from different buffets until we feel like we're going to throw up, then head back to the beach. The colors in the sky are bright and beautiful, a mix of blue, orange, and red, with the hint of the sunset slowly peeking out. The mood has lightened since stuffing our faces and I turn to him from my beach chair.

"One favor?" I pull out my phone.

He groans jokingly.

"Just a few selfies. To commemorate this."

"What is 'this?'"

I point to the sunset. "That. Things to remember. Our first-ever outside-the-States trip. You know, cheesy stuff like that."

Steven humors me with a grin. "The colors are actually unreal."

"Right!" We both lean into the frame, the bright colors dimming our faces. I take exactly two photos of us, one picture of the sky and the waves, then toss my phone back into my tote.

Steven looks past me at something with a hint of mischief. "Be right back," he says, jogging off. He doesn't come back right away so I grab my phone again and take a few more videos of the waves, of the resort, of the calm that I feel. I wish I could hold on to this, but I already know the second I'm on my way back to New York, this feeling of freedom is going to be gone. I'll be back in a cramped apartment with my demanding little sister, my disappointed mom, my injured dad, and I know it'll be hard to breathe.

Out of habit, I open Instagram before remembering to stay off it. But it's too late. I see everything and I'm sucked in. So many people have commented and DMed me, wanting more content, more stories, more everything. The desire to please and to give my followers what they want eats away at me.

Suddenly, I want to kick myself. How could I be doing this again, when last time it led to Jojo's . . . incident? I can still hear her cries and feel that same panic. I try to remind myself that she's okay now and focus on this moment, closing my eyes, evening my breathing. But I've never hated myself so much. I force myself to thrust my phone deep into my bag. When I open my eyes again, Steven's right in front of me, holding two virgin strawberry daiquiris and giving me an arched eyebrow.

"Meditating?" he jokes.

"Sort of," I say. "You ran off to get drinks?"

He extends one of the fancy glasses to me. "Take one," he says, again with that mischievous tone.

"Okay," I say warily. I take a long sip, and gasp when a sharp taste touches my tongue. "Steven Yoonho Chang!" The Korean mom in me awakens and I shoot him a look. The taste of alcohol in this daiquiri is mild but it nicely balances out the oversweetness of the virgin version.

"Good, though, right? Admit it." He takes another long sip of his as I shake my head.

"Yeah," I admit. "How did you even get these?"

He sits back on his chair and slouches into a reclining position. "A dude left his band out so I went over and took it. I mean, it's easy enough for him to get a new one. Us, not so much." He grins like an excited kid and I can't help but laugh. It *is* kind of fun. Getting drunk with Audrey and Alan was a different experience. Not as fun, more stressful, more regrets. But with Steven, everything feels like the dream day that you think can never be that good, but ends up being even better. It's because of how safe I always feel with him.

I raise my glass. "Cheers."

Our glasses clink and he grins. "Cheers!"

"Is this your first drink?" I ask him.

He shakes his head.

"Wow," I say jokingly. "Remember when we promised we'd have our first drink together?"

"Yeah, but is this *your* first drink?"

"Um . . ."

"Ha. Didn't think so," he retorts.

"How'd you know?"

He shrugs. "I mean, you've gone to a few parties and events with your influencer friends, so I just figured."

"This feels different, though."

"Maybe because our parents could be anywhere. They'll probably ship us to Korea to live with relatives we've never met if they catch us," Steven jokes.

I look at him earnestly; perhaps the rum is affecting me already after a few long sips. "If we were there together, though, it'd be really fun," I say.

He grins, nodding. "Yeah, it would be," he agrees. Then he lies back down on his chair and slurps his drink.

"Want my cherry?" he offers a few minutes later. I take it from him and smile at all the small ways Steven's always thought of me over the years.

"Want my pineapple?" I ask him.

"I'm good. But look," he says, pointing to the pamphlet. "There's a salsa dancing class soon."

"But you don't dance," I tease. "And neither do I."

"A first time for everything," he says, grinning. "Let's go."

"Okay. After our drinks." We cheers and down the rest of our cocktails. "I could have another one of these," I say.

Steven lifts up his wrist, showing me his band. "I got you."

The class takes place in a small lounge area outside one of the bars. Patrons have already gathered and the music is loud and wonderful.

Steven orders two more cocktails and we sip on them, trying to act years older than we are. People who are actually twenty-one and older surround us, moving to the music. Turns out it's more a dance *session* than it is a class. There's a band performing and salsa dancers taking over the area. They invite people to join, and couples and friends on girls' trips gather around to dance.

Steven leans into me so I can hear him above the music. "Come on, act like you're twenty-five!" he urges me jokingly.

"How do twenty-five-year-olds act?" I shout back.

He shrugs, the grin still on his face. "Confident?"

"You first," I challenge him.

"Fine," he says loudly. Then, he starts walking backward to the center of the circle, his eyes never leaving mine. He gestures for me to follow and I shake my head, trying to hold back a laugh at his stilted movements. He saunters back to me, then takes my wrists, lightly pulling me in, and I don't resist. Confident twenty-something-year-olds. That's us, and the second daiquiris are definitely helping.

I throw my head back, laughing as we both play into our roles. We follow the beat of the music and look at the dancers, trying to mimic their movements. He takes my hands and our legs move in sync, forward then back again in an intoxicating rhythm. He spins me away from him, then pulls me back in and into his arms. Steven holds me for a beat longer before releasing me and everything in me aches to be held longer. I look at him, wondering if he's feeling the same wild emotions for me that I've been having for him, if it's mutual. Or if it's just the alcohol making his eyes sparkle when he looks at me.

I don't know why it took me so long to realize that I'm into him like this. Or maybe I just needed this trip with him to admit it to myself. Maybe without Aruba, I'd still convince myself we're just friends. Life has so many fillers: school, work, extracurricular, classmates, family. It's easy to neglect what's hiding in the depths of your heart.

The music slows down and people start pairing up like a slow dance at school. We look at each other awkwardly, then, shrugging, Steven extends his hand, palm open, waiting. I look at it, then at him, and every inch of my body feels nervous. I smile and take it. He closes his hand on mine, pulling me gently toward him. We're swaying slowly together, my arms around his neck, his hands holding the curve of my back. This close, everything feels more heated. Our bodies are lightly touching. My brain rushes back and forth between telling him or shutting up. But I know I need to tell him how I feel. Because it's real.

"Steven," I say, looking up at him. "I need to talk to you about something."

"Yeah? What's up?"

He looks sweet, but he looks oblivious, like he has no idea what's coming. And that's when I stop myself. Everything hits me fast. Whether it's the alcohol making me overthink, or the sobriety freshly hitting me, I can't tell, but all I realize is that I *kissed* his neck yesterday and he hasn't brought it up. And *he didn't kiss me back.* Maybe all the things I've been reading into this are just things he did because he's a thoughtful friend?

"Hello?" he says, snapping me out of my spiral. He looks at me with a pleasantly confused face as he waits for me to share whatever it was I was going to say.

Of course, I chicken out. "Do you want to watch the sunrise with me tomorrow? Um. As a friend-date," I ask, using his words.

He chuckles. "Can you even wake up that early?"

"Oh, come on. I can!" I protest. "So . . . yes?"

He gently rubs my back, in the subtlest of ways. "Yes."

The slow song comes to an end and my heart drops. I don't want to pull away. I want to stay this close to him, but when he begins to loosen his hold on my waist, I do the same. I hate it. I want our bodies to be as close as possible. All the time.

By the time I'm back in our room, all the lights are off. Whether my parents are asleep or just pretending to be is unclear, but the quiet is better than whatever the alternative would be. I look at my angelic sister sleeping next to me and all of me aches from the pain I've caused her. I vow to find ways to make it up to her.

A few hours later, a small body jumps on me. Jojo pushes away the hair that's stuck on my face and peels open my eyes. It's the worst yet cutest thing, the way she tries to "gently" wake me.

"Hi, sissy," she whispers.

I giggle and open my eyes fully. "Hi. I missed you, Jojo." I hold her, nuzzling her little neck and breathing in her Jojo smell. Steven and I agreed to meet at six, so I have half an hour to get ready and spend quiet time with her. We lie together for a while, her enjoying the attention, me trying to express how sorry I am. When it's time to go, I leave Jojo with our iPad and let her watch her favorite shows while she waits for my parents to get up. I'm confident she'll wake them up herself very soon.

Out on the beach, Steven lays out a beach towel he brought, close enough to the shore where our feet can play in the water but not so close that we have to avoid the waves.

"It's so quiet," he says, staring at the sky as it shows the first signs of dawn.

"I love it." I hand him the coffee I brought for us.

We're seated side by side, but I inch my body even closer. Today is the day I'll tell him. I won't chicken out this time. Our palms are digging into the towel as we lie back to stare up at the sky. Then, very slowly, I lightly place my pinkie on his hand and hold my breath. He doesn't move. And the longest minute of my life begins. He can't not notice this. It's too obvious. Finally, after what feels like an eternity, he looks at me.

"Hi," he says quietly. *Knowingly.*

"Steven." It doesn't matter how he feels. Just that I need to be honest with how I feel. I'm out of breath and nervous and he's looking right at me. "I need to tell you something."

He cocks his head. "Let me go first."

I freeze.

And before I can respond, it happens.

He kisses me.

It happens so fast that I pull away first in shock. But Steven is composed as ever.

"I'm sorry I took so long." He closes the gap between us, taking my hand. "Can I kiss you again?"

I lean my head on his shoulder. A wave of relief washes over me and I sigh. "I thought maybe you didn't feel the same way."

He dips his head as I lift mine to meet his eyes. "I did. I do. And you made these the best four days of my life."

We kiss again, slow enough so I can feel everything as it happens. His hands hold my waist, just like when we were dancing, but it's tighter, more urgent. One hand moves to the small of my back and I press further into him as we explore each other with increasingly desperate kisses. His mouth finds my neck and my hands find his hair and everything feels fast and urgent. We're hungry to hold on to each other, like our bodies have been longing to touch each other like this since the start of time. When we slow down, Steven gently runs his fingers through my hair as he kisses me in different places. I'm giggling quietly, mostly out of shyness. *Steven*, the friend I've known since before I was born, is *kissing* me. Steven, the boy that I'm beginning to see now as a man. As my first love.

"I can't believe I'm kissing you," he says softly, his mouth still lightly pressed against the side of my head.

"I never thought something like this would happen," I tell him earnestly.

"Did you want it to?" He tucks a tendril of hair behind my ear.

I nod, even though "want" feels like an understatement. It feels like our souls have known this desire our whole lives and now, finally, our bodies get to follow. "Yeah, I did. A lot. Did you?"

"I've always wanted this to happen." He says this softly and leans in to hold me for another kiss.

But I know I can't be with him freely yet, not with this guilt consuming me. I close my eyes, ready to tell him that I had a moment of weakness, and that's why Jojo got hurt. That I broke my promise to him, that I'm sorry, and that I hope he can forgive me.

I'm scared.

What if he doesn't want to be with me after I confess? I toy with the idea of not telling him, but it just feels wrong. It's Steven, and I don't want any more secrets between us. My hands feel clammy, but he doesn't seem to mind it.

I take a deep breath. "Steven?"

"Yeah?"

"I, um, I—"

"Wow," he breathes. He finds my hands and we continue looking out over the horizon. "Look, the sun's about to come up." We sit side by side and watch in awe as the sun begins to illuminate the sky. It's still dark, but second by second, the vibrant colors thin out as the whole sky turns into light. Before I can continue again, Steven lies down and pulls me gently toward him and we lie there, side by side in this perfect moment. He turns to face me and we start kissing again like we can't get enough of each other. The full weight of him hovers over me gingerly, and every touch feels more intimate. The towel is too small for the both of us and I can feel sand inside my clothes, but I don't care. I hold my breath, wondering if something more will happen. And with Steven, I think I'd be ready.

I realize that it was never that I wasn't ready with Alan. It's that it had to be Steven. Our gazes are fixed on each other and neither one of us makes a single movement, perhaps wanting to savor every bit of this moment. He brings my arm above my head, holding me there, and—

"Sex on the beach? How original," a familiar voice says above us.

CHAPTER TWENTY-ONE

My head jolts up to look at the person standing near our heads. Once I see who it is, my entire body goes rigid.

"Oops, am I interrupting?" Alan has a faux-innocent look on his face.

Steven climbs off me and says nothing, but his movements are stiff.

"How . . ." My words can't even fully form. "Alan, *what* are you doing here?" I look at Steven, desperate to tell him he has nothing to worry about. That I'm his. "Steven, I didn't tell him to come here. I swear." I need him to know I'm not like his dad; I'm not a cheater. But the warmth that was exuding out of him a moment ago is all gone.

Alan glances at Steven, too. "Oh, that's fair. She didn't. I just came as a fun little surprise." He turns to me, grinning. "You missed my birthday party. So I brought the party to you. Me, I'm the party."

Steven looks only at me. "You've been texting him the whole time?" The light in his eyes is gone, too. He looks so cold and stoic that I can't seem to speak.

I shake my head vigorously, but Alan cuts me off.

"Nah, dude, I just saw her here on Instagram."

I freeze.

"Have you been posting?" Steven asks quietly. "After you said you wouldn't?"

"Steven . . ." It's like my mouth is broken.

He doesn't bother staying and walks away before my body reacts. I rush after him and grab his arm. "I tried to tell you. I really didn't mean to—"

He yanks his arm away. "I should have known, Char, that to you, I'm just a safe choice. A backup, right?"

"You know that's not true." My voice is desperate. Desperate for him to understand, desperate to apologize.

"Then do *you* want to explain why you've led a guy on enough that he thinks it's cool to surprise you while you're on a trip with your family? Or would you rather tell me why you've been lying to me about posting this whole week? Was it for the sponsorships? Or the likes?" His eyes look bloodshot. He says *likes* with so much contempt. "Word of advice? Don't pretend to be there for someone when all you care about is yourself."

"Whoa, whoa, whoa," Alan cuts in. "Hey, man, calm down. It was just a friendly little competition over our girl Charlotte. I wasn't trying to cause anything. Relax."

Steven stops glaring at me for one second to look at Alan. "There's no competition here. She's all yours." And then he storms off. Just like that, like the past twenty-four hours meant nothing to him.

His words cut me so deep I can't go after him. I watch him, getting farther and farther away from me, wishing I had the strength to grab him and explain everything. Alan clears his throat. "Are you okay? That was a little dramatic."

I turn around to face him. "I'll repeat my question. *What* are you doing here?"

"Well, I was in the area with some friends, saw your post, thought it'd be fun to make a surprise pit stop and hang. Didn't think I'd find you so fast."

I shake my head, frustrated and confused. "What do you mean, you were 'in the area'?" I say.

He looks at me sheepishly. "One of my friends took us to Curaçao on his jet, which isn't far from here, so he dropped me off here for the day. They're all still there if you want to join us."

I don't respond. A guy that I barely know flew here on his friend's private jet and showed up . . . just to surprise *me*?

"Look," he says, taking my arm. "I felt bad about how things ended last time. I was just caught up in the moment, you know? It's fine if you want to move slow. And I really was just busy after that."

"Alan, I'm over it. I don't want to talk about that." I lightly pull my arm out from his grip.

"Come on, Char. I came here for you."

"No, Alan, *you* come on. Why are you so obsessed with winning me over when you don't even like me enough to want to commit?" I recall his messages from Sylv, the girls on his stories. I don't get it. If you like someone, you want to be with them and them alone, right? He doesn't like me. Not truly.

"What if I'm willing to commit now?" He asks this so tentatively that I know he's not.

I sigh. "Alan, you don't even *want* to commit. And it doesn't matter. I've moved on, okay?" I slouch back to the sand and sit on the towel.

"What does this Steven guy even mean to you?" He sits down next to me, the very spot Steven was sitting in not even ten minutes ago.

I shake my head. "You don't really want to know. You just feel bad for me."

"Eh, kind of, yeah. But I also didn't think I'd show up right when you were about to do it with someone on a beach. Sorry I ruined that moment."

I laugh. It comes out unexpectedly. Whether out of bitterness or confusion, at least I'm not crying.

He chuckles, too. "No, seriously! I'm sorry I got in the middle of whatever was going on."

I look at him with raised eyebrows. "No, you're not."

"Yeah, not really," he says with a grin. He shrugs. "But I *am* sorry you're so upset. To be fair, you didn't tell me you guys were, like, in love."

Another sigh escapes me, loud and slow. "You're not the one who ruined it. I did. I promised him I'd be off Instagram while I was here. And it was an important promise."

"He still didn't need to be such a dick about it," Alan says.

"Can we just talk about something else?"

"Well, I'm just saying, he shouldn't be this angry about me

showing up. It's not like you had any control over it. I surprised you, not the other way around."

I lie down on the towel, covering my face with my arm. "I told you, that's not why he's angry."

"Fine, but you really think he would have acted like this if you told him you posted one measly photo online and said hey, sorry? He's mad because I surprised you during a, let's say, inopportune moment. As if that's your fault."

I lie there, unmoving. I can't believe Steven took off without even giving me a chance to explain. Being an influencer comes with its own type of pressure. He was asking a lot of me to disconnect completely like that. A small flicker of anger grows in me. It's small, but it's there. Maybe Steven wouldn't have gotten this angry if I'd told him before Alan showed up. Maybe he wouldn't have given me up so easily. *She's all yours.*

He nudges me. "So . . . my friend's picking me up later today for a party on the other side of the island. You can join, but I'm stranded here until then. And if you really don't want me near you, I'll leave. But otherwise, can we just hang? It's only for the day."

For what it's worth, he still came for me. And I have a strong feeling that an offer like this will never come to me again, from Alan or anyone else. Who on earth would I ever meet that has access to a private jet and surprises me on an island on my vacation? I shake my head, smiling to myself from the ridiculousness of it all.

"Fine," I say, pulling myself up. "Let's go."

The whole morning, I'm wary of running into Steven or my

parents. But we stay toward the end of the beach, out of sight. Right after lunch, Alan tells me he's booked something for us to do, and that a driver is on their way.

"I don't think I should leave the resort, Alan."

"Why not? It's safe, don't worry. The driver is picking us up, dropping us off, picking us up again and bringing us back to the resort. You have nothing to be worried about, I swear."

With a lot more convincing, I finally agree. The whole drive to the surprise excursion, I'm terrified of getting caught by my parents. But there's no way they could find out. The resort is massive, and my mom and I are avoiding each other. The drive there is bumpy and unfamiliar, but when we pull up, all my fears disappear.

I'm in awe of what I'm looking at. Amid a deep and vast ocean, volcanic stones have created a naturally colorful pool that remains untouched by the crashing waves surrounding it. People are jumping off the geological formations and cameras are out everywhere. It's a relief to see—the freedom to document this beauty. Alan's on top of it before I am.

"Say hi, Char," he says, grinning at me with his phone pointed.

"Oh my god, show the pool!" I say to him. Its deep colors are unlike anything I've ever seen. I get my phone out, too. Might as well at this point since Steven's not around to care anyway. I take photos of the natural pool and the way the light is hitting the water so everything looks even more heightened in its beauty. The green looks emerald, the blue looks turquoise, the dark blue looks purple. It's stunning.

"Here, give me your phone," he says with a daring tilt to his eyebrows. "Jump in."

It's high, but I'm determined to fully live this amazing experience. He starts the video as he shouts a countdown from where he's standing. I run, and before I chicken out, I jump. I scream as my body hangs in the air for a split second before I plunge into the depths. I open my eyes under the water just to see everything. I don't care about the stinging. Fish are swimming around me and it's like this pool is giving a different energy from everything outside of it. Everyone here seems so undisturbed, so happy even. Jumping in has given me an endorphin rush and I tell Alan to join in. He puts our phones in waterproof bags, and as I count down, he dives into the water and comes up with a big grin.

"Holy shit," he says, wiping his face. "I need to do that ten more times."

"Give me your phone and do it again," I say, matching his grin. "I'll film you this time."

After a few more rounds, he suggests going together and asks someone to film us. Even though I did it already, every time I'm at the top, my stomach fills with nervous butterflies. Alan holds out his hand to me. "Jump in together?"

I look at it tentatively before taking it, and we soar, landing in the water with a giant splash. He comes up out of the water and our faces are very close to each other. He's looking at me with the same intrigue that we shared on the 7 train the first time we hung out. Right before he—

"Think of this as a goodbye, okay?"

"A what?" I begin to say, but he presses his lips on mine and the way he deftly moves his tongue and takes me in feels otherworldly. It's definitely what you'd expect if you've ever fantasized about kissing a movie star. But it's not the same intimacy that I shared with Steven. I manage to pull away after two seconds.

"You're too good at this," I say, shaking my head but inevitably also smiling. "But I'm not the one you're meant to be with."

"What if you are?"

We make our way to the edge of the pool where we can rest on the rocks. "You know it's not me, though. You just want . . . someone."

"Yeah, I know. It was fun, though," he says, mischievously grinning.

I still appreciate how Alan is able to take life so lightly. He's always had it good enough that he can do whatever he wants, whenever he wants. I'm relieved there's no animosity now, despite the chemistry we shared. But I also know that he's not the one for me, because the one I want is currently somewhere back in the resort refusing to even speak with me. I may be angry at Steven right now, but I also can't deny that I'm in love with him. And I'm determined to make it right.

When we get back to the resort, Alan and I pause outside the entrance, ready to part ways.

"You know, Charlotte. Despite the other girls, I did like you."

I smile at him and nod. "I know. I liked you, too. But . . ."

He shakes his head. "Let's just leave it at that. Friends?"

Alan extends his hand and I take it, shaking it. "Friends," I say, meeting his grin.

"All right, well, I have a party to be at. If I'm not there, people won't have fun."

And just like that, he's gone, and I know what I need to do. I head to the receptionist in search of pen and paper.

◆◆◆

I spend the next hour writing a letter to Steven. I don't know when or if I'll ever give it to him, but it feels cathartic to explain my side. It also gives me the strength to sit down at the same table as him without breaking down, because my dad and Carol-eemo wrangle all of us to commit to a final evening meal together, despite the tension.

"To our last dinner!" Carol-eemo raises her champagne glass and my mom and dad follow suit. Steven and I lift our Shirley Temples.

My dad nods. "To more vacations." He pats my knee a few times. "We missed you today, Charlotte. You feel okay?"

The live music drowns out our conversation and I lower my voice so only he can hear me. "No, I feel horrible, but I don't want to talk about it, Appa."

He nods, a look of concern settling on his forehead and eyes. He silently cuts up the fish and plates it for me.

Throughout dinner, I look at Steven sporadically, hoping we'll lock eyes at some point. We never do. His eyes look a little red and I wonder if he's cried. I've only seen him cry twice and if I'm the reason he did today, I don't think I'll ever forgive myself.

I'm ready to avoid my mom like the plague, but surprisingly, she doesn't give me death glares or passive-aggressively insult me. We avoid eye contact and eat our meals without talking to each other. My dad must have really talked to her.

It's an uneventful final night, which I don't mind, given my whiplash morning. Today felt three days long. Most of dinner is spent with everyone's attention on Jojo as we all avoid our issues with each other, but at least she loves it.

The next morning, everyone is up early and we make it to the airport just in time to board. I'm restless the entire flight home and pass the hours reliving the final day. How perfect it started, how weird it got, how badly everything ended with me and Steven, how my mom and I are still not speaking. During the final hour of the flight, I get a calendar reminder that it's time to upload my second post with Lavish & Pearly. I close my screen. I thought having a lot of money to give to my family would change things for the better and make everything easier. So why is everything still so messy?

CHAPTER TWENTY-TWO

When we're home, I try to distract myself by posting an "Ask Me Anything" prompt. An hour into unpacking, I take a break and return to the AMA to begin answering questions. It's perfect timing since I got a ton of new followers after Alan shared videos of us in Aruba. It's a boost of validation to see all the questions that have come in. A ton of them are in regard to Alan and I being together, but I quickly clarify we're just friends. People want to know more about my trip. Did I go anywhere else? Do I have more photos? Was it a vacation or a work trip? Both? Who did I go with? Where did I stay? There's also a lot of basic questions about my life: if I plan to stay in New York, where I want to go for college, what my hobbies are, what books I've been reading lately. Two hours into answering questions and the exhaustion hits me harder than I thought it would, so I give up for the night and head to bed.

In the morning, everything comes back to me in a quick and ugly memory. I open my phone to text Audrey then remember . . . we're still not speaking. In fact, we haven't talked in days. Was it just a fight? Or is our friendship over, just like that? What was our friendship based on? I thought we had connected instantly, that we were friends beyond the world of social media connections, but maybe not. I could have just been honest from the beginning. Maybe then Audrey would've understood. But how could I betray my parents' private problems? Regardless, I should have at least been upfront and *told* her I'd be taking the sponsorship.

It's weird to think I've only known her for a couple months, but quickly felt so comfortable around her that it's even weirder to not text her for this long. I throw my phone back onto my bed and give up.

"I'm *spiraling*," I tell my reflection. I get ready for school and focus on French-braiding my hair and tying it with a wannabe Sandy Liang bow that falls past my waist. "Just text her." Talking to myself is never *not* weird.

My phone buzzes again to remind me that I need to post my outfit for Lavish & Pearly. I clear out a part of my room where the light is coming in and take pictures of my outfit from different angles. From these images, you can't tell that I feel hollow inside. Before I head out, I upload one to Instagram and tap share. If people see these photos of me, do they think I'm living the dream?

At school, it's like Steven and I never even met, let alone kissed. He doesn't talk to me, and I don't approach him. I carry the letter I wrote in my hoodie pocket, though. In case I change my mind and decide to give it to him.

Post vacation, school feels extra stuffy, so I grab my sandwich and water and sit on the steps outside. I browse through my phone and my insides tighten when I see the number of tags in my notifications. Almost like a too-good-to-be-true feeling. And it turns out I'm right.

Most of them are not kind comments.

People post about how they knew I was a sellout, with the partnerships I was doing, with all the sponsorship I was suddenly feeding everyone, that all I cared about was being paid by big brands and I lost my authenticity. It's not all bad, though. Some people try to defend me, saying everyone has their own story and reasons. But it's not enough.

My stomach feels like it's curling into itself. I don't know why, but I methodically look at each tag with a level of masochism I didn't know I had. Too many people have tagged and reshared photos of my post, hating on my "willingness to be tokenized." Maybe I haven't built up enough of a platform to have those super-loyal followers. Or maybe, when it comes down to it, people can't help but put others down. Maybe we all want to, all the time, but we know it's not morally acceptable. And any chance we get, we pounce.

The number of comments and shares continues going up and up, until it surpasses any of the engagement on my other posts. My vision feels clouded by my tears but I jolt out of the moment by my phone's vibration.

I look up at the sky. It's like God knew I needed this.

audrey

Char, are you okay?

No . . . can we talk?

Thirty minutes later, I've ditched school and am ringing the bell to Audrey's apartment. The door opens and relief spreads across my chest at the familiarity of seeing my friend. "Hey," she says, a little awkwardly.

"Can I come in?" I ask. She nods and opens the door.

We settle on the couch and I launch right in. "Look, I know you have every right to say you told me so. But—"

"You don't owe me anything. I shouldn't have been so judgy with you to begin with."

I smile a small smile. "Well, you did warn me." I take a deep breath and choose to be vulnerable this time. "I tumbled into this world to make more money for my family. My parents aren't doing well financially and it's been taking its toll on us, so when this partnership landed in my inbox, it was just too hard to resist. I just did what I thought I needed to do. But as your friend, I knew it was shitty."

"Listen," she says, sighing as she opens a bag of Hot Cheetos, "it can get hard in this industry, you know? To trust people. I've been burned a few times, so I get it. Opening up to people isn't easy, especially when it's about family." She pauses as if debating sharing something further, so I wait. "Just so you don't feel so alone . . . my parents don't actually live together in Canada."

"Oh. Are they divorced?"

"Basically," she says, laughing a little. "They're still legally married, but my mom got her own place when I was like ten. Haven't lived together since, so when I visit, I just split my time between them."

"I had no idea, Audrey. I'm sorry."

"You couldn't have known. But maybe from now on, no more secrets?"

I smile with my puffy eyes and dried-out cheeks. "Deal."

Audrey helps put together a PR strategy for me, assuring me that all of this will die down soon enough. She shows me some messages she gets from haters on the daily and reminds me that we just need to build up the talent to ignore them and focus on the good.

"But why do you think this second post got all this flack and not the first?"

She shrugs. "The algorithm is a thing of mystery, honestly. Maybe the first post didn't really have a ton of momentum. There's no use trying to figure it out, though. You just have to focus on your resilience and move on, you know?"

I nod, but it sounds so much harder to do for me, and eventually, I tell her I need a break from all of hating. I just don't think I'm as strong as Audrey is.

So, with *Gilmore Girls* playing in the background, I update Audrey on everything: Steven, Alan, Aruba, even my parents, and how perfect the kiss was with Steven before the great demise. She's giddy with me, giggling at the right moments, sitting up for the juicy details. It's such a relief to have her back in my life and I finally got to have this moment: of sharing in girly gossip with a friend who asks me all the questions about a first kiss. I even share how confusing it was to be with Alan, who seemed so into me but also not at all, not in a true way.

She nods knowingly. "He has a bit of that reputation. He's not a bad guy, but, he sort of changes his interest by the season." Then her eyes get big. "Not to make it sound like a fling! I didn't really say anything in the beginning because, for what it's worth, he *did* seem a little different with you."

"No, no, I completely get it. That's how I felt with him, too." We share a cozy blanket and fast-forward to an episode with Jess and Rory.

"Yeah. No one knows why, but he's never really been in a real relationship before."

"It was fun, though," I admit.

She laughs at this. "And I'm sure the making out didn't hurt," she adds. "But you should definitely give Steven the letter."

I recline fully on the chaise. "I'm pretty sure he hates me."

Audrey shakes her head. "Trust me. If everything you shared is true, he definitely does *not* hate you."

It's an afternoon of the medicine I needed, but I dread heading back home. It all feels so banal, being back in my cramped apartment while I avoid my mom. When I get to my building, my legs refuse to go into the elevator, so I sit on one of the lobby chairs.

"Not going up, Ms. Goh?" Teddy asks with a knowing smile.

I sigh. "I'll have to eventually."

Thirty minutes later, I drag my body up to our floor. And when I get to the living room, my parents are seated on the sofa and my mom has her phone in her hand, opened to something.

"Um, hi," I say, trying to evade eye contact. But my mom's eyes are laser focused on me and I look at my dad for help.

"Seoyoung-ah," my dad says in Korean from his seat, ever so calmly and tenderly, "why don't you sit down now?" From his tone, I know this can't be good.

"What's going on?" I ask.

"Sit," my mother says. Short commands in Korean freak me out levels beyond English. Something about the intonation strikes a different chord. And as I do, she slams the phone on the coffee table face up, and I jump. On the screen is the video of me and Alan leaping off the rock formations and into the natural pool in Aruba, playing on loop.

I take a deep breath as quietly as I can. *Shit. Shit shit shit.* "How . . . did you even find—"

"Does that matter?" Her voice is eerily quiet.

I shake my head no.

"Did I do something wrong?" She's speaking in that angry Korean whisper.

I look at her, feeling uneasy with her mind games. "What?"

"You lied to us . . . for how many months now? Pretending to win contests, making us proud of your grades, of the tutoring you weren't doing, only to humiliate us today when a mom at Jo's school showed us a version of you I've never known, fooling around with people we've never heard of. I must've done something really wrong to have deserved all of this, right?"

My throat feels tight. "I did it to help us." My voice comes out almost in a whimper. "I knew you wouldn't understand."

"I learned a big lesson today," she says, too calmly. "That I've failed as a mother. Because the most disappointing thing as a parent is the moment you realize you have no idea who your kid is or what she's doing with her life. To think you've been living this lie right under our nose . . . in this home . . ."

Tears stream down my cheeks and I taste the salt on my lips.

My mom pierces me again with her words. "You should be ashamed of the person you've become, selling yourself online like that to a bunch of strangers."

I ball my hands into fists to keep them from shaking, feeling like I'll implode if I don't get my words out. I talk slowly, trying to contain my growing rage. "It's my *job*. I do it to help support our family."

"Your job is to listen to us," she says.

An uncontrollable laugh comes out of me. "When it comes to school and grades, you want me to be this obedient student and daughter, who only does what she's told, to be 'just a kid.' But when it comes to Jojo, I'm her other mother. I have to take her to dance class and cafés and keep her entertained inside free museums and feed her ice cream or put her to bed or watch her while you're busy or stressed. On top of that, I have to sit here and listen to all your dumb dreams, all your regrets, all your goals. You have *no idea* what I go through. Don't tell me not to feel responsible and to only focus on school when *you're* the one putting all that responsibility on *me*."

My mom looks too stunned to speak. She just sits there, looking at me, like she's only noticing who I am for the first time in her life.

"That's enough," my dad says. "Seoyoung-ah, I think you should go to your room. We'll talk more later."

"I don't want to talk to you, Appa. You're part of the problem. If you helped with Jojo more, if you remembered the dad you used to be to us, maybe we'd all be a little less tired and stressed." My words come out angry and dripping with venom. The look on his face is heart-wrenching. I slide out of the seat and close the door to my room before anyone can follow. Not that they do.

I cry until I'm dizzy. Until I feel like I'm drained of fluid and my cheeks hurt from the salt. Despite the ache I feel, my mind is screaming to protect what I've built. I blindly upload a bunch of photos from Aruba, desperate to move forward. I try to put aside my emotions but it's impossible as I scroll through comments, DMs, and repetitively tagged posts of people boycotting the brand and even me.

 She caved for the attn of white ppl

 i bet she always wanted to be mainstream tbh

 I hope you remember your values and don't just post whatever offer comes your way because you can't resist the money. I'll be unfollowing you now but wish you the best.

No one knows the full narrative except for me, but it doesn't change the fact that I'm a sellout, just like everyone says. Even my mother.

An hour goes by and there's a knock at my door as it opens gingerly. "Can I come in?" my dad asks in Korean.

I don't say yes, but I don't say no. I know I hurt him. That he still comes in to talk to me after how I treated him is what makes me soft inside.

"Why are you so upset, my ddal?"

I swallow the lump in my throat. "Because Umma doesn't get it. I was trying to help the family by earning money."

He takes my hand in his and pats it. "That's not your responsibility."

"She can't expect me to help out with everything but not care about our financial problems. I care what I care about. And I wanted to make money for us."

"Aigo, Charlotte. You don't need to worry about that."

"Don't I? You're not able to work and the more mom works, the more I have to watch Jojo. I'm working no matter what, so I might as well get paid."

My dad sighs and I know our logic is on different planes. I wish I could get him to understand me, too. "You shouldn't have lied to us, Charlotte." He's still holding my hand.

"I know," I tell him quietly. "Appa, I'm sorry I said—"

He tuts lovingly and holds my hand tighter. "Appa will get better, Charlotte," he says, switching to English. "Not just my body, but heart, too, okay? My mind . . . it feel too strong, sometimes. Like I cannot beat the bad thoughts."

I shake my head. "It's okay, Appa. I'm sorry."

He smiles brightly even though I know that's not how he feels right now. "So, do you like it? Being Instagram influencer. That's what it's called, right?"

I smile a little at this, then sigh. "Sometimes. But it's messing with me."

He lets go of my hands and crosses his arms. "How?"

"I feel like everyone's always judging me but how can you know someone through curated content? I keep feeling like I have to prove myself. The real me."

"How long have you been doing this?"

I chew on my lower lip, afraid of how honest I should be. "Um. Like two years."

He gives a small whistle. "Was it different then?"

I nod, relieved that he's not pressing. "In the beginning, I didn't even care what anyone thought. I was just trying to help our family. But now it's different. The more sponsorships I got, the harder it became. I thought I would finally have it easier once I started getting paid, but I feel like people are always criticizing how I look or my choices or the brands I work with. It's endless. How can strangers be so mean?"

He pats my back a few times. "Seems like lot of energy for not-nice people. Maybe you should do cost-benefit analysis," he says, chuckling.

I smile back, appreciating my dad's humor in all this.

"Seoyoung-ah, we be okay. I promise. Appa looking into jobs I can do from behind a computer, so you don't need to worrying about our family's finances. I can still work in construction but more behind the scenes. Your mom and I, we're both adults. Not you."

I nod.

"And if you don't want judged by strangers . . ." He trails off. My dad was never the type to tell me what to do with my life; that was my mom's role. "Just focus on yourself, okay?"

"This isn't how Umma feels, though. And I know it."

"She's angry, Charlotte, because her ddal lie to her two years. That's not easy to reconcile," he says gently. "Give some time, okay?"

◆◆◆

In a few hours, everyone's asleep but me. As much as I wish I could end my night, it's hard to fall asleep when my mind won't rest. I scroll through Instagram again and spend my time in the dark, poring through comments on my vacation post and rereading hateful messages—dissecting them, seeing if there's truth. Although there are some kind and supportive notes, my focus is on the criticisms.

Lmao not her trying to cover up her lack of azn support

its worse cuz shes not even addressing it

yall this is fake news

maybe try sponsoring brands you actually align with?

maybe she aligns with yt ppl lol

Outfit choices eh

cancellllll

I'm not sure when I started caring so much about what strangers said on the Internet. I'm not sure when I started spending all my energy digging myself into a hole of self-loathing and finding comfort in its grave. Even in my room, alone, I feel watched. I feel like I can sense a hundred unrecognizable profile pics covering my walls and closing in on me. I close my eyes and focus on feeling my body, on breathing slowly, on trying to erase floating faces laughing and seeing my whole life, unfiltered. I reach out with eyes closed for objects, to touch and ground myself in my present reality, and I focus on the cold metal frame of my bed against my hands. But my soul feels like it's already taken off and I don't feel present.

I'm in another world, one where everyone's staring at me, looking through photo after photo on my feed, looking through my Highlights and Reels, judging me, pointing, commenting, picking apart every bit of my life, thinking they know everything that goes on behind closed doors. I force myself to open my eyes and remember this is all in my head. But no matter how many times I repeat it, I don't feel grounded. I clutch the sides of my bed until my nails are in pain from the pressure.

"I'm safe." It's weird to say it out loud, but it helps me. I feel one beat of a normal breath. So I keep going, looking at my eggshell-colored ceiling. I count five slow breaths.

"I'm fine."

"I'm grounded here."

One more deep breath. "It'll be okay, Charlotte."

I almost believe it.

CHAPTER TWENTY-THREE

When I wake in the morning, I still have a loose grip on the side railings of my bed. I can hear distant shouting, but it's so high-pitched that it might as well be right next to my ear. I can tell by her footsteps that Jojo's running in excited circles in the living room. I feel far from my family in a way I've never felt before. It's a little bit jarring and a little bit sad. My mind still feels trapped inside Instagram but my body is in bed.

My eyes wander to my calendar and I'm reminded that Jojo's recital is today. It's the last thing on my mind but definitely at the forefront of Jojo's. I can hear her practicing yet again—feet stomping and jumping, and her squealing as she dances along, following each beat.

I texted Steven last night, asking to talk. I stared at my phone for an entire minute, waiting for a response. And then thirty. I check again now, but the most recent message is still the one I sent.

I join Jojo in the living room. "Hi, sissy girl," I say, greeting her with a smile.

"SHARTY!" She runs toward me and wraps her small arms around my hips. "Today's a special day," she tells me sweetly.

I kiss the top of her head, the way my dad does to me. I smile and use my Dramatic Voice. "I know. Big day, right?"

She nods shyly and whispers, "I can't wait."

I look at the hanging wall calendar with the big red circle around today, dotted with heart stickers everywhere. *Jojo's Recital Day!* It's written in every room of the apartment. I know it's a big day for her, probably thus far the most exciting day of her life, so I try to match her joy and avoid eye contact to not give away my lethargy. My mom joins us after we migrate to the kitchen, where I plate Jojo's breakfast—yogurt, crackers smothered with peanut butter, and fresh fruit. She looks at me as if she doesn't know what to say.

"Hi," I say, breaking the silence.

"Good morning."

I can't read her expression. Her normally c-permed hair is thrown back into a short ponytail, which usually means she hasn't had time to blow-dry it or is too preoccupied with other things. But otherwise, her face gives off nothing except maybe a layer of softness that didn't exist yesterday. Or maybe it's defeat.

"You didn't need to make breakfast for Jojo," she adds, looking at the plastic plate I've now covered with food.

"I've been doing this for years." I shrug. "Where's Appa?"

"He's preparing for an interview later today."

My ears perk up, and I want to know more but my mom reaches over and takes the plate, diverting her attention to an impatient Jojo. I already know she's not going to say much about it. He's had interviews before, and she's gotten excited before. Then disappointed.

"He's going to meet us at the recital at five. Are you going to come from school or coming home first?" Her voice is cordial but not warm.

I feel anxious just thinking about it. Sitting in a room, next to my parents, in a room full of other families. It's the last place I want to be. "I don't know yet. I'm heading to school."

"Okay." A moment later she adds, "Have a good day," with her back turned.

I look at the clock. It's barely seven in the morning and I wonder if she notices that I'm leaving almost a full hour and a half before first period and she's letting me be. That, or she has no idea what time my school really starts.

I buy a muffin and a hot coffee from a cart near school and sit down to go through my emails. When I scroll, I see an unread one from Lavish & Pearly that I'm not surprised by. But I'm not ready to open it either. I focus on my cornbread muffin instead.

It's about halfway through eating it that I know I can't stand to go to school today. The thought of bearing through seven hours of lectures and questions overwhelms me and I know I'll panic being confined by those walls. I toss my muffin and coffee in the trash and jog toward the subway before I think twice about my new agenda.

I promise myself that, just for today, I'll only focus on *me*.

Fifteen minutes later, I'm at Chanson. It feels different coming here alone, just for myself. I get a piece of red velvet cake, a deca-dent cheesecake éclair, and a hot mocha from the barista. A table full of deliciousness, all for me. I take out my letter and a pen to continue writing my note to Steven. Maybe one day, when we talk again, I can give it to him. But for now, this will do.

Two hours go by. Even though I'm full, I order another hazelnut éclair to go, and head toward my next destination not far from here. It's a place I've never let myself go in before, because I was always afraid the temptations would be too hard for me to resist.

A woman inside Anthropologie greets me and offers me a shopping bag. I thank her and take it. As I browse the store, I'm not sure what I'm looking for, but for once, I let myself pick something. Anything. Whatever calls out to me. I could spend the whole day here, but I have another stop I want to make later. I'm not sure how much time goes by; it's probably lunchtime at school right now. But my phone is buried in my bag, and I have no intention of unburying it.

I try on three different jumpsuits, four sweaters, a few dresses, and a lot of accessories. I like the sweater but I put them back for now. I idle in the home goods section of the store, imagining stocking our kitchen with holiday plates. Then I see something that catches my eye. It makes me do a double take, actually, how similar it looks. A black baker boy leather cap that reminds me of the one that I tried on at *Fall into Florals* where I met Audrey, where all of this really started. I take it to a standing floor mirror and try it on. I'm hesitant, convinced it can't be as good. But it looks even better than the one I wanted at the event. And even though I told myself that today, I'd splurge, I'm giddy to see that it's on sale for 30 percent off. It's the one thing I buy, and I leave the store wearing it.

Three stops on the E later, I'm standing in front of a bakery with the best macarons, bar none. (Not even Steven's.) I've only had Ladurée's macarons a few times before, but always just one and only packaged in a paper bag. Today, I pick out a bright red box with *Ladurée* written in a beautiful shimmery silver and slowly choose eight different flavors that sound appealing to me. Seated in a plush chair inside the café, I gingerly take a bite out of the pecan pie macaron. If I close my eyes and focus on the flavor, I can pretend like my life is dandy and easy. One deep breath. Two deep breaths. It feels cathartic.

Finally, I open the email from Lavish & Pearly, ready to face it. With all the backlash, I had a feeling this was coming, but it doesn't make it any easier to read it.

> Dear Ms. Goh,
>
> Thank you so much for your participation with our brand. Given the recent situation, we've decided not to renew our contract. However, we will still honor the agreed-upon fee and wish you all the best in your future endeavors.
>
> Best,
> Lavish & Pearly

This is what I get for trying to work with people I was told not to trust. Reputation is reputation for a reason. I toss my phone back into my bag and fiddle with my macaron box. I choose a rose flavor this time. If I could go back in time knowing what I know now, would I boycott them like my friends did? Or would I cave again? I'd like to think I wouldn't be a sellout, but if I thought that the money would help my family . . . I'm not sure there isn't anything I wouldn't do. Still, I feel relieved to be done with them.

But today, I won't worry about that. I finish all of my macarons and it feels decadently gluttonous. There's a Citi Bike dock near me, and before I overthink it, I unlock one of the e-bikes and let myself be carried through the city and I head uptown and over the Queensboro bridge.

It's a long ride before I dock the bike in an open station. Eleven miles. I walk around my old neighborhood, unfamiliar now but carrying the weight of so many memories. The streets of Elmhurst haven't changed, though the surrounding establishments have. The nail salon my mom used to work at is gone, as well as the grocery store my dad was a cashier at. Now it's a juice bar, which feels out of place. But the park my dad used to take me to is still there.

I walk a little further and see a new-looking pharmacy where the bodega used to be. I walk in and buy a bottle of flavored water. Roaming my old neighborhood, it feels only right that I contribute somehow.

I wander through the streets and compare how different it is to LIC. The homes here are real houses, not two hundred and sixteen units in a tall building. There's no culture of extreme high rises and *What's the latest, tallest building in all of New York?* vibes here, just people living their lives. And even with doors all closed, there's a warmth I feel from the streets. Whether it's the neighborhood or my memories playing up nostalgia is up for debate. Eventually, after topping my previous week's step count by many miles, it's way past school hours and close to five p.m. I know I need to leave right now if I'm going to make it to Jojo's recital on time.

These are moments when journals are useful; when you can write down thoughts that are too ugly to say out loud or to anyone else. I grab a worksheet from my backpack and use the back side.

> I can't go to Jojo's recital. I don't want to be anywhere
> near anyone I know right now. Jojo's going to be crushed.
> Devastated. But I can't bring myself to go.
> I'm so sorry, Jo.

Just for tonight, I'm letting myself be selfish. It's the most inconvenient night to choose myself, but if it was convenient to choose me, would it really be choosing? I get back on a bike and ride around, putting on my earphones and blasting music into my eardrums so loudly I don't hear cars and trucks honking and whizzing by. It's weird how fast time goes when you're doing absolutely nothing. I don't know how many times I circle the vicinity, but soon the sun is almost down, my phone is still off and my stomach is making noises.

There's a taco truck not far ahead with flashing neon TACO lights on it. Perfect.

Two tostadas later, it's dark. I wash down my food with an orange Fanta (the superior flavor) and head to the overpass nearby, the one where so much of my childhood was spent. Back when Steven and I used to live close to each other, we always met at this specific overpass because it felt like we could see everything. A memory plays in front of me when I reach the middle of the bridge: I was wobbling on an old inherited bike and screaming as Steven held the frame and ran alongside my pedaling.

You're doing it, you're really doing it!

He screamed it so loudly I was startled, then started laughing uncontrollably and eventually fell off. He felt so bad, especially at the sight of my scraped and bloody knees and elbows, but I didn't. I felt like the luckiest kid in the world because someone's entire attention was on me and celebrating what I was doing.

I sit on the concrete ground and send well wishes to the patients at the Jamaica Hospital Medical Center in the distance. Then I dangle my legs above Van Wyck Expressway and spend the next hour watching the sun set over Queens.

CHAPTER TWENTY-FOUR

"Good thing you're here," a familiar voice says.

I jump. Steven's long legs are next to me, so I stand up to face him.

"W-what are you doing here?" My voice is strained. Hurt. Surprised. The memories I have of Steven are nothing like the Steven I know right now, the one who passed me off to Alan like I was some secondhand item he was done with, the one whose eyes got so red with rage who yanked his arm away from me back in Aruba.

He hesitantly takes a step closer, as if I might tell him to back off.

"I'm sorry, Charlotte," he says. He takes another step. "I'm so, *so* sorry for what I said in Aruba. You don't owe me anything. It's just when I saw Alan there, I just got super . . ." He looks for the right word.

"Triggered," I finish for him.

He nods. "That. It wasn't okay, I know that. So, I'm sorry," he says again.

I study him. He looks haggard, like he hasn't slept in days. It's probably how I look, too. And he came all the way here to find me.

"I'm sorry, too. I broke my promise." And before anything could interrupt us again, I pull out the letter from my backpack. "I wrote this that day and a little more later. Read it."

He takes it, studying it. "Right now?"

I nod.

We both sit down and he opens the letter.

Dear Steven,

I messed up. I know I did. But I didn't think it'd lead to . . . well, what it led to. So there are some things I need to tell you now before any more secrets get in the way of us.

First, I was on my phone the night Jojo almost drowned. I'd been feeling super pressured by all the social media stuff and it got to me. So, I caved and posted some photos from our trip. That's why I got distracted and didn't see her run off. I wanted to tell you right away, but I was so afraid you'd hate me for breaking my promise. But I hope you know I do take your promises seriously, and that I won't make that mistake again.

Also, Alan is just a friend now. I realize that I was never really into him like that . . . not like the way I'm into you. With you, it's something else. I guess there's no better time to say it, especially since I don't even know if you'll ever get this letter. With you, it's a soul thing. I think I'm destined to be with you.

I was always afraid to be more than your best friend, because I didn't want to risk losing you if it didn't all work out, and something like only 2 percent of high school relationships end in marriage. And I can't imagine a life without you in it. But maybe it's not really living if we don't get to experience our heart's greatest needs. And hopefully, we'll be in the 2 percent. I want to try.

This life feels so stressful sometimes, and I wonder if it'll ever get easier. But at least if we have each other, we can face everything together. I hope you want to be with me, too. Because I'm pretty sure I'm in love with you, Steven Yoonho Chang.

Charlotte

He folds the letter into thirds and takes my hand, holding it tightly.

I never noticed how big and long his fingers got. When we were younger, Steven used to be shorter than me. He had this perfect bucket hair and round glasses. His fingers were a little stubby then, even though his face was always lean.

He presses his lips into my forehead. "I went back to therapy."

I meet his face in surprise. "You did?"

"Yeah. Clearly, I needed to. Did I say how sorry I was?"

A smile breaks free. "A little, yeah."

He looks so relieved at my smile. "Well, I'm sorry. Really, really sorry. I can't believe I yelled at you. The person that means the most to me in this entire world."

"I should have kept my promise," I say.

Steven shakes his head. "You did nothing wrong. I shouldn't have asked you to just be offline like that when I knew that it was becoming your paid job. I just . . . I think I was in a sensitive space with the whole Panama thing, and I kept thinking about how I remembered seeing my dad for the first time online, with her," he says sheepishly. "I hope I didn't ruin this already?"

"No, definitely not." I zip up my jacket as the wind gets stronger.

"Good," he says. "Because I think I'm destined to be with you, too. And also—"

My cheeks are dry from the cold and my nose feels pink. I'm impatient to kiss him so I cut him off as I press my mouth to his. The shock of the heat from his breath amid the cold air sends shivers through my body and Steven kisses me back as he slides his hand under my coat, gripping my waist. We slide our legs out from over the highway as he pulls me on top of him. I'm seated in between his thighs with my legs wrapped around his waist and I move his hands under my shirt. His hands move to the elastic of my bra, and he pulls his lips away to look at me for permission.

I'm barely breathing, nervous about being caught, but no one is on this bridge but us. The nearest commotion is the thousands of cars driving under us. I manage a nod before his fingers undo the hooks. With all the gentleness in the world, he glides his hands over my bare breasts—lightly at first, and then firmer caresses. I wince from his cold hands, but I'm shaking from the delirium of him touching me.

He brings his mouth down to my neck and sucks the skin and I feel like my lower lip might start bleeding from the bite of holding in this pleasure. The need for him is blinding. I arch my body into him and can feel him *there* under me, and our hunger for each other feels wild and incoherent and perfect.

Our tongues are madly exploring each other and all our sounds are muffled by the traffic and our bodies. When we finally come up for air, our lips are swollen and we're sweaty, despite the evening chill. Steven leans his head against mine.

"What I wanted to say," Steven exhales, "is that I am *definitely* sure I'm in love with you, Charlotte Seoyoung Goh."

I curl into him and his arms wrap tightly around me. I turn my head just a little to see him. "How'd you find me? My phone is off."

"Well, your mom started losing her shit when you weren't in any of your usual places. And then I remembered what you said about this overpass."

"So you went Sherlock Holmes on me?"

"Exactly."

I smile, shaking my head in disbelief. Never did I think anyone would find me here. I'm blown away, completely in shock, and grateful all at once.

"Do you remember what you said?" Steven asks.

I rack my brain until it hits me. "That when I was here, it felt like we were—"

"On top of the world," he finishes.

He lets go and leans back with his palms against the concrete, reminiscing. "You'd go on and on about how on this specific overpass, everything felt so small."

I belly-laugh at this. "This overpass is *so* mundane."

"That's what *I* told you, but you said it wasn't."

"I did?" The moon gets brighter in the sky as the night gets darker. Steven looks illuminated.

He nods. "Yeah. That this overpass is the one you see on the way to the airport, so the air is happier here, whether you're greeting someone who's coming or you're escaping. That both are good. And that cars are going so fast you feel like you're in a constant time warp. That—"

"Seconds don't matter," I say, remembering everything.

"Yep."

"Clearly I didn't think about all the sad reasons you could have going to an airport," I say, laughing again. "I can't believe you remembered all that," I whisper.

"Of course I do." He sits up, wiping his debris-dotted palms on his jeans. "Thank you for the letter."

"Thank you for coming to find me."

He wraps an arm around my waist and closes the gap between us, meeting my lips again. He's warm and tastes like croissants and home. I try to focus on everything in this moment right now and everything that had to happen for all of this to begin. When we pull away from each other, I'm already ready for more.

"I would go through universes to find you again and again," he says, dipping his head to kiss my cheek.

His bold declaration makes me shy and embarrassed. We hold hands and sit in silence for a little while.

"My dad told me not to worry about the family. Isn't that ridiculous?"

Steven nods. "How can you *not* worry? They're our parents."

"Right. Do you think they never worried about their parents?" We're facing the sky, speaking louder to cut through the noise under us.

"No. They definitely did. Probably way more than us."

"Yeah, because they had it so much harder," I say. "Like sweatshops and minimum-wage-jobs hard."

"Yep. But even if our future kids have it super easy, do you think they'll worry about us?"

I gaze at the hospital and think about all the families inside and about his question. "Yeah," I say finally. "I think so. I think that's in our DNA."

"Like a virus," he jokes.

"The Immigrant Family Strain," I joke back, eyes wide at my brilliance.

We laugh hysterically like we've done so often before, except we never let go of each other's hands.

Eventually, I know I need to turn my phone on and deal with what's waiting.

"Thinking of your mom?" he asks.

I nod. "Do you think she even notices I'm gone?"

Steven wears a face of guilt. "I texted her once I saw you," he confesses. "She was *freaking* out."

I groan and look up at the infinite sky.

"She loves you, Char."

I nod. I think I know this. I'm relieved that they know I'm safe. "Thank you. I guess I'll just focus on trying to get Jojo to forgive me."

"That's going to take twenty of Chanson's Messy Croissants," he says, laughing.

"Oh my god, that's the bare minimum. You don't know it, but that girl can hold a freaking grudge. She once ignored my dad for three days because he forgot her ice cream from the grocery store."

Steven belts out a laugh. "Scary."

"Extremely."

"But you're her favorite person, so I think she'll let you off the hook a little more easily," he says, taking my hand again and kissing the back of it. His gestures are so sweet and simple.

"I think *you're* her favorite person," I tell him.

"No way. She actually once reminded me that I was number two on her list," he says, then imitates Jojo's voice. "Sharty one, okay, Steeben? You two."

"I'm so lucky," I say while laughing. A surge of longing and a heart full of regret for missing her recital fills me and I want to go home and hug her. "Let's head back," I tell him.

After all of this, I'm ready to see my family again. And to make some changes.

◆◆◆

It's way past Jojo's bedtime by the time I get home. I stop in front of our apartment door to take one deep breath. Then two, then five.

I know everything that'll unravel behind this door won't be fixed overnight and I dread the long path ahead of me already, but I know it needs to be done. So, I go inside. My mom's voice immediately meets me from the living room.

"Charlotte?" The urgency, the panic, the weight of sadness hit me right in my lungs. I hold my breath, unsure of what'll happen next.

"Hi," I say tentatively.

My mom rushes to meet me and grabs my shoulders before I have a chance to fully shut the door behind me. Her hands feel around different parts of my body, checking for traces of something wrong. She touches my forehead to check for a fever and when everything is clearly intact and not injured, she grabs my shoulders again and looks at me straight. I look back at her, noticing how red her eyes are, how swollen they are, and how exhausted she looks.

Guilt twists inside me. "I'm sorry," I mumble.

She hugs me. It's been a long time since my mom's embraced me like this, with this much longing. I try to keep my emotions at bay, looking up as tears begin to slowly fill my eyes. Inhaling and slowly releasing, I gather myself, ready to do a whole lot of explaining. But then a sound comes out of my mom—a foreign sound. And then the sleeve of my shirt suddenly feels damp.

My mom is crying, and it's a heavy, deep sob. It's powerful and all-consuming and it takes over me, too. My emotions come flooding back at the touch of my mother's tears soaking my shoulder. Together, clutching the other, it's a moment of relief for us both. Our sobs are guttural, heart-wrenching, and vulnerable. My mom is the first to pull back. She holds me, arm's-length apart, pushing my hair out of my face, touching my cheek, as if she can't believe I'm right there in front of her.

"Seoyoung-ah, I thought—" She can't even get her words out before choking up again. Taking a breath, she starts over. "I thought something had happened to you. Something . . . something I can't say out loud," she says in Korean. "Because of what you said, back in Aruba. That you thought I wouldn't care if you drowned. I thought you . . ." Her eyes, bloodshot still, scrunch up, and through her tears she communicates her deepest fears and worries to me. "I thought I lost you," she whispers.

Clarity comes over me as I realize what she's getting at. "Umma, I'm so sorry," I tell her again, unsure how to apologize fully, feeling stupid with just mere words. "I wouldn't . . . I couldn't do that to you. It's just been . . . hard," I say, swallowing the lump in my throat that continues to come up.

She shakes her head back and forth, back and forth. And then again and again until she can find her voice. "Umma is sorry," she says in Korean, in between heavy cries. She says it multiple times. *Umma is sorry. Umma is sorry. Umma is so sorry.*

When both of us calm down a bit, my mom offers to make us some tea. I watch as she puts on a hot pot of yujacha, making mine extra sweet. I look at the teacup I used to drink out of when I was younger, when my mom had time for tea parties. I felt fancy holding the Villeroy & Boch china adorned with flowers and I'd pretend I was the queen and she was my lady-in-waiting. As if reading my mind, she puts it in front of me, smiling sheepishly. "Been a while, huh?"

I nod. "Smells the same, though."

"Do you want to talk about it?" she asks. *It* feels loaded. What would it cover? Sneaking around in Aruba? Being in love with Steven? My private influencer life now out in the open with my family? Being canceled by my online community? How I've felt for years toward my own mom?

"I wouldn't know where to start," I answer quietly.

"We can start anywhere . . . and make our way through it slowly."

I chew on my lower lip, trying to figure out what I feel the most in this moment. She waits patiently, drinking her citron tea.

"I'm jealous of the mom that you are with Jojo," I finally say.

She nods, like she was expecting this. "I put too much on you. You're only sixteen." She laughs a little, shaking her head. She changes to Korean because I know it's easier for her to communicate her deeper feelings. "It's just Umma treats you more like a best friend, the person I tell everything to. It doesn't mean you need to carry any of the burden of what I carry."

"I'm *not* your best friend, Umma. I'm your daughter." I bite my lip, hoping this doesn't sound too harsh.

We sit in silence for a bit and she doesn't say anything, which makes me feel worse. I want to take it back immediately, but how can I when I mean every word of it?

Finally, she rubs my back and kisses my temple. "I'm so sorry, my baby," she says in Korean.

At the threat of tears, I say the other thing at the forefront of my brain. "And I feel so bad for missing Jojo's recital."

She laughs loudly at this, throwing her head back. "She's three. It was hardly a real recital," she jokes. "I'm sure she'll get over it."

It's the first time I feel this flicker of relief spreading through me. The promise of a little more balance, at least for the foreseeable future. And it's only after I feel this ounce of relief that I realize how completely exhausted I am.

"Go, go, go sleep," she says to me in motherly Korean. "It's so late." She shoos me off the sofa, taking the teacup from my hands and pushing me toward my bedroom.

I rub my eyes but turn around when she calls my name again.

"Do you want to go to the Met tomorrow?"

It takes a moment for her offer to sink in. I really can't remember the last time we spent time together like that. "All of us?" I ask.

She shrugs. "Your call, baby."

"Yeah. I do. Maybe just you and me, though," I say, smiling. "There's a lot more I want to tell you."

I go to bed that night, a feeling of gratitude welling up inside me. Despite everything that's happened, I'm surprised that getting through to the other side wasn't as painful as I thought it'd be.

For the first time in a long time, I feel hopeful.

CHAPTER TWENTY-FIVE

I'm relieved it's the weekend because I still don't feel ready to be back at school just yet. Even though I've only slept a few hours, I wake up like my REM cycle brutally decided to end. It's not even six a.m., but it feels much later.

Shuffling into my house slippers, I grab my laptop and crawl back into bed. For the next hour, I make new choices. I don't know if they're better ones, just that they're different. I think only time will tell if they were the better decisions. It's a lot of apologizing via email, a lot of explaining, and a lot of studying contracts the best that I can. Nothing is hugely problematic, thankfully, and then, without any attempt at makeup or filters, I snap a few pictures and pick the most normal-looking one. I write a lengthy caption, pouring my honesty out as best I can. I read it, edit it, and read it again. When my thumb hovers over the Share icon, I realize I'm nervous. My fingers are shaking a little, not fully ready to let go.

There's a gentle rap on my door. I glance at the clock. There's only one person who would ever be up this early.

"Come in," I say.

"Sharty?" Her head peeps through first, the rest of her little body toddling in after.

I slide off my bed fast and kneel down so I'm face-to-face with my whole world. "Unni is so sorry she missed your recital, Jojo. I'm so, so sorry," I tell her. "How can I make it up to you? Do you want ten Messy Croissants? All-day *Bluey*? Ms. Rachel? *Paw Patrol*? Name the price of your forgiveness. You got it."

Jojo pauses, a slow grin spreading across her chubby face. "*Ten* Messy Croissants?" she asks eagerly.

"Anything you want, Jojo. I'm so sorry I wasn't there. Were you really sad?"

I think about every twirl, every position she practiced, each plié and relevé she focused on perfecting as a three-year-old. I recall the hungry desire I saw in her eyes as the teacher showed what a proper arabesque and pirouette look like, promising that she too could one day perfect them, as long as she practiced. She wouldn't stop trying all evening at home, and I see these images flash through my mind, how much she loves ballet and pours everything into it. And I had missed it. For no other reason than that I cared too much about wallowing in my own misery.

"You saw it already, Sharty," she says in such a grown-up, matter-of-fact voice that I'm convinced she's matured in the last two days I barely interacted with her.

"I . . . did?"

"All my practices! You were there."

I love how kids her age aren't overthinkers yet. That they just say whatever they mean, good or bad. I hug her tightly, kissing her head. "I'm still sorry," I whisper. "I'm sure you were so beautiful and strong up there, Jo."

She plays with my hair, patting it lightly. "Do you want to see it again?" she whispers back.

I square her shoulders in front of me and put on my most serious expression. "YES. PLEASE!"

An eager squeal escapes out of her and she runs out of the room. I join her in the living room, and we work together to create a stage. I drag out chairs and put them in a line while Jojo grabs her stuffies and places one on each, leaving the center chair open for me. We run to her room to grab her recital costume and I help her into her tights and her shimmery tutu. I even slick her hair into a bun and add her favorite pin in the front.

Finally, I connect my phone to the living room TV and turn the music on as she gets into position. I sit on the edge of my seat as I soak in each wobbly twirl and plié and watch in awe as she jumps and points toes outward and lifts her arms en haut. I don't blink, not wanting to miss even a single moment. Pride swells through me, and seeing her perform with all that she has for me, an audience of one, gives me the confidence to do what finally feels right. When the dance ends, she performs a reverent ballet bow and I stand up, applauding and cheering.

When she runs to grab some snacks, I open my phone to the queued post, newly inspired by Jojo, and tap Share.

Hi. I know a lot of you must hate me. I know I didn't handle things as well as I should have. I know I've disappointed you, and I'm sorry. To each friend who has supported me and sent encouraging DMs, thank you. I've read and found comfort in each message. I can't get into the details of my recent choices, as the reasons are highly personal, but to anyone I've upset, to anyone who believes that I don't support my fellow AAPI community, I'm deeply sorry. The last few months have been mentally taxing for me, and I've seen myself spiral into dark spaces I wasn't sure I could come out of. As a result, I've decided to delete my account for the foreseeable future to focus on regaining healthy habits and nourishing my relationships and my soul. If and when I come back into this space, if you're still open, I'd love to see you here. And I'll be healthier, for you, for me, and for our community.

Sending all my love, Charlotte 🖤

I sigh slowly, relief and anxiety pumping through me, entangled. I send Audrey a quick text, asking to get on the phone to catch up sometime today if she's free.

"What now?" Jojo asks. "When can we get Messy Croissants?"

I grin, loving that toddlers take up your entire attention. Loving that when I'm with Jojo, it's hard to focus on anything else because of her vibrant and demanding energy.

"How about tomorrow, after church?"

She nods and asks me to turn on *Bluey*. I laugh loudly, knowing she's working her magic to get everything she wants. And I oblige. We spend hours like this, welcoming the sunrise and cuddling on the sofa together. A buzz jolts me out of the world of Bluey and Bingo and the parents that are so perfect that they must be animated.

audrey

Yes, def! Saw your post.

Big hugs. Hangout next week?

♥ def. thanks audrey

With my phone already in my hand, I give in to my temptation and open Instagram one last time and scroll through the comments. My eyes and brain devour them, and I'm reminded how addicting it is. I don't let myself read the nasty comments, but I'm glad to see it's mostly supportive. But one comment catches my eye instantly. It's from Alan.

Happy for you. Really.

I tap the heart icon then delete the app from my phone. It's done. And though nothing seems different, it's like there's a slight shift in everything. The good kind.

By late morning, our home is bustling with the usual chaotic weekend noise. My mom is blending a smoothie, my dad is cooking, and Jojo is begging my dad to let her help. Despite her "help," which mostly consists of loud singing, my dad makes blueberry pancakes for us, courtesy of a recipe he says is from John Legend. We all laugh at this but compliment his pancakes and help ourselves to more servings. My dad updates us on his interview, telling us how well it went and how good he feels about it.

"Feels very promising," he says in Korean, pouring maple syrup on his pancakes. Then he looks at me pointedly. "But regardless, no one needs to worry about that. Everything will be okay," he says, smiling meaningfully.

I smile back and nod. I think it's a little unrealistic that my parents still expect me to never worry about them. But I can pretend not to. I can let them be my parents and let myself be a kid, at least for one more year.

Steven texts me after breakfast, asking if I'm free.

YES! free now

but going to the met with my mom later:)

An hour later, we're at Gantry Park walking along the water. It's a little cold, but it's the kind of brisk air that whips problems away into the wind and disappears, leaving only simple joys. He casually grabs my hand and I duck my head just a little to hide the blush creeping up on my face. He nudges me, knowing this already. I nudge him back.

"Shy?" he jokes.

"Shut up," I joke back.

"Happy, though?"

"Super happy."

We spend our walk with me updating him on my new choice. "I'm feeling a slight withdrawal, to be honest. But it's freeing."

He *hmms* thoughtfully at this. "I think life is better without it, anyway."

I roll my eyes, but I'm smiling. "Of course *you'd* say that. But I agree."

Steven smiles back. "I talked to my dad. Told him I wasn't ready to go visit him in Panama."

I squeeze his hand. "You didn't talk to your mom about it?"

He shakes his head. "I already knew I didn't want to go. I miss him, but I'm not ready. Not yet."

"When you're ready, I can go with you if you want."

"I'd like that." Steven kisses the side of my head. "So, how long do you plan to stay off social media?"

I shrug, looking at children scootering past me and parents chasing them. "I don't know. Until it feels okay to be back on. Whenever that is. But if I do, it won't be for the money," I add.

"Makes sense. Should I make you like an Instagram withdrawal patch?" Steven jokes.

"And what exactly would that patch consist of?"

He looks at me mischievously. "A *lot* of kissing. Maybe some movies. A lot of books."

"I might be busy, actually," I say, teasing him.

"Oh yeah? Doing what?"

It's my turn to look at him slyly. "I applied for a job."

"You *did*?"

"Yep." I'm grinning. "At a bubble tea shop close to Court Square. I should hear back soon."

He pats my back cheerfully, half in sarcasm. "Look at you! A regular teenager."

I shove him lightly, but I'm excited. I want this.

He makes a face, like he's in trouble. "In other news, I told my mom that we'd be cooking Sunday dinner tomorrow."

"What! Still not sick of my doenjang jjigae?"

Steven laughs. "Let's try something new. What about those BCD spicy tofu stew packets? It comes with the sauce and everything."

I can already imagine our parents forcing themselves to eat our stew, trying to pretend like it's delicious and I burst into laughter. "Why did you even offer to cook?" I ask, half in panic, half in curiosity.

"Honestly? Cooking together sounded romantic."

I purse my lips, so I don't look like I have a hanger in my mouth. He's so cute. "Can we also make a dessert together, then?" I imagine us in the kitchen, cooking and kissing. Maybe with me, Steven can bake when he's happy, too.

He puts his arm around me. "I already have all the ingredients for the world's best hodduk. It's the perfect ratio of cinnamon to brown sugar."

"Sounds perfect. Gooey cinnamon wins every time."

We walk toward a corner of the park where you can see the entire city skyline and he looks at me with this sort of in-awe expression. "I hope we're doing this same thing in another five years," he says, holding my waist a little tighter.

I plant a kiss on his cheek. "I hope we're doing this same thing in another *fifty* years."

The sky is blue, with no clouds in sight. It looks like an enormous canvas, waiting to be drawn and painted on, worn in, and loved on. It mimics how I feel. With only one year left before our futures take us wherever they take us, I want to do it right. It's so cliché, how snapping so many photos all the time takes us away from moments like these: blue skies, orange leaves, yellow petals from ginkgo trees scattered loosely on the ground. How our phones dilute the intimacy of the moments we want to keep for ourselves. And seeing the empty blue canvas above me, I feel nostalgic already for what I've lost, partnership opportunities I could have had, a future that will now never be known.

But I also feel wildly hopeful, like what lies ahead might be dreamier than anything I've ever imagined. These last few years, I felt like I was drifting away, barely tethered, constantly trying to find a place—even a digital one—where I could keep my feet planted. Who knew, this entire time, the place I was searching for was right here. I look out over the East River and breathe in the salty air, and for the first time in a really, really long time, I finally feel grounded, like I'm right where I'm meant to be.

I nudge Steven and challenge him to race me back home. "Ready . . . set . . ."

"*Go!*" he says, grinning.

We take off, running as fast as we can through New York City, feeling like nothing could ever stop us.

ACKNOWLEDGMENTS

To anyone who's ever hated social media, I feel you in my core. But! This isn't a hate letter to social media (because who of us doesn't gain knowledge and the best recipes and fun toddler activities from amazing influencers?). Rather, it's an encouragement to us all to remember to put your phone down and be present.

So many thank-yous . . . Where to begin?

To Jenny, my editor. For pushing me to make this story the best it can be, and for advocating for me.

Jim, for always being here through it all, and always with a smile. Thank you for making your magic happen so I can keep writing.

To the wonderful team at Penguin that I get to work with: Felicity and Shannon and everyone else on the marketing, publicity, and sales team; Krista and Joy and everyone on the design team. It takes so many people to create a book. Thank you.

Sarah, for your check-ins on motherhood and writing, for sharing about the Quarry Rock hike. For the kindness you pour out always.

Ruth, this past year and this book's journey were made so much better because of you. You, your prayers, and this friendship sustained me. Now teach me to draw like you!

Jesse, your unhinged books give me joy. I wish you didn't live in Singapore. Consider moving to NYC. Thank you for being my fellow unhinged mom and writer friend.

Maurene, for your guidance, encouragement, and friendship. Maybe one day we will have the courage to leave behind our toddlers and meet in a state in the middle of us, drink wine, and write and gab all day in a beautiful hotel.

Frances, for being my author unni. Thank you for always thinking of me.

To Lucy. And CJ, Kazumi, Babe, Anders, Tyrinne, Christy, Mags, Theresa, Wes, Viv, Chitra. I can't believe my fortune to know you all and get to call Yu & Me home. I'm trying so hard to not burst out a deep love letter spanning pages because I have to keep this appropriate, you know. I love you all. So stinking much. Thank you for being a home for my books, but mostly thank you for being my friends.

To Yurie, for always being the most excited person in my life in all the small and big things.

To Jen, for loving my book babies. I can't wait to love YOUR BABY.

To Annice and Carol, for always being my source of laughter.

To my carnal lust house: You are my lifelines. I cannot survive without our friendship. Wo ai ni, Linds. Wo ai ni, Mels.

To Appa, for always sharinanag about my books to everyone you meet.

To Umma, who always believed I could do anything I wanted. I dream big because of you.

To Unni. This book is for you. I'm so proud of how far we've come. Love you, Sissy.

And always, my husband. What a whirlwind 2024 we have had, with so many uncertain seasons. Through it all, you've remained my rock, and I still consider myself the luckiest.